Bro Amazing

Bro Amazing

The Bro Series

Alby Blake

Gaming Handles

Miles = Thrower

Helix = Hel

Quintin = Arrow

Lionel = Faker

Ethan = Ender

Content Expectations

- Foul language, dirty talk, and spicy situations
- Free use, including sex while asleep and dub con situations
- Anal play, including lube, toys and cocks
- Toys, both electronic and non-electronic
- Sharing, including one-on-one sessions and group sessions

Chapter One

The flyer is vague beyond belief, but I'm desperate. I can't keep chasing my dream of being a full-time writer while at the same time affording rent. Prices are too high, even for a studio apartment. I'm at the stage where I need to either admit defeat and apply for full-time jobs, or any of my current books need to suddenly jump onto the bestseller lists. Really, though, even if that happened today, I'd still be in this exact position since it takes two months to get paid in this world.

I'm on my last bit of savings, so my options are: get a job that pays straight away and give up writing—at least for now —or find some way to live for free. Which is a ridiculous notion in a city this size. Living cheap is silly enough.

But then I saw the flyer on the lamppost. *Wanted: Live-in girlfriend, includes free room and board.*

It's probably a scam, or the guy is creepy. I mean, why would someone advertise for a girlfriend? What's wrong with them? And to go so far as to pay said girlfriend via room and board? There has to be a serious catch. It almost doesn't sound like they want a girlfriend so much as a ...

No. I shut that thought down real quick. Not going

there. I don't have any other options that will allow me to continue to pursue my dream though, so I need to at least check it out. I can always leave if the interview gets too creepy or if I feel unsafe.

I can picture the headline now: *Romance Author Clarissa Clarke Missing; No Potential Suspects.*

I should at least let someone know where I am so that if I go missing, they can tell the police where to start looking for my body. I pull out my phone to text my friend Sasha.

I'm going to a roommate interview. Wish me luck, I type, along with the address. No need to tell her that the interview is not only for being a roommate, but a girlfriend as well.

Good luck! Sasha texts me back almost immediately. *I'm in the middle of packing up a ton of books today since my direct sales have been crazy.*

Yay! Get it girl! I add in some celebration emojis, but I don't feel any of it. I mean, I'm happy for her because she works super hard and deserves every bit of this success, but I've worked hard too and have barely gotten any page reads.

This is yet another reason why I don't want to get a job and give up my dream of being a full-time author. I've already put so much into this career and if I give up, it'll feel like all of my compromises have been a waste. I'm a good writer, I know it. I just need to work harder.

And maybe stop comparing myself to my friends who are having more success than me because we don't write in the same subgenre.

Sasha writes high-heat romantasy, while I've been focused on clean or fade-to-black small-town romances. And while hers fly off the shelves, mine have been collecting dust.

Maybe I should try writing in Sasha's line of romance.

The only problem with that idea is that I don't really

have any experience in the bedroom. I had a boyfriend for a while, but when I got serious about being a writer, that fell to the wayside because he didn't understand what it's like to have a passion and follow a dream.

Stopping outside the address on the flyer, I look up at a front door with slightly peeling paint and one of the numbers a little crooked, almost like it's barely clinging to the door. Even the little bit of front yard that exists is covered in weeds, giving the whole place a slight air of dejection.

This house looks exactly like how I feel lately. But it also looks like whoever lives here could murder me and dump my body in the nearest ravine. I'm already conjuring an image of an older man with a beer belly in a sweaty white tank top, sharpening the blade of his machete as he prepares to chop me up into little pieces.

I really should leave. Give up my dream and continue to live my life, at least.

A group walks past on the sidewalk and one of their shoulders hits my back, shoving me toward the steps.

"Watch where you're going," says the man gruffly as he hurries on down the sidewalk.

I frown after him. I was literally standing there minding my own business. He's the one who ran into me. I swear, people in this town are getting worse.

Now that I'm standing on the little front walk, made of cracks and half-covered with grass, I suppose I should take the next step up to the door. The passing stranger was rude, but it was probably my sign that I should at least try every avenue to succeed before I give up. This is only an interview, and I can always leave.

I tuck my long, pin-straight, brown hair behind my ears and smooth my hands over my best pair of jeans, straighten my shoulders, and climb the steps up to the front door.

There's no bell or knocker on the door so I use my knuckles and wait, when a new thought occurs to me.

What if the flyer and the job is real, but the guy already found a live-in girlfriend and just hasn't gotten around to taking down the flyers yet?

Oh man, this is so embarrassing. Maybe I should leave. Thousands of other people have given up on their dreams and survived. I could too. It'd be sad, but it'd be an existence.

Or I could come back to a career as a writer later when I'm retired and don't need to worry about income so much.

I'm halfway down the steps to the sidewalk when the front door opens to reveal a tall man in black sweatpants and a graphic tee. The shirt has some sort of cartoon character on it I don't recognize, and his deep red hair is kind of sticking up from his head as if he just woke up.

"Fuck, we almost didn't get the door, you knocked so quiet. We had a debate about if it was the wind or a ghost or something before we decided to check," says the guy, rubbing his face as if it's too bright out here. "You here about the position?"

He still hasn't introduced himself, but he points to the flyer still in my hand. He's lanky, young, probably early twenties, about my age. He can't be the one from the flyer though, because someone his age, and dressed the way he is, probably can't afford to cover room and board for himself, let alone a live-in girlfriend.

"Uh, yes?" This is a bad idea. I should walk away right now. "Is the guy who's hiring the, uh, the girlfriend here?"

It's super embarrassing to say those words out loud and have someone else hear them. I can't believe it's come to this. Admitting that not only am I single, but I'm desperate enough that I'll live with someone even more desperate. Desperate enough to put up flyers. Who does that?

"Yeah, come on in." The guy gives me a weird look before heading down the hall, expecting me to follow. "Hel! I owe you twenty bucks. The flyer worked."

I glance around the street behind me in case anyone is around to see me go into this house alive so they can testify to the police later at my murder trial. But the street is empty. Not my lucky day.

Reluctantly, I step inside and close the front door behind me. The entire place has a slightly forgotten feel about it, as if no one has really noticed that it's here for a long while. Do I take off my shoes? This is someone else's house, and I can't remember if I saw the guy who answered the door wearing shoes or not.

He sticks his head out of a doorway up ahead. "Come on, we need to interview you."

"We?" I decide to leave my shoes on in case I need a quick getaway.

Stopping in the doorway where the guy disappeared, I come face to face with the little detail they left out on the flyer.

Chapter Two

Five guys, all of a similar age and style of dress, stare back at me from an array of computer chairs. The room is completely dark—if there are windows, they're covered in blackout curtains. The only light is from the monitors of their computers. Multiple ones in front of each chair. The only thing on the screens are screensavers of different animated characters who I also don't recognize.

I can't say anything. I'm completely stunned, more nervous than ever, and absolutely confused. I don't even know where to start with all the questions I have now.

"Hi, I'm Helix," says one of them, a lanky guy with a man-bun and shaved sides, getting up and reaching his hand out to shake. I take it automatically. "I'm the one who put up the flyer. This is Miles"—he points at the one who answered the door—"Quintin, Lionel, and Ethan."

"Oh. Okay. I'm ... " I glance around the room again. There's a weird vibe in here and I don't want them to have any identifying information about me, like that my name is Clarissa. Everyone is staring at me. Maybe my lipstick is a little smeared? I don't normally wear makeup since I sit at a computer all day and don't see anyone else, but I figured for an interview, especially one for a live-in girlfriend, I should make the effort. "So you're the one looking for a live-in girlfriend?"

"No, well, yes." Helix looks briefly over his shoulder at the other guys. "We're all looking for one."

"You're going to hire five girlfriends to live here with all of you?" It's a good-sized house from the front, but ten people living anywhere together is going to be crowded, especially because I work from home. Maybe it's a lot bigger on the inside though, or the others don't actually live here and are just hanging out here for the day.

"No," Helix draws out the word. Slowly, as if judging my facial expression, he says, "We're hiring just one girlfriend, to share, among all five of us."

"All five of you?" I sound stupid repeating Helix's word back to him, but it's taking my brain longer than it should to compute the implication of his words.

"Yeah, doesn't it say that on the flyer?" Helix takes the paper out of my hand and looks it over. "Oh, it doesn't. Looks like I forgot to include that part on there. Oops. Oh well."

Oops? That's a pretty big detail to have left out. Dealing with one boyfriend who is paying you to be their girlfriend is awkward enough because what if you actually can't stand each other or you don't like him? But *five?* Five is just too many.

"She looks like she's about to pass out, Hel, get her a chair," says Quintin, the rich deep tones of his skin highlighting the tendons in his arm as he gestures.

Helix grabs the empty computer chair and swings it around so the seat hits the back of my knees, forcing me to collapse onto the seat.

"Are you okay?" Helix leans down so we're face to face, but he doesn't touch me. "Do you need water?"

"I'm fine." I should leave. I should go back to my apartment and look for normal jobs.

"Why don't we go over some of the aspects of the job then?" says Miles, leaning forward in his chair, watching me.

I must have heard Helix wrong. Or misconstrued his words. He couldn't possibly mean being the live-in girlfriend of five guys at once.

"Good idea," says Helix. "So like the flyer says, room and board is included."

See, he's talking about practical things that are on the flyer, and there was nothing about all five of them being the boyfriend on the flyer. My imagination must be overreacting again.

Helix is cut off by Quintin, who says, "Does it really say that, or did you forget to put that on there too?"

"Zero out of ten," says Lionel. He has dark, wavy hair down to his shoulders which should not work on anyone, but pulls it off. He's good-looking, thin and kind of lanky like the rest of them as if they're not used to doing physical labor. They're probably stronger than they appear though.

Actually, now that I'm thinking about it, they're *all* pretty attractive.

"Powerspike," calls Quintin, cupping his hands around his mouth to amplify his voice.

Is this what they're always like? Bickering and mocking each other? That would be a lot to put up with in roommates. It's too weird in my mind to think of them as potential boyfriends. Eyeing them up as roommates is much easier, and keeps me breathing.

"Fuck you both. Of course I did," says Helix, but he covertly glances at the flyer. "Anyway, you'd have your own room, and we'd do all the grocery shopping. Well, we order them online and they're delivered. We don't really cook, kind of just eat whatever, whenever."

"Although if you cook, we wouldn't stop you," says Lionel.

"Sure, yeah, that'd be nice, but not a requirement," says Helix. "We don't want to make expectations too high or no one is going to say yes to us."

"Just saying," says Lionel, "it'd be nice to get a home-cooked meal sometimes is all."

"I do know how to cook, a little at least. Nothing really impressive, but I can get by." What am I doing? They're interviewing me to be their live-in girlfriend, and I'm over here offering to work extra. I can't believe I'm this hard up for money that I've come to this.

These guys haven't even asked me any questions about myself and I'm not sure how much they want to learn, yet they're already asking how much extra I'd be willing to do around the house. Although from the little bits of the house I've seen so far, this place is in more than a little need of TLC.

This whole idea is crazy. I should just get up and walk out while I still can.

"Oh, sweet!" says Lionel, bumping knuckles with Quinton in the chair next to him.

"Moving on." Helix gives Lionel a second look before turning back to me. "If you have dietary needs, we'd accommodate that as well. The one limitation would be that this room would be off-limits because the equipment is quite expensive."

"And we don't want our chairs adjusted," adds Quintin.

"Oh, yeah," agrees Miles. "That would be the worst."

"She'd fucking drain tank us," mumbles Quintin. "I don't champion if the positioning is off."

"What do you do in here?" Before we get any further in

this ridiculous farce of an interview, I need to ensure these guys aren't doing something illegal. This neighborhood isn't the greatest, but it's still a big house and close to public transport, so it must be pricey. How can they afford to support themselves and cover my living expenses too? I mean, whoever takes the position as their live-in girlfriend, not necessarily me. I haven't made any decisions yet.

The guys all share a look before Miles offers, "We're e-athletes."

"I don't understand." They answered very simply, but it definitely wasn't clear.

"Look, that isn't important. We don't expect whoever accepts the position to understand what we do or show an interest in it," says Helix dismissively.

"At least for any of the right reasons," mumbles Lionel.

"Okay," I say uncertainly. They sound super jaded, but if I'm not allowed to know everything about their job, or not expected to, then they can easily be left in the dark about my own job.

It's always awkward when people learn that I write romances. They either look at me like I'm pathetic or become a bit lecherous. Very few people have shown they're actually cool with what I write, which is why I spend most of my time writing alone or with others, particularly my critique group.

Although my critique group has never been too impressed with my writing. It's yet another sign that I'm not succeeding in my chosen career field.

"We work a lot and sometimes at odd hours of the day due to the worldwide aspect of our jobs. So you'll have to be able to entertain yourself when we're busy. Basically, if we're in here, we're not to be disturbed," says Helix.

Which means lots of time to do my own writing undisturbed by them.

"What, um." I have to ask the big question, but I'm scared. "What is required of the, uh, the girlfriend aspect of the ... flyer?"

If I say *job*, it makes it sound a little too salacious for my ears. Which is why I've always shied away from writing the spicy stuff that sells, sticking more to fade-to-black romances.

Helix tugs on his ear, glancing around the room at the other guys. "We would require all the, uh, conveniences of a girlfriend."

"But one who respects our space, and is more there when we have some free time for that sort of thing," adds Lionel, crossing his arms.

I can feel my eyes bugging out as my brain struggles to process what they're saying without actually coming out and saying it. I could pretend I'd imagined it a moment ago, but now they're talking about it again.

"So you, all five of you, want the physical benefits of a girlfriend without the emotional labor? And the compensation is just room and board?" The very idea of this is egotistical and disgusting.

Besides, while I don't know much about this type of job, I'd imagine putting up with five different guys all the time would deserve more than just room and board as compensation. And then being ... *used* by all of them? I swallow hard at the thought.

"Yes," says Helix, biting his lip.

I can't believe these guys thought someone would actually agree to this. I can't believe I actually came here and have been considering taking them up on this offer. I never would have started this stupid interview process if I'd fully known what they expected.

I'd assumed it was one guy. Maybe pretend to be his girlfriend for friends and family, maybe to impress his boss.

I'd read about that sort of thing in books, but this is taking it too far. They'd expect me to let them have sex with me whenever and however they like? I feel faint at the very thought.

"Okay, I've heard enough." I stand up quickly, and the chair rolls back a little with the momentum.

"So you'll take it?" asks Helix, standing as well. I can hear the hope in his voice.

"No, I need to go." I can't contemplate the idea of going from no boyfriend to suddenly having five, and basically being paid to service all of them sexually at their own whims. This whole situation is too ridiculous. I need to get out of here before they decide I can't leave.

"But we haven't even shown you your room yet," says Quintin.

All five of them follow me out into the hall as I hurry to the front door. Luckily, they don't try to grab me or restrain me. They let me go, which is surprising since they outnumber me and could easily overpower me.

"That's okay, I don't need to see it." They hadn't even locked the front door. "Good luck finding someone."

I don't really mean it, but saying the nice thing is too ingrained in me and it just slips out. I check over my shoulder every few steps as I hurry toward The El, but there's no one there. And they don't have any of my personal information to track me down, so I should be safe.

They hadn't even asked my name or anything about me. They don't care about who their live-in girlfriend is so long as she leaves them alone most of the time and spreads her legs whenever they ask.

Chapter Three

"Yes, I understand that rent is supposed to be paid monthly." I roll my eyes to the ceiling since my landlord can't see me over the phone. "What I'm asking is if I can get a small extension for this month."

"And I'm telling you, you need to either pay or I'm going to find a new tenant who can pay," he says, enunciating each word as if I'm an idiot. "This is a business, not a charity."

Pinching the bridge of my nose, I ask, "When do I need to pay by?"

"Like every month, you need to pay by the seventh. If you can't do that, you need to move out by the eighth. Now get the money together, and stop calling me begging for an extension." He hangs up without a kind word.

At this point even if I could apply for and get a regular, full-time day job, I wouldn't get paid soon enough to cover the rent. Who knows if whatever I'd get paid would even cover it. My landlord keeps jumping the rent higher and higher every month, it seems, to keep it in line what he calls "market inflation." Really, it's just increasing it until no one can afford it.

I could ask Sasha if I could stay with her for a little

while, and she'd say yes, but having to see every day how much better she's doing in life than me may push me over the edge. And she'd also see how much of a failure I am right now.

What I need is a miracle.

Dumping my uneaten bagel in the trash, I shuffle the bills that have accumulated on the counter into a pile to make room for the dirty plate. Things have kind of gotten away from me around this place as I've tried to write more in order to make more money. Basically, at this point I need not only a miracle in the short term, but maybe to switch to writing something different, something sexy, for the longer haul. But I have so little experience with that, I'd need to do a ton of research.

Uncovering the flyer from those guys looking for a live-in girlfriend, I stare at it. I don't know why I kept it. I should have thrown it out the minute I left their house last week.

It's a terrible idea to let any guy pay me to be his live-in girlfriend, let alone five guys I don't know. To basically let them use my body however they want for as long as I live with them and let them pay for everything.

It would solve my financial situation for right now though, and they didn't say there was a minimum time that I had to live there. Maybe I could stay with them while I save up a little bit of money again to live on my own. It's not like I'd be spending anything on bills, I'd only be making money.

Maybe finding the flyer tucked into this stack of unpaid bills is supposed to be some sort of sign? The universe telling me not to give up on my dream because there's a way to make it work?

Great.

Although, I do need more experience if I want to write something spicier and more to market. I could gain that experience from the five of them, if I really committed to this role. And an artist needs to give everything for their art. I think I read that somewhere. So it wouldn't be them using me so much as all of us using each other.

This viewpoint makes the whole idea a little more palatable, though it's not like I can see any other choices at the moment. Moving back home or in with Sasha would both be admitting defeat, that I can't survive on my own, that I'm not good enough.

I can't do that. Not yet.

I need to become a live-in girlfriend.

Before I can talk myself out of what I'm about to do, I grab my coat and head to the train. As I step onto the platform, though, something occurs to me and I nearly falter. What if, because I've waited so long, they've found someone else to fill the position? Or they won't accept me because I turned them down the first time? Or I'm not pretty enough? What if my reaction to the whole thing tipped them off that I am nowhere near as experienced as they probably want their shared girlfriend to be?

Even as all these doubts cloud my mind, The El rattles on. I have to at least go and see at this point. I'll just have to be humble and nice and convince them I'm the woman for the job.

Unless it's already taken. Then I don't know what I'll do.

I practice my speech, laying out my entire argument why they should hire me as their live-in girlfriend as I walk from the train station to their house. Moving in with them will be worth it in the end. It has to be.

Keeping in mind that the last time they told me I knocked too softly, I bang my fist against the door before stepping back to wait. Either way, once this door opens, I'll know my fate. I'll either become a live-in girlfriend, or a washed-up writer sleeping on someone's sofa.

The door flings open, startling my speech right out of my head. It must be one thick door for me not to have heard any movement on the other side.

"You guys need to take a fucking turn answering the door sometimes," Miles yells back up the hall. As soon as he sees it's me though, his face lights up. "Wow! You came back."

"Um, yeah." Forget just my speech disappearing, all of my words seem to have fled as well. I can't chicken out now. It's this or sofa city. "Is the position still open?"

"It is. Does that mean you'll take it?" Miles's eyes grow bigger with each word.

"If I can move in today or tomorrow." I close my eyes and take a breath. I've just sealed my fate.

"You can move in right now." Miles backs up into the hallway. "Come on in, I'll show you where your room is and get you a key."

"There isn't anything else you want to ask me before we all live together?" This whole thing still sounds super sketchy and like a bad idea, but there's really no going back now.

"No." Miles scratches his head and looks up to the ceiling. "I can't think of anything."

"Well, my name is Clarissa." How could he have overlooked such a big question? I thought computer people were supposed to be smart.

"We've just been calling you Hot Girl, but Clarissa works too." Miles leads me upstairs, pointing to each door as we walk down the hall and telling me who sleeps in each room. My head is spinning because I'm actually *doing* this. There's no way I'm going to be able to remember this. All I'm taking in right now is that this upstairs hallway is just as dark and dingy as the last one.

I just need to keep breathing. Everything is going to be

okay. So what if I'm moving in with five strange guys I met because of a flyer. And so what I'm now trading my body for a place to live. At least I'm going to be able to continue to follow my dream of being a full-time writer and get the experience I need to write higher heat books. That's what I need to keep reminding myself of. I'm still a good girl. They aren't using me, I'm using them.

"And this one here will be your room." Miles opens the door at the very end of the hall. "It's the only one with an en suite, and we thought it was only fair for it to be yours."

Miles looks a little sheepish as he admits this last part. I'm not sure if it's because they wanted to do something nice for me—or whoever their live-in girlfriend was—or if it's because of the room itself. It's not a bad room, but it's not great either. Empty. Basic and boring. Very beige, with some faded paint rectangles where past tenants had pinned up posters. Overall, though, I could do a lot worse for a free room.

Well, not free. I'll definitely be paying in one form or another. At least for a little while.

"It's great." I force a to smile even though I'd rather curl up in a ball and cry. "Thank you. It's really sweet of all of you to let me have my own bathroom as well."

"You're welcome." Miles blushes even deeper. "We could help you move if you want. I mean, we don't have an ARAM until this evening. Until then we're just co-oping against bots."

Although I have no idea what Miles just said, they're clearly making an effort to be sweet, at least for now. For some reason, their kindness makes me want to cry even more.

"I actually haven't started packing yet." Yikes, I have so much to do. I can't believe this is actually happening. That

I'm agreeing to this ridiculousness. "I didn't know if you'd gotten someone to move in or not already."

Miles looks down and toys with a loose trim board with the toe of his shoe. "You were actually the only one who showed up to even ask us about it."

My first thought is, *That's because all the other women in this town have way more dignity and self-preservation than me.* But it's clear Miles doesn't see it that way. He sees it more as being rejected, and I can't help but feel bad for him. The flyer was kind of creepy, but maybe they just didn't know of any other way to find a personal connection since so much of their lives seem to be online.

"Well, their loss is my gain." Oof. No wonder my career is suffering if I use cliché phrases like this.

"True." Miles smiles a little more, but it's not the same as when I first walked through the front door. "Let's go tell the guys."

I follow him back down to the first floor and he peeks his head into the computer room. The other gamers don't even look our way, completely focused on their screens. All I can see are different colors moving around fast. And even though they're all wearing headphones, the room is nearly deafening with the clacking of keyboard keys. Loud, fast, and hard.

"Faker, you're overextending and these creeps will collapse on you." Helix pulls back one of his headphones and asks, "Who was at the door?"

"Clarissa. She's agreed to be our girlfriend and move in," says Miles, a note of pride in his voice.

The computer screens all freeze as the guys turn in unison to look my way.

"Hi." I wave awkwardly because I really don't know what the protocol here is. I'd always imagined if I were ever to move in with a boyfriend it would be a moment for hugging and excitement. But I don't know these guys. And there are five of them.

"The flyer worked," says Quintin in awe.

When no one else says anything, I decide it's time to go. If this is going to be my future, I might as well start right now. Besides, I need to be out of my current apartment and have it cleaned by end of day tomorrow.

"Well, I'm going to go get started on my packing." I point to the door—as if they don't know which way I'm about to go in their own house. "I'll try to start moving in tonight so I can have everything settled at my apartment tomorrow."

"We have an ARAM tonight so we can't help you then," says Lionel immediately.

"That's what Miles said, and that's okay." I'll need someone to help though, and I can only think of two people who will be willing to help me on such short notice. I don't want to make the call, but I will. I'm annoyed that I'm having to make so many unpleasant choices lately, so many things I wouldn't do under normal circumstances, but I need to keep the end goal in mind. It will all be worth it when I'm a full-time author with an amazing career.

"You'll need a copy of the key," says Helix, reaching into his pocket and producing a set of keys. He finds the one he wants and starts pulling it off. "This way you won't have to interrupt or bother us."

"Thanks." I can't decide if this is sweet or annoying. How many guys will give you not only a key to their place almost as soon as they meet you, but their own key at that? Although Helix is also making it clear that their little game and their needs are above mine even when I'm doing them this favor of agreeing to be their live-in girlfriend.

Well, they're also doing me a big favor, but they don't need to know that part. This isn't a normal relationship where we tell each other everything and confess our deepest secrets. This is a business exchange.

They're all staring at me. Am I supposed to kiss them goodbye or something? I don't want to drag this out any longer than necessary. And I'm not ready to take so much initiative, even if they are handsome. This all feels so quick and sudden. I've just met these guys.

"Okay, good luck with your game. I'll see you later."

"Oh, and Clarissa?" calls Helix when I'm only a few steps from the gaming room. "You get on birth control."

"Uh. Okay." I practically run down the hall and out the front door, desperate to be out of there and away from their intense gazes. This is going to be difficult, but at least I've solved my problem on my own like a big girl without having to call my parents for money.

Although I'm about to call them to borrow their truck. And maybe ask for help carrying my bed frame. I'll just have to figure out how to explain my new living situation to them.

And then there are Helix's parting words.

Chapter Four

It's crazy how fast someone can pack up an entire apartment when they're threatened with eviction. It's all very motivating.

"Thanks again for helping me move," I say the next day, carrying one end of my mattress while Dad carries the other up the stairs.

"Any time, sweetheart, you know that," he grunts.

"Maybe next time give us a little more notice?" asks Mom, lugging a box up behind us. "If you'd told us earlier this week when you found out, we could have gotten a few more people to help us."

"Sorry, with all the planning and packing, it completely slipped my mind." I hate lying to my parents, but I don't want them to know how bad my situation is. If they knew, they'd try to convince me to move home and give college a go. Most of my friends went that route, but it's not for me. I want to be a writer.

Or they would try to give me money. Which they definitely don't have.

"Our daughter has a lot on her mind, love," says Dad, always willing to protect and defend me. I can do no wrong in his eyes. "She has all of her stories and business things, and then the day-to-day stuff too. I'm sure it's a lot to keep track of."

His words are sweet, but they cut even deeper than if he'd agreed with Mom. They can't find out that I'm broke or about to move in with five guys I met because of a flyer. It'd break their hearts.

"All I'm saying is, then we could have picked a day that her new roommates would be home to help, is all," rebuts Mom. To her the world is black and white and it's everyone's duty to help everyone else. And she is not okay with anyone shirking their portion of the heavy lifting of life.

"They have a weird work schedule." *Please don't ask what they do for a job*, I think. That would not impress my parents. "And I had to work around when my critique group meets."

"Well, I hope we at least get to meet them some day," says Dad, lugging more boxes up the steps to stack them carefully in one corner of my new room. It's a bit of a disaster area, but Dad's trying to keep it as organized as possible so we can still move around in the small space. Chicago is not known for its spacious bedrooms.

"I'd like that." I smile at my parents. We're all sweaty from the heavy lifting, and because it's the last nice day between summer and fall, but they came through for me when asked and I love them all the more for it. I even mean what I say. I've always been close to my parents and would love for them to know my roommates. But only as roommates, and I'm not ready for them to meet before these gamers know that I'm keeping my parents in the dark about this single small aspect of my life. I don't want them to let anything slip in front of them.

Okay, maybe two aspects of my life, since I'm not going

to tell them about my slight genre shift, either. They're already weirded out that I write romance books with fade-to-black love scenes. To tell them I'm going to switch to high-heat romances with all the spice might give them an aneurysm. There are just some things we don't talk about in our family, and my sex life or sex fantasy life are definitely on that list.

"Do you need help setting up anything else? Or unpacking?" asks Mom, eyeing the towering stacks of boxes along the wall.

"No, I'm good. Thanks though," I assure them. "We already have the bed set up and I'm not sure exactly how I'm going to arrange the rest of the room yet. There's no rush though, I can do a little bit every day as I make those decisions."

It's starting to get late and I'm not sure how long this ARAM my new roommates mentioned takes because I don't know exactly what it is. My parents need to be out the door and on the road before they finish and come out of their computer room, though.

"We have a long drive, then," says Dad, pulling me into a hug. He's sweaty and so am I, but there's so much love in these arms. "We love you, sweetheart. You call us if you need anything."

"Thanks, Dad." I completely believe him. My parents would rescue me the way they think I need rescuing, but I want to do this on my own. Prove to myself that I'm an adult and can stand on my own two feet.

Well, with the help of my five new boyfriends.

"Take care of yourself, Clarissa." Mom pulls me into the quickest hug imaginable. She turns away to head downstairs, but I swear I catch her wiping her eyes behind her glasses, even if she is trying to be discreet about it.

I follow my parents to the front door and wave goodbye

from the top of the stoop as they drive away. As soon as they turn a corner and are out of sight, I close the door and slump against it. I'm absolutely exhausted from rushing around and doing an entire move in one day.

Trudging back up the stairs, I dig through the boxes labeled "bathroom" until I find my shower things. Right now, I'm really grateful for having my own en suite so I don't have to worry about interacting with any of my roommates or being caught unprepared.

As I wash the sweat from my body, I think that this house might be a little run down, but at least it has amazing water pressure.

Once I'm clean, I feel better. I have a place to live and a path forward. However, because my packing was so chaotic, I can only find a hand towel to dry myself off. Unpacking is definitely moving up on my list of priorities.

Walking out into my bedroom to look for one of the boxes with my clothes, I am met with a sight that has me scrambling to cover as much of myself with my tiny towel as possible.

Ethan is standing in the middle of the room looking around as if it's a museum and not my bedroom.

I guess their whatever-it-is is over then.

"Can I help you?" I try to remember if I'd closed my door or not. I'm so tired though, I can't remember. Either way, my door is standing wide open now. And I don't want to tell him off for not knocking if I'd left the door open in invitation to anyone passing by.

"So, are you our girlfriend now?" Ethan has a soft voice. I realize this is the first time I'm hearing it. He looks even more uncertain than I am about this situation.

"I ... guess so?" I dig a little through the nearest box for anything I can use to cover myself up while glancing back at the bathroom. Which option would hide me quicker?

"I pentakilled today," says Ethan, fisting the ends of his sleeves over his hands.

He says it so simply, I can't help but stop my search and look up. "Is that good or bad? Because I don't know what that means."

"It's good." Ethan nods, more to himself than to me since he's still not looking at me. "Can I kiss you then?"

Clearly we're starting right away with all the benefits of being in the middle of a relationship. None of the get-to-know-each-other first dates. Just right into the deep end.

Unless Ethan really means he only wants a kiss, and nothing more.

Part of me wants to say no. I've had a rough day, making a big, life-changing decision and moving my entire life into this room. But this is the agreement. I'm their girlfriend and I need to make myself available as they requested.

"... Okay." I suppose there's no better time to hold up my end of the bargain and start my own research. I can do this. I just need to pull on my big girl pants and kiss this stranger I just moved in with.

Except I guess I can't pull up my big girl pants, because I can't find any of the boxes with my clothing in it, but the point still stands.

"Okay," repeats Ethan as he shuffles over to where I'm standing, still shielding myself with the hand towel.

Ethan places his hands on my bare shoulders. It's a little bit shocking—I knew it was coming, his touching my bare skin, but it's still a surprise. He's focused on my lips, and I can't help but stare at his own. At the way he bites his bottom lip a little in anticipation, so when he moves closer there's the tiniest markings where his teeth were a moment ago.

He's moving so slowly, it's making me more anxious, and I just want to get this first time out of the way. Thinking about something and prepping for it is painful. Let's rip the BandAid right off this entire situation so I am no longer freaking out, and can no longer back out.

Leaning forward ever so slightly, I meet Ethan's lips with my own. I capture his mouth in a kiss that's both tentative and warm. His lips are plush and the perfect amount of moist, with a slight hint of mint. It makes me wonder if he made the effort of a special trip to the bathroom to use mouthwash and rolled on a sheen of lip balm.

He's not a bad kisser.

I slip my tongue along his lips and Ethan eagerly joins, taking this kiss deeper. I thought I wouldn't like it, that I'd have to treat this as a job. But if one of the very few first dates I've gone on gave me a goodnight kiss like this, I would have agreed to a second date so fast. It only feels natural to wrap my arms around his neck, letting my fingers delve into the back of his blond, wavy hair.

Gasping a little, I realize I've dropped my towel to my feet and am completely naked before this man whom I've essentially just met. Ethan slips his tongue past my lips and the student becomes the master as he explores the possibilities of our kiss. He's either a quick learner or has plenty of experience.

Initially, I'd been cataloging feelings for my writing, but now I'm just experiencing it. There's so much more to explore, to research. How deep into this situation am I willing to go, and how fast? Am I going to hold my new supposed boyfriends off for as long as possible, thereby denying me access to hands on research? Or am I fully committing to this new path that I've chosen, starting right now?

My hands run down the front of Ethan's shirt until they land on the drawstring of his pants.

Ethan breaks off our kiss but doesn't back away. "Are you sure?"

"You're my boyfriend, right?" My heart flutters and my hands shake, but I keep my eyes trained on Ethan's lips. Eyes are too personal right now. This is business, and I need to sleep with this man to become the author I deserve to be.

"Yes," he whispers, and I swear his breathing nearly stops, it's so ragged.

Gathering all my courage, I undo the tie of Ethan's drawstring and slowly push his waistband down. I've agreed to this exchange and I'm not backing down. I'm collecting all the research material I possibly can because I'm determined to be a good writer. And this will be the best way.

Before Ethan's sweatpants reach the floor of my new room, he fishes in his pocket and pulls out a condom. *At least one of us is prepared.* The back of my hand brushes against the bulge in his boxers and ... he's more than prepared. He's ready for action.

Rotating my hand, I cup him in my palm, but he's too big. I can feel my own breathing matching his. It's been a long time since I've dated, let alone slept with someone. And here I am, about to get down and dirty with a practical stranger. This is so illicit and wrong. I've never done anything like this. I've always been the good girl.

It's about time I let myself get a little dirty. So I push his boxers to the floor too.

Ethan's hands are everywhere, never settling. There's an edge of desperation in his movements, like he's afraid I'm going to disappear. Not that I blame him. I'm just as fumbling as we fall back onto my unmade bed. We're both nervous, and this is our first time together. It's best to get it over with.

Ethan nudges my legs apart to fit his hips between my thighs, and I help him slide on the condom, both of our hands shaking. This is happening. I'm doing this. Wrapping my hand around his cock, I measure how many fingertips don't touch and I'd have to stack both of my fists to cover the entire length. Before I can get too intimidated and back out, I shift my hips to line him up with my entrance.

"Fuck," he breaths out as he slowly slides inside me, his hair flopping forward to brush my forehead.

It's tight, but somehow the wrongness of this whole situation has excited me, and I'm wet and ready. Ethan presses in until our hips are locked together and I'm filled with him. All I can do is breathe and appreciate the feeling of fullness. This is what my characters will feel every time they're with their own boyfriends.

Ethan's hands brace on either side of my shoulders as he pulls back a little bit, only to slam into me completely.

"You feel so good," groans Ethan. "I want to make you feel good too."

It does feel amazing to have a strange man pressed so close against every inch of my naked body. But I could feel better, and I'm used to getting myself off since I don't date anymore.

I slip my hand between our bodies, his shirt gaping down to graze my bare chest, and as soon as I brush a single fingertip over my clit, I'm gasping. It's so different to touch myself while at the same time being filled with a cock. Especially when the cock moves again, dragging the fullness in and out.

"That's so hot," whispers Ethan, pushing up to watch the way my fingers play with myself as his cock disappears inside my body.

He speeds up, fucking me faster in quick, shallow thrusts. I work my clit in tight circles, matching Ethan's pace and watching right along with him. I can't believe this is happening. It feels so overwhelming and encapsulating, as if there's a huge bubble inside of me that's about to burst. It's never felt like this before when I go solo late at night. Is this what I've been missing out on? If that's the case, I should have bought a dildo years ago.

Ethan's cock twitches inside my pussy and I swear, it's getting even bigger. Tilting my hips, I lean into the feeling and give myself over. An obscene moan escapes my lips as I cry out in release, my hand falling to the side as I ride the wave of pleasure.

Ethan's cock strokes my pussy through the final tremors before he collapses on top of me, crushing my body beneath his. His weight feels good, comforting even, as the after-tremors of my orgasm flutter through my limbs.

Only when he rolls off me do I register that it's a bit cold in here, naked and with the window open. It'd been so hot earlier in the day, but with the sheen of sweat on my body, it's too much. Great, the whole neighborhood probably heard us. I'm itching to pull a blanket out of a packing box and cover myself up. To hide my nudity and embarrassment.

I just had sex with a complete stranger, and even worse, I enjoyed it. What kind of person does that make me?

Ethan sits up and looks back at me over his shoulder as he ties off the condom. He's biting his lip again, sending covert glances down at my naked body while he gathers his discarded clothes and pulls them on.

"Thank you." He hurries out of the room, the door still wide open.

Shoot. I don't think we remembered to close it before having sex. Did I seriously fuck a stranger with my bedroom door open and four other guys in the house? Yet more people I have to worry about having overheard my sex-noises.

I don't have a lot of experience with boyfriends, and

absolutely no experience with one-night stands, but I'm pretty sure that's not how this is supposed to end—with the guy hurrying away as if he's embarrassed. I'd been hoping at least *they* would know how this whole situation is supposed to progress. They're the ones who put up the flyer.

I'll have to ask if they had a live-in girlfriend before, and how they had it work with her if they did. So many questions I should have asked before moving in, but my choice is made. I need to focus on the future and what I'm getting out of this situation.

Sitting up, I dig through my boxes for a notebook, pulling on the first pieces of clothing my hands land on as I search. Then I close my eyes and mentally relive my encounter, however brief, with Ethan. I write down how it felt to kiss him, and where his hands traveled over my body, cupping my flesh. My blush deepens even with the memory as I jot down little details about him caging in my body as I lay beneath him on the bed, his hands bracketing either side of my head. And the moment his cock entered and stretched my pussy, filling me over and over again.

It's so embarrassing to write these private thoughts and feelings down, but thankfully no one will ever know or see it. I need to write it all down so I don't forget all the tiny details. The slap of his hips, or the few times my fingers trailed from toying with my own clit to brush his shaft as it slid in and out of my wet pussy. Even using these words is embarrassing, but I need to get comfortable with them. If I'm going to be a respected spicy romance writer, this is what will be expected of me. And I'm determined to begin as I mean to go on.

I'll have to figure out what type of story I'm writing, besides a steamy one, but that can wait until tomorrow. Once my room is a bit more unpacked and I know where my laptop actually is. I've already made so many decisions today, I can't make another.

I don't even want to go downstairs and tell the guys, my new boyfriends, that I'm all moved in. Mostly. I just want to fall asleep and pretend I'm not using my body to get ahead in my writing career, and that I'm not depending on men to support me financially while I do it.

Chapter Five

When I wake up the next morning, the house is quiet. I decide I might as well make myself comfortable since I don't know how long I'll live here, and will probably spend a lot of time in my room. I can't imagine it'll be comfortable hanging out in the living room with all the guys. There will probably be a weird line between this being a job and my actually being able to actually relax as a person in my own house.

I'm resigned to spending most of my time between these four walls, so I'm setting everything up to be as conducive to working as possible. It'll be good to just focus on my writing —after all, that's the whole reason I'm putting up with this ridiculous agreement. I'll write an amazing, super hot romance using all the techniques the gamers downstairs teach me, and I'll earn enough money off it to move out and live on my own again, this time as a successful author.

It's not until my stomach rumbles for the third time that I brave stepping out into the hall. I've been on edge all morning and avoiding going down to breakfast. I need to learn from these gamers, but it's nerve-wracking. I just met them. They say we're dating now, but this isn't how things normally work. And I know they said food is included, but do they have anything good in the kitchen? More questions I should have thought to ask before I moved in, but there was no time, what with my being evicted from my last apartment.

The stairs creak as I sneak downstairs. I live here now so I shouldn't have to sneak, but I'm hiding from my new so-called boyfriends. I mean, Ethan showed up in my room last night to fuck me. Obviously they know I'm here.

When I reach the bottom of the stairs, I realize I have no idea where the kitchen is in this house. *Time to explore, I guess.*

I follow the main hallway farther back into the house, taking in the general shabbiness of the place. Do they not see it, or do they not care?

The door to their computer room is open, and even though I'm not supposed to go in, I can't help but take a peek. It's dark, save for a few bright neon rope lights glowing. I have a laptop that I love, but I could never imagine setting up something like what they have. So many cords and screens. And cameras, for some reason.

The house is still silent, and I wonder if they're even home. If I'm here by myself, I really will feel ridiculous for having spent so much time hiding in my room when I could have been snooping around to figure out who these guys I'm living with really are.

I continue following the hallway and eventually end up in the kitchen. It's actually pretty spacious, with lots of counter space around the walls and a big table in the center of the room. It's not as messy as the rest of the house, but there are still dishes piled in the sink even though there's a dishwasher not two feet away. But I'm not their maid, so it's not my problem. Their flyer said nothing about cleaning up after them, and they didn't say anything about it yesterday or at that first interview, so I'm not doing it.

They probably would have gotten way more responses to their flyer, though, if they'd simply been looking for a live-in housekeeper. Not that that would help me research for my book, but it sure would've been less weird.

A box of cereal is sitting out on the counter, but I peek through the cupboards to check what else they have. It's surprisingly well-stocked. Not necessarily with ingredients, but with snacks and ready-to-eat items. None of my normal go-to choices, though. I'll have to either pick up a few things for myself or figure out where they keep their shopping list.

Cereal it is, then. I shouldn't complain—it's not like I expected gourmet meals. And I can at least appreciate the peace and quiet of being alone.

Except one of the guys—Lionel, I think—chooses that moment to walk in. *Welp, there goes my peace.* He's the one who told me they couldn't help me move, which didn't exactly give the impression that he's the friendliest of the group. Hopefully he just grabs something and leaves so I don't have to be Miss Sunshine this morning and make small talk. I'm not sure if our arrangement means I need to be sweet all the time and make them think they're special and that I really like them, or if I can be myself so long as I put out for them.

But Lionel does not just grab a granola bar and leave. Instead, he shakes coffee grounds into the coffeemaker, filling the room with the warming scent of happiness. At least the soft bubbling of the percolation breaks the awkward silence as I cast furtive glances to where he stands at the counter, watching me slowly eat my cereal as if I'm not panicking on the inside that he's here and I don't know what's going to happen. We aren't characters, and I'm not in control of this scene. *An author's worst nightmare.*

"I heard you already started the job," he says, leaning back against the counter. Watching me.

Not sure what to say to that, I take another bite of my cereal and try to pretend I'm not blushing like crazy. He must be referring to last night with Ethan, and I'm not sure how I feel about that. Or how he found out. Are the gamers talking about me? Comparing notes? Way for them to take an already weird situation and make it even worse.

The best way I can handle this is probably to act as if I'm not panicking. They hired me to do this as a job. There is nothing more between us.

"That's why I'm here, right?" At least, that's why they think I'm here. There's no way I'm going to let them know about my little notebook. They still haven't even asked what I do for a job. If they don't care about me as a person, they don't get to care if some of their moves make it between my pages.

"So if I told you to get down on your knees for me right now, you would?"

I slowly pull the spoon out of my mouth, shooting a reflexive look at the front of Lionel's pants. I'm not actually interested in Lionel's crotch, or in him, or any of them. They're just my contractual boyfriends for while I'm living here. Nothing more.

Is this what it's going to be like the whole time? Me going about my regular everyday life and them asking me to drop whatever I'm doing to service them? I suspected I wouldn't love this job, but I didn't think they would be demeaning and demanding.

The coffee is ready, and I still haven't said anything. But Lionel hasn't said anything else either. He pours himself a cup of coffee, doctoring it up with some of the sugar from the bowl sitting out on the counter and giving me a break from his fixated stare.

If I were one of the characters in one of Sasha's romantasy books, what would I do? If I'm going to do this, to live with these guys and write explicit books, I need to channel my new, sexually confident characters.

Straightening my shoulders, I set down my spoon. Before I lose my nerve, I cross the room and kneel at Lionel's feet. He finishes stirring his coffee and turns back to me, nearly tripping over my kneeling form. There's a flash of surprise across his face, and his eyes darken. He takes in my position slowly as he blindly sets his mug on the counter. All of his focus is on me, kneeling at his feet, waiting for instructions.

"Well, go on then," he says, glancing down.

The wood floor is hard under my knees and the bulge in his pants grows as the moment stretches out. Even if this wasn't his plan, he isn't going to say no.

I've never given a blow job before. The only boyfriend I've had was more of an only-missionary and only-in-the-dark type of person, so everything I know about oral sex has come from reading sex scenes at my critique group. I'm on completely untried terrain.

I reach up, my hands disappearing under the hem of Lionel's shirt as I gently hook my fingers into the waistband of his sweatpants and pull the elastic away from his stomach without actually touching his skin, then inch the fabric down. It feels awkward to undress someone, especially in a kitchen. But glancing up, I see that Lionel's hands are braced around the edge of the counter and his focus is completely on my movements.

I'm expecting a second layer—boxers, briefs—but he is completely naked beneath his sweatpants, and his stiff cock springs forth, startling me. I can't help but glance up at him, waiting for him to laugh, but he's completely serious as he bites his lip and watches my reaction.

He's so big that I'm not sure how he'll fit in my mouth, let alone anywhere else. I could still back out, tell him I'm not interested and return to my cereal. But then I would have to move out. The agreement was that I have to do all the girlfriend things, and Lionel apparently expects his girlfriend to suck his cock in the kitchen. *None of this is real,* I remind myself. It's just a fantasy for them, and a research project for me.

If I were a character in a spicy romance novel, I would suck this cock so good.

Gingerly, I run my fingertips over his hard length, testing his girth and weight. It feels both velvety soft and completely solid.

"Lick it," says Lionel, his voice gruff.

I've never tasted a cock before and suddenly I'm swallowing hard, more nervous than I should be. *People do this all the time. I can do it.* Remembering how the characters in my critique partners' books do it, I slowly lean forward to run the tip of my tongue along the vein on the underside of his cock, from sack to head. I treat it like I would an ice cream cone on a hot day, licking up all the little drips as it slowly melts before swirling my tongue around the tip to make the ice cream spiral up into a perfect point.

It tastes a little salty, not at all like ice cream, but it doesn't taste bad. If it was ice cream, it would be more like a salted caramel than the mint chocolate chip I usually get. I lean in to taste his cock again so I can really judge, rolling the flavor around on my tongue.

When I flick my tongue over the tip, Lionel groans, a deep rumble in his chest that reverberates through my body. I want to make him do that again. To balance my learning to enjoy having his cock in my mouth with his enjoyment of my sucking him off. I repeat the flick to see if he'll groan again.

"Less teasing," he says, and my nipples harden at the

command. "I want to see your lips wrapped around my cock."

Okay, maybe cocks are more like popsicles than ice cream cones. I wrap my hand around his hard shaft, my fingers unable to touch, angling him just right for how tall I am on my knees. I'm not sure how I'll fit something this wide in my mouth. I lick my lips before stretching them around Lionel's cock. My mouth feels stuffed, and I've barely taken any of him in.

He's so big, he's flattening my tongue so I can't swallow, let alone breathe.

"Just relax. You can take it." Lionel strokes my face.

I bet he can feel the pressure of his finger on his cock through my cheek. The idea of him stroking himself through me has my thighs clenching, and I inch a little closer to take in more of his impressive length. Hopefully I'm doing this right, and Lionel is enjoying his blow job. From how hard his cock is, I assume so. What's really surprising is that I'm not hating it.

Slackening my jaw, I'm able to ease another inch into my mouth. It's still difficult to swallow, and I suck hard so I don't embarrass myself with the amount of saliva threatening to drip down his thick shaft.

"Fuck," groans Lionel. "There's nothing teasing about this. You're no OTP."

I have no idea what that means, but it's clearly a good thing. I like to be good at things. The vibrating pleasure between my thighs increases with his words and I redouble my efforts until the tip of his cock hits the back of my throat, cutting off my airway completely, and I'm gagging.

Only when I'm desperate for air does he pull back enough for me to gasp a breath before shoving his cock back into my throat. Then out in quick strokes. His hands slide into my hair, holding my head in place, and my palms are glued to Lionel's hips. I want to reach around to grip his ass, to touch more of his bare skin, to hold him close ... or maybe I want to reach down between my own legs and see exactly how wet I am. I shouldn't be, but I am. Just like last night, the illicitness of this behavior has me soaked with my own arousal.

"Such a good girl. I'm so close," he groans.

His grip on my hair is tight as he moves my head on and off of his cock, and I'm loving every moment. The feeling of letting go and allowing my body to just exist in this moment. There's a freedom here in not having to do everything myself. My palms are no longer resting on Lionel's hips, but pressing, urging him on.

Footsteps approach, and all my good feelings evaporate in a flood of panic. No one can see me doing this. We need to stop before we're caught.

"Shh, it's okay," says Lionel, still fucking my mouth. I try to protest, but I can't make a sound with his cock down my throat.

"Well, good morning," says a voice.

I'm not sure who it is, because my eyes are squeezed shut in embarrassment at being caught giving one of my new boyfriends a blow job, and even worse, at the fact that I've been enjoying it. What if whoever it is can tell how much I like having a cock in my mouth?

"Fuck!" Lionel slams his hips forward once more, and ropes of cum slide down my throat, his cock pulsing against my lips. "Yes, it is absolutely a good morning."

As soon as Lionel releases my hair and slouches back against the counter, I'm on my feet, swiping my hand over the saliva and cum mingling on my chin and dashing out of the kitchen. I can't look any of my new roommates in the eye now because I don't even know who came in on us. I'm blushing and completely turned on and I hope to everything they didn't notice.

Closing my bedroom door, I lean against it, blocking any of the gamers from following me. My knees and jaw ache, and I wait for the regret or guilt to sink in, but all I feel is embarrassed at getting caught.

And at how much I enjoyed it.

Lionel called me a good girl.

My hand sneaks down inside the waistband of my jeans. I imagine his voice telling me I'm a good girl as my fingers slide over the soaked gusset of my cotton panties. This is what his words do to me. The way he held my jaw open with his big cock. The way he gripped my hair and fucked my face with no way for me to stop it.

I slip my underwear to the side and my fingers slide right through my wet slit. *They never need to know I'm doing this.*

As my fingers delve inside my pussy, I imagine they're Ethan's cock again as Lionel calls me a good girl. In practically no time at all, I'm coming so hard I see stars.

Chapter Six

Two days later, I still can't believe I did something so brazen as pleasure Lionel in the middle of the kitchen. Of *course* someone walked in on us. We weren't even trying to be subtle. The fact that I hadn't been able to see who it was at the time, and never looked up as I dashed back to the seclusion of my room, has turned whoever it was into a stranger. Obviously I don't really know any of my new roommates, so they're all strangers, but this was a faceless one. A random man watching my "boyfriend" shove his cock as deep down my throat as he could get it.

Every time I think about it too long, I start getting warm and squirming at my desk chair until the temptation is too much and I sprawl on my bed and touch myself as quietly as possible so none of my new boyfriends hears me. Afterward, I feel like I've done something wrong. These gamers hired me to take care of their needs, not my own. I didn't even fully realize I *had* needs like this.

At least all of these bubbled up, conflicting feelings have been great for my writing. I've produced more work in these two days than I have in the last few months. Everything going through my mind, every flicker of emotion and physical sensation that's gone through my body, has ended up on my pages, experienced by a character.

I'm nervous about what my critique group will say about this change in my writing. I haven't told them I'm switching from writing sweet romance to high-spice. It's already uncomfortable for me to read and discuss the explicit scenes they've written, and now it's going to be mine. They'll all know that I've thought about these fantasies.

At least they won't know that I've actually lived them.

Slipping out of the house to come to critique group is the first time I've left my room since the kitchen incident. That's how I'm thinking about it—*the kitchen incident*. I've been surviving in my room on snacks I'd brought from my old apartment. Writing, masturbating, and snacking on a loop has become my new normal.

Honestly, I'm kind of surprised that none of the gamers barged into my room, or even knocked. They hired me for a job that I'd barely started before I went into hiding. How can I look them in the eye again, though?

That's a problem for later, after critique group.

My train was late, so the other ladies are already chatting at our regular table. I slide into my normal seat as quietly as possible so as not to interrupt. I'm just lucky that they let me be part of their group. We all write slightly different subgenres, and they're all further along in their careers than me. As in, they're all actually making money.

Critique group always meets during happy hour because a drink or two helps make it a little easier to discuss the sex scenes in their books. I'm going to need at least one or two extra myself today, since my own sex scenes will be on the table.

Maybe literally, one day. There is a table in our kitchen. I wonder if any of the guys has ever considered using it for—

No, I scold myself. *I'm here to focus on work.*

The conversation stops as I slide into my seat, everyone's heads swiveling in my direction. "We have to talk about your new pages," says Angela, a small-town romance author.

I snag a menu from the table even though I get the same thing every time. I need a moment before I have to look my critique partners in the eye.

I don't like being called out in this way. Normally the other ladies keep talking for a few minutes, not even acknowledging my arrival. But discussing our work is why we're here, so I force a smile. "I'd like that very much. Thank you."

"Oh, my god! Your pages this week! Am I the only one who needed a minute to take care of themselves after reading that?" Maddie, who writes billionaire romance, fans herself theatrically.

"Do you want to go first?" Sasha pulls out her stack of our weekly writing submissions. There's red ink all over the page. "It's not bad." She pauses. "For a first attempt."

My stomach roils at the sight of all that red ink, but this is why I'm here in this group. To get feedback from authors whose opinions I respect. I want my writing to be the best it can be. These ladies are helping me achieve my dreams. They want the best for me too.

"Ooo, yes. Let's order our drinks, and then I need to talk about these pages." Maddie pulls out her copy of my chapter. There's a few markings in the margins, but nothing terrifying like what Sasha's copy has on it.

"Agreed," says Angela. "Drinks first. I'm going to need them before we get to my new pages. It's been a rough week."

My shoulders relax. I'm so nervous to hear what these ladies think of my new writing. It's so far from my normal style and I wrote it so fast, I'm not even confident about what's on those pages. All I know is that every word was inspired by Ethan, Lionel, and whichever stranger watched me choke on cock on the kitchen floor.

The other ladies order cocktails, but I take a house wine. It's on the happy hour list and the cheapest option, and I'm broke. I may need to have two today to get through this ordeal. But people need to read my work at some point in order for me to make it as an author, and there's no sense in me having started down this path of new sex acts if I'm not going to use them as inspiration.

It doesn't take long for our drinks to arrive. Pulling out my own copy of my chapter, I get my pen ready to note down any and all comments my critique partners are ready to dole out.

"Well, I for one would love for the new book boyfriend you're writing to just step out of the pages and take care of me like that." Angela laughs and fans herself. "I had to read your chapter twice this week. The first time I raced through with such enjoyment, I needed a second time to catch the one or two places that could be a little stronger."

"I'm glad you like him," I say, blushing. "This is my first attempt at spicy writing so any advice you can give would be appreciated."

Angela shows me her copy of my pages and points to the first circled paragraph. "This section here seems a little redundant—you don't need to describe the layout of the room as the characters change positions. And this section here," she points to another circle, "was just a bit quick for me. Even if the characters are rushing through the act, that doesn't mean the writing of the scene should be quick. We still want to draw the emotions out with more about the inner feelings and thoughts of the FMC."

"Thank you. That's very helpful." I jot down notes in the margins of my own pages by those sections. I'm so glad

Angela is giving me concrete things to improve and not making me feel bad about the change in my writing.

"This is quite different from your normal work," says Sasha with an appraising look as she sips her pink cosmo.

"Yeah." I shift a little under Sasha's gaze and take a large gulp of my wine, but both Angela and Maddie have friendly, open faces, and I remind myself that they're all here to help me succeed. "I wasn't making much money with the sweet romances, so I thought I would try writing a bit more to market. And readers seem to want the spice."

I don't want to come out and say, *Hey, I saw you change up your business strategy and I wanted to do the same. I don't want her to think I'm copying her. That could jeopardize our friendship.*

"When I was doing my research for my new genre, I did a spreadsheet with all of the statistical data for each genre so I could find the gap between want and supply. Did you use my method? Are you subscribed to all of the reports so you can get the monthly updates on all of the analytics?" Sasha glances over her copy of my chapter, with all the red ink. "If you're not going to do it properly, there's no sense in even getting feedback on something that won't sell anyway."

"Umm." I glance to Maddie and Angela, who both roll their eyes at Sasha's comments. "I thought I would just try writing what I already enjoy, just adding more spice for the readers."

I take another sip of my wine. Sasha's comments hurt because not only is she my critique partner, but I see her as a friend too, and I want her to be proud of me. Yet she's making me feel like I haven't done enough. I wish I could tell her that I'm doing a lot behind the scenes to get these pages to be so amazing, but I'm not about to tell anyone about my current living arrangement.

"I like that," says Maddie. "If you're enjoying yourself,

the reader will sense it and enjoy themselves too. I think that really came through in this chapter."

"I'm just not sure that will be enough," says Sasha. "The research I did showed that I needed to switch from contemporary to romantasy to make a name for myself." Sasha pauses, laying her hand on the table and leaning forward. "I'm only saying this because I want you to succeed."

"And I really appreciate that. I'll look into it more." I probably should do that, but dipping my toes into the reality of writing sex is hard enough. Shifting into a different subgenre at the same time would be too overwhelming. Instead of relearning just part of my career, I would almost be relearning the entire thing.

Although, while Angela and Maddie do well as authors, Sasha is the most successful of all of us. Maybe I really should do what she says and switch from contemporary to a more specific subgenre.

"You've clearly done some of your research though," says Sasha, almost reluctantly. "Your sex scenes aren't terrible for your first try. And you've never had a boyfriend since I've known you."

Here it comes. Sasha is going to ask me how I've been researching these scenes, and she's going to try to pry it out of me. It's going to be so embarrassing. Not only can I not get a boyfriend on my own, but now I'm sleeping with five guys for money. Well, room and board, but same difference.

"You've probably started watching porn," suggests Angela. "I've been telling you to watch for ages. Didn't I tell you? Great inspiration."

"And reading other high heat books," says Sasha, giving Angela a sideways look.

"Oh sure, books too. Anything, really, to get the blood

flowing to all the right places," agrees Angela, doing a little shimmy. "First the blood flows, and then the fingers fly."

"You're talking about fingers flying on the keyboard, right?" asks Maddie, barely holding back a laugh. "Not on anything else?"

"Like I said," says Angela with a smirk of her own. "First one, and then the other."

By the time we've finished with everyone's chapters for the week, happy hour is about to end so we order a second round of drinks to take advantage of the cheaper prices. I normally only have the one even though they're cheaper, but I'm not paying rent anymore and my new chapter went well, so I decide to splurge a little.

Besides, a second glass of wine will be the perfect excuse for the glow I feel radiating from me. This critique session was the first time my critique partners have recognized me as a good writer instead of the little author they take pity on to make themselves feel better, even as they gatekeep all their trade secrets.

To be their complete equal is a dream. Even just listening to their critiques of each other's work is helpful. I'll go home tonight with a mental list of positions to maybe try with my new boyfriends. Attempting them in real life before making my characters do something similar would probably be best.

Maybe by the end of my second drink I'll have the nerve to ask my critique group if they think the same way. Or maybe because I had such limited sexual interactions with my high school boyfriend and am only now experimenting with sex, my mind is more tuned in to the possibilities—at least more than before.

This is definitely something to consider. Will the guys change just my writing, or will they change me too?

"So what made you decide to make such a sudden change to your writing?" asks Sasha the moment Maddie and Angela step away from our table.

"I've been contemplating it for a while," I say, playing with the stem of my wineglass. This is, of course, not true. It wasn't until I saw the flyer that the idea started playing over and over in my head. "And I just sort of decided that you were making good points when you were talking about the market, and what did I have to lose? So why not give it a try and see if I'm any good at writing spice."

"And turns out that you're a natural." Sasha eyes me over the rim of her cosmo.

"Thanks." While it is still technically a compliment from Sasha, she doesn't really sound impressed with my writing. Especially given that she marked it up so much. "But like everyone pointed out today, I still have aspects of writing spicy to work out."

"Mmm," murmurs Sasha. "You never did say earlier, what are you using for research?"

"Oh," I hesitate. "Just like what you all said. Well, not the porn part, but reading other books with higher spice. Noting how those authors set things up, not only in the bedroom, but between the couples, so I can learn from their techniques."

That part is true at least. I did read two or three high-heat books, or at least I tried. I was so convinced someone was going to catch me out and tell me I shouldn't be reading such filth in the exact voice my parents would use that I stopped, but I do mean to start again. Maybe it will also give me a better grasp on what the guys expect from me.

"We should buddy read then." Sasha sets down her glass and looks me in the face as if daring me to refuse her offer. "We can do our research together and that will make it easier on both of us."

"Yeah, sure that sounds good." Now I really will have to read these books, and get brave about discussing the intimate details of book sex with Sasha so she doesn't realize that I've been doing hands-on research with my new roommates.

Maybe before I discuss the scenes with her, I can come up with a way to suggest the moves to my boyfriends —just so I don't come across as a complete novice to Sasha.

"Perfect." Sasha checks her phone. "We need to get moving if we're going to make our train."

"Actually, I have a little bit because I need to take a different train." I won't have anyone to ride home with now that I've moved, which makes me a little nervous safety-wise, but Sasha and I got off at different stops anyway so I suppose it doesn't affect too much.

Maddie and Angela slide back into their seats in time to say goodbye to Sasha.

"Are you going somewhere else after this?" Sasha gathers her things, eyeing me curiously.

"Oh, a date perhaps?" asks Angela.

"You're still so new to town, you have so many options for good dates. Tell us all about him," says Maddie, leaning toward me in hopes of some good gossip.

"No, nothing like that. I just moved is all. Since my lease was up and I didn't love that place enough to renew." Sort of true. My old apartment wasn't the most amazing thing ever, but I would have renewed if the rent wasn't going up outrageously because living alone was fantastic. Although my new roommates haven't been loud, and we haven't had any issues yet. I did just move in, though, so there is still plenty of time for that to happen.

"Well, that's exciting still," says Angela.

"Not as exciting a date, but fun," agrees Maddie.

"Wait, is this the address where you were going the other day?" asks Sasha, pulling up the text message on her phone. "I thought you were afraid they were going to kill you, yet you've already moved in?"

"Yikes, that's a quick turnaround on impressions," laughs Angela.

"How many roommates are there then?" asks Maddie.

"Five." I laugh a little to make it seem funny and not intimidating. "But they keep to themselves mostly so it should be fine."

Again, technically true. They have kept mostly to themselves, except for the sexy times.

"Well, they say don't shit where you eat," says Maddie, "but maybe they have friends they could introduce you to and then you really could have a date."

"Yeah, sleeping with roommates always gets messy," agrees Angela.

"Lots of new changes then," says Sasha, bringing the attention back to her. "Anyway, message me this week with your next research read and we can go through it together with an author's eye."

She leaves me to listen to Angela and Maddie bemoan their own lack of decent date prospects until it's time for me to catch my own train.

Chapter Seven

It's such a relief to have that first critique session with my new work over. I hadn't realized how stressful it was going to be to take critiques about a new heat level.

As soon as I step inside the house I'm tempted to creep upstairs to my room and hide away, but because tonight's critique session went so well, there will be higher expectations for my next set of pages. Which means I need to do more research. Which means I should probably put in some face time with my boyfriends.

Dropping my bag by the foot of the stairs—if I bring it to my room, I know I won't come back down—I venture deeper into the house in search of my roommates. Maybe they're shut up in their computer room again where I'm not allowed. Or upstairs in their own individual rooms. I'd consider either option lucky, but then I wouldn't be doing what I need to here. Collecting inspiration for my books.

There's a lot of chatter and noise coming from back near the kitchen, so I head that way.

And ... no one is there.

However, there is a door that's partly opened. I'd thought it was a pantry or broom cupboard, but now I see that it seems to be a basement. This is an older house, and I'm sure it's going to be super creepy down there. *The things authors do for their careers.*

Closing my eyes, I take a deep breath, then open them and start down the stairs. Hopefully there are no cobwebs. Or mice.

The steps are a little rickety, and as soon as I'm part way down, I squat down so I can peek between the railing bars to see what I'm walking into, hoping none of my roommates sees me first.

It's dark down there. The walls are dark. The ceiling is dark. The floor is dark. There's an oversized black sofa in the middle of the room facing a projector screen. Helix stands by the screen, pointing things out using big sweeping hand movements. The others watch intently from the sofa, but I'm not sure what they're watching. It must be paused at the moment because nothing is moving. It's almost like a big map with weirdly bright colors in the corners, blues and purples.

I can't tell if they're working or not, but they never said I couldn't come down here. Of course, they hadn't shown me that this room exists, either.

Though they'd also never shown me that the kitchen exists, but I'm still allowed to use it.

It doesn't matter. I stop arguing with myself and scoot a little farther down the stairs to see better.

"You can come down and join us if you want," says Miles, glancing over at where I crouch on the dark stairs.

I stand and force my legs to carry me down the stairs into the room. The only light in the room is from the projector screen, and I'm careful not to trip over anything as I make my way through the dark. I'm not sure where to sit, and finally settle on perching on the back of the U-shaped sofa.

Maybe my new boyfriends don't know what to do either now that I'm here in their space. Maybe they aren't as confident as I thought. Maybe they're also figuring this out as we go.

"So ... what are you watching?" It's the most basic question I can think of to ask. It's not like I can ask what they want from me, or why they let me hole up in my room for a few days and didn't pressure me to give up any of the benefits they'd hired me for, even though I desperately want the answers to those questions.

"We're going over game footage for the next team we scrim," explains Helix, looking around the group for backup.

"This way we can see what their go-to moves are. Learn their patterns and weaknesses," adds Quintin. "Choose our champions wisely so we can counter their damage."

"Oh, like the way football teams analyze their own games or the games of the teams they're about to go up against." I didn't realize gamers would do the same. I mean, from how much they seem to play their game, I assumed they were serious about it, but I didn't realize it would go so far as this.

"Yes, exactly like football teams," says Helix, pinching the bridge of his nose in annoyance. "Because esports are real sports."

"Oh, yeah, of course." I shift uncomfortably on the back of the sofa. I didn't mean to insult them, but I've never met an esport team before them. I've never even met a single player. Or at least not someone who openly admitted to being a professional esport player.

There's an awkward silence that none of us seems to know how to fill. But if I were trying to date these guys for real, I would take an interest in what they do for a living. I try again.

"So have you found any weaknesses you can exploit?" I ask, then wonder if I shouldn't have said anything else. I'm completely in the weeds here, and I don't want to be in the way. I'd rather they keep going, pretend I'm not here, and let me listen. It'd be its own type of research.

"The other team tends to counter jungle, so we're going to choose champions with ward abilities to block off not only the jungle entrances, but the gank paths too," explains Helix, pointing out different areas on the map. "Of course, each of those potential champions have weaknesses of their own, and we'll need to weigh out if they're worth the risks."

"That sounds like a difficult choice." I've got no idea what they're really talking about, but it does sound complicated and like they're making a big decision. However, it's just a silly game, so I'm not sure why it matters.

"It really is," agrees Miles. "Their team often chooses the same characters each time though, so that at least helps."

"It'll be a clown fiesta no matter what," says Quintin, looking around at his teammates. "You know *they're* not having a strategy meeting right now."

"Don't be toxic, Arrow," complains Lionel. "We need to stay on top of our play. If they want to be feeders, that's their choice."

"This next scrim will help prep us for the next rank game," Ethan points out in his soft voice. "It's all part of the training so we can make it to the top."

"Yikes, this all sounds a lot more complicated than I thought it would be." Who knew computer games could be so involved? I'd thought they sit down, bash a few monsters, steal the flag, and then declare victory. But apparently there's actual strategy to this game.

"That's why this pays so much," says Helix. "It's a lot of work and a lot of effort, but if you can make it, it's worth it."

"Is that why you all do it?" I find myself wanting to understand these guys I find myself living with. What brought them together? What holds them together as a unit?

"This is what we enjoy," whispers Ethan.

"Why would we want to be stuck in a cubicle all day when we can play games we're good at and get paid?" adds Miles as if it's the most obvious thing in the world. Which, I have to admit, is a fair point.

"But aren't you stuck inside all day anyway? I didn't see any windows in your computer room and there's no light in here." I look around at the darkness to make my point.

"It's different." Helix shakes his head. "This is our choice. When it's your choice, you're willing to do anything to chase your dream."

His argument sounds a lot like the one I've used to justify my current situation.

Maybe we have more in common than I thought. Maybe ... I could actually be friends with these guys. It'd make the sex a lot less awkward.

Or maybe it'd make it more awkward.

"Speaking of being stuck inside all the time," interjects Lionel, "you've spent a lot of time shut up in your room lately."

Heat rises in my face. I knew at some point they would call me out and demand all the benefits they've missed out on over the last couple of days.

I shouldn't have come down here. I shouldn't have sought them out. I'm not their friend, I'm their hired sex toy.

I mean, hired *girlfriend*.

"So it's not like you can talk because you haven't gone outside in days," Lionel continues, interrupting my panic spiral.

"Maybe I've left every day," I counter. "You've all been so focused on gaming, you never noticed."

"Your shoes have been in exactly the same position. If you'd left, they would be slightly different," says Miles.

"Maybe I have multiple pairs of shoes." I don't know why I'm arguing. But I am surprised by the interest they've taken in my whereabouts. I wonder how far their curiosity stretched. Did any of them walk by my room and listen to hear if I was inside?

Were any of them were tempted to come find me for sex?

Did I *want* them to barge in and say, "This is happening now!"? Did I *want* them to leave me no choice in the matter?

"Do you have multiple pairs of shoes?" asks Quintin, snapping me back to the present.

"Of course I do." Everyone has multiple pairs of shoes for different occasions and weather. "But ... you're right. I didn't go out. I was working."

I hope they'll let me leave it at that. What else can I say? That I was avoiding them and the sex that I'm certain they want from me?

"At least you get to work from home instead of having to go into the office. But even that little bit of freedom wouldn't be enough at some point," says Helix. "Not for me."

"Nor me," says Lionel.

"Same," adds Ethan as the others nod in agreement.

Well, *that* was certainly easier than I thought it would be. Either they have absolutely no real interest in me as a person, or they really can't imagine that anyone else would decide to pursue a career outside of the normal nine to five.

"Where did you go tonight?" asks Quintin.

The other gamers all shoot him a look, as if they can't believe he is asking me such a question, and then return their focus to me. I guess he's paying even more attention to my shoes than Miles. I'm not sure if that's weird or sweet.

"Did you go out with a guy?" asks Miles, his voice sharp. "Because we've hired you to be our girlfriend, and it should go without saying that that means you can't be dating other people."

I can't help but roll my eyes.

"I met some girlfriends for a drink. We usually meet at least once a week to catch up with each other."

And to talk about sex and romance and imaginary characters who live in our heads.

Lionel smirks. "So you're going to come home tipsy at least once a week?"

Miles frowns at Lionel and then focuses on me. "Is that safe?"

I start to protest that I'm allowed to go outside by myself.

"No," says Miles, shutting down anything I was about to say. "I mean, like, safe to walk home alone after drinking. Should one of us go meet you and walk you home, or did your friends walk you?"

I open my mouth again to protest, but immediately close it again. I'd been prepared for Miles to say something controlling, like that I can't talk to any guy without the team's permission. Instead, he's worried about my safety.

"I'm good," I say. "It's not far from here to the train station."

"Well, if you change your mind, let us know," says Miles, sitting back on the sofa and switching his attention back to the projector screen and Helix.

I could take this as an out and head back upstairs. I did come down here to spend some time with them, and I have.

But I know this wasn't really what my goal in coming down here was.

"Mind if I join you then for the rest of your strategy session?" I move around the edge of the sofa and squeeze myself between Quintin and Miles. It's the most room I can see on the sofa even though they barely shift over for me, and if I hadn't been drinking, I wouldn't have tried it, but the wine has made me brave.

"Uh, sure," says Quintin, looking around at the others to see what to do. "But why?"

"You've all hired me to be your girlfriend, I should try to understand what you do for your job." That sounds plausible enough.

"Does that mean we should take an interest in your job? And all the personal details of your life?" asks Ethan, leaning around Quintin.

"Nope." I stretch out my legs and rest my feet on the coffee table in front of me after making sure there isn't any food on there, just cans of energy drinks. If they don't want their drinks near my socked feet, they can move them. "That's not how this works. You hired me to be you girlfriend, so we'll keep this professional and sexual."

Chapter Eight

Fuck, I didn't mean to say that. Maybe I should not drink a second glass at critique group ever again. My mouth will be writing checks my body won't want to cash.

Or maybe I do. Drinking is supposed to bring out the truth, right?

"If you say so," says Miles, scooting the slightest bit closer to me on the sofa. There was barely any space between us already, so now we're pressed against each other from shoulder to hip.

And they say men don't listen. Miles clearly heard the last word I said. *Sexual.* He is cute in a nerdy way. He's not someone I would normally check out from across the room, but up close, really looking at him, he's attractive. Maybe something could happen between us tonight. For research, of course. And because of our agreement. Work stuff, that's all.

I lean in a little myself, letting my shoulder brush against his. It's a bit pokey, not padded with muscle, but I don't mind.

"I suppose we should keep going with our strategy session then?" asks Helix, looking around at the others, but pausing longer to stare at me. He must see something that answers his question as I stare back patiently, because he turns back to the map on the screen and points out different landmarks.

The rhythm of Helix's speech is calming as he methodically goes through attack patterns their upcoming opponents have launched in the past. Add in the darkness of the room and the second drink, and I could comfortably stay here all evening.

I'm sure it doesn't help that I've barely slept these last few days, wondering if any of my roommates will come in when I'm asleep to access their benefits. Then working my fingers to the bone typing—and touching myself—all day as I compile my notes on our sexual escapades and translate them into my new book. But tonight I got good feedback from my group, and I'm confident my new story is awesome. I've earned a chance to relax.

Miles kisses my forehead and I'm in such a happy, drowsy haze that I tilt my face up to him and kiss him full on the lips. *There's nothing wrong with it,* I sleepily think. *He's my boyfriend.* Granted, the others are all sitting around us, watching. But it still feels right.

It's slow and coaxing, with a hint of tongue. Just a hint that it could turn deeper at any moment, should one of us decide to take it there. With all of the other gamers around us on the sofa.

The thought that they may be taking notes of their own amuses me, and I decide that I want more than a chaste kiss.

Twisting, I turn so I'm facing Miles directly, climbing into his lap. With Ethan, we were both nervous and clumsy as if it were actually our own individual first times. With Lionel, it was commanding and overwhelming. And in both cases, even though I was accepting of what was happening, I also kind of felt like I didn't really have a say in it. But this here with Miles, it's my own choice. I *want* to explore, to gain new experiences. The other times were testing, required. This is *my* choice, and I'm chasing it.

Miles is already hard beneath me as my knees bracket his hips. I can feel everything through my thin leggings as I grind on top of his sweatpants. There is still no finesse in my approach. I haven't learned that yet, but I know exactly how thrilling it feels now to feel in control and desired by a man. So much so that he doesn't seem to care we're not alone.

Even though I'm in control, Miles is right here with me. His hands frame my face as we kiss, and now his tongue is involved, darting past my lips, fucking me the way he will soon with his cock.

Possibly with an audience.

When Lionel and I were walked in on in the kitchen, I was startled, but in the days since I've realized how much the idea of being watched turns me on. I never thought I would want that. And this time, it's not going to be a surprise.

Besides, they're all going to get a taste of me at some point, so they might as well get a sneak peek. And they're all going in my books, so the world will get their very own sneak peek at these men, and what they're like between the sheets. And on sofas. And the kitchen floor. And wherever else they'll have me.

Somewhere beside me, a phone starts beeping. Not just one, but several. An incessant noise that isn't immediately stopped.

Miles groans beneath me, but it's not a *thank goodness this is finally happening* type of groan, it's an *I'm being interrupted and I don't like it* one. This is made all the more clear when his head drops back against the top of the sofa and he doesn't let me follow. Even though I really want to keep kissing him. Who knew making out with a guy could be so much fun?

The sudden silence of the room when the phone alarms stop going off is almost deafening. I look around and see that every guy is holding their phone—not to film my scandalous antics with their friend, but to check the time.

"It's time to boot up," says Lionel. "Get your blood back in your brain."

They all stand except for Miles, who is still wedged between my legs and beneath me. I'm so confused. My brain is a haze of horniness.

"Can't I at least come real quick? Just so I can think straight?" Miles's hands land on my thighs, keeping us both in place.

Not that I want to move at the moment. The "real quick" part doesn't sound great, but right now I'll take anything I can get. My body wants more. More of everything that Miles could give me right now.

Helix checks his phone. "Looks like the other team is already logged in. We can't keep them waiting."

"Fine." Miles throws his head back again in disappointment for a moment before tapping his hands to my thighs twice and lifting me off his lap. "Don't touch yourself. We're going to finish off these guys quick, then I want us to finish together."

"Bummer for you, man," says Lionel to Miles as they file upstairs. "Clarissa's real good, and you're missing out."

"Fuck you," grumbles Miles.

Left in a heap on the sofa where Miles dropped me, I watch them disappear from view, leaving me in the basement. I can't believe Miles was able to so easily lift me off him, and I *really* can't believe that I was the one voting for him to not go to work so I can get off.

And what's with his comment about not touching

myself? He can't be serious. That's not a rule I'm about to agree to, now or ever.

Although I never would have thought that was something I wouldn't easily be able to adhere to. I've never considered myself particularly sexual, but ever since sleeping with Ethan and especially since giving Lionel that blow job, I've been turning to my vibrator daily. Never would I have thought that toy would become one of my favorite possessions, almost rivaling my computer.

I wait until I'm certain my roommates are shut away in their computer room before rolling off the sofa and heading up to my room. I'm no longer tipsy now so much as high on the combo of wine and good feedback. And horniness.

My body is still humming with pent-up sexual frustration, and my vibrator is just sitting in my bedside table. Miles would never need to know, and I don't have to obey him in everything.

Glancing at my closed door, I pull out my pink battery-powered friend. *No, none of my roommates are going to walk in.* They're all working, and while I don't know how long their games take, I'm fairly certain they can't be this quick.

I change into my pajamas and climb into my bed, a soft buzzing fills the room before I slip the toy beneath the blankets. The vibration is soft and fluttery, but I move it in the same rhythm Miles had been moving beneath me on the sofa. I pretend the toy is his cock, teasing me through my leggings. I imagine him peeling them off me until I'm completely bared to him. Helping me back onto his lap so I straddle his naked thighs, his cock hitting against my bare pussy even better than it was through our clothes.

I'd look to my left and Quintin would be right there, sitting beside us fully dressed, admiring the way Miles and I tease each other. We'd be teasing Quintin too, letting him watch but not touch. If I were to turn to look around, all of my roommates would be watching the way my legs are splayed on either side of Miles's thighs.

"Let them watch and be jealous," Miles would say. Then he'd notch the head of his cock at my entrance before guiding my hips down, watching me slowly be impaled by his cock.

I up the power of my toy's vibration as I imagine Miles filling me. So many eyes on us. Would they line up, waiting their turn to be next? Would I rotate through being fucked by them each individually, continually arousing the others around us until they all needed a second turn to stick their dick inside me? Or would they all demand attention all at once? Could I handle it? Do I want them to use my body for their pleasure until we're all exhausted and unable to move?

"Yes!" I cry out as the vibration directly on my clit becomes almost too much and throws me over the edge. My hips buck automatically, riding the waves of pleasure, and I wish Miles's cock was really driving in and out of my fluttering pussy as the orgasm rushes through my limbs.

Everything is fuzzy and pleasant now that I've come. My hands barely have enough strength to keep hold of the vibrator, so I let it fall to the side. I should get up and jot down a few notes, but the slight buzz from drinking and the haze from that orgasm is too much. I'll never be able to pick up a pen.

Rolling over, I curl up on my side. Miles never needs to know that I came upstairs and took care of myself. There won't be any consequences but a good night's sleep. And he definitely will never know I thought of him while I masturbated. It will be my little secret.

Well, maybe mine and all of my readers'.

Tomorrow, I'll spill the beans on the pages. Tonight, I'm

going fall asleep pretending that it was Miles who took care of all of my needs.

My blankets flutter a little, letting cool air into my warm bed. I shiver, trying to resist the urge to wake up and gather my blankets tighter, but the slight breeze of cooler air is over in a moment.

It's the feather-light touches down my arm that jolt me awake. I freeze, terrified. There's someone else in my bed.

"Someone isn't playing fairly," whispers Miles. The touches turn from startling to soothing. "You should have at least hidden the vibrator before falling asleep. You weren't even trying to not get caught."

"You're not the boss of me." I slowly open my eyes. It's dark, but I can make out his features as he lays on the pillow next to me.

Reaching out, I let my own fingers brush against Miles's bare chest, checking that he's real and in my bed. That this isn't another fantasy my brain has dreamed up to help me climax.

I flatten my hand. Yup, no shirt, just warm, solid chest. Now I want to inch closer to see if he's wearing anything at all. It's still a little surprising that he's here.

"How did your game go?" I keep my voice low. This house is pretty well-insulated and sound doesn't carry, but it's the middle of the night and we're in bed together. I feel like this calls for whispering.

"Is that why you did it?" His fingers trace the bottom hem of my sleep tank, inching the fabric up. "You were mad I didn't let you come downstairs on the sofa with all of my friends watching? You had to come up here and take care of your needs yourself?"

There's another flutter of cool air behind me as my blankets are adjusted. I try to turn to look, but Miles catches my lips in a kiss. It's slow and possessive, more languid than the way he'd kissed me earlier in the basement. This one melts me, making me want to sink deeper into my mattress. Into his chest. To stay cocooned with him in these blankets all night long.

"It's not fair that you got to come already and I didn't," he continues. "Do you know how hard it was to concentrate on protecting my teammates when I knew you were up here, wet and waiting for me?"

Miles's hands inch my sleep tank higher, and he breaks our kiss to pull it over my head. I shiver a little, bare in front of Miles for the first time. It's dark in here so I'm not sure how much he can actually see, but he's touching everything. Nothing is off limits. I'm his girlfriend.

Another set of hands slide around my hips from behind, and I freeze again.

"You didn't think I would miss out on watching Miles fuck you, did you?" asks Quintin, pulling my hips back a little so I'm pressed up against him.

Quintin's hard cock presses against my ass through the thin cotton of my panties and his chest is bare against my back. My brain feels fuzzy, unable to process this information. Two of my new boyfriends are in bed with me. At once. I'd guessed they would enjoy their girlfriend benefits together at some point, but I thought I'd have more time to acclimate to our pseudo-relationships before we'd take the next step to group activities.

Before I have a chance to answer, I hear a soft buzzing. I recognize the sound, but I can't figure out why I'm hearing it now.

Until there's the solid touch of my pink toy against the front of my panties.

"Tell us, did you think of me while you were playing with yourself?" Miles teases my toy over the fabric, never settling in one place.

He isn't setting the toy right where I want it. Right where I need the vibration. I'm already warming to being sandwiched between two of my roommates—and that kiss! I want more. I shift my thighs a little to give Miles better access, silently asking him to give me what I want.

Quintin's hand slides down to the inside of my thigh and lifts my leg a little. "Go on, tell Miles what you imagined. Are you still fantasizing? Or is this exactly what you want?"

"Yes," I whisper. I'm not sure which question I'm answering. Maybe I'm answering all of them. And as soon as the word hangs between us, the head of the vibrator slides across my clit, the fabric dampening with the attention.

"Thank you," Miles says. The power of the vibration kicks up a notch and begins to focus on my clit. "You deserve a little reward for your honesty."

He holds the toy there in that one sensitive spot, and it's overwhelming. The few times I'd masturbated before moving into this house, I'd always tease myself and ease into the climax. This is like going from a bicycle to a race car.

"Too much." I reach out to touch Miles's arm, even as my hips arch into the vibrations. Instead of pushing Miles and the toy away, I'm pulling them closer.

"You can handle it. You're doing so good right now," says Miles, kissing my forehead. "Let's try a little more."

"Let me help you out there, Thrower." Quintin shifts his arm so he's holding up my leg, and there's no way I can move away from the intensity of the toy. It's a lot, but then

Quintin's fingers glide across the gusset of my panties, moving the toy away.

I want to cry at the absence of the vibrations against my clit. I was so close, and now the edge feels so sharp. The only thing I can do is lean my head back against Quintin's shoulder and breathe.

"You're so wet for us." Quintin chuckles in my ear. It's such a dirty sound, made sexier by the fact that he's my roommate and there are two of them here in bed with me. "Let me slide her panties over for you, Thrower, so she can really enjoy that toy. She did choose it over waiting for your cock."

"Clarissa is so lucky to have us," says Miles, moving the toy back to my clit, now with nothing between the toy and my sensitive bud as Quintin pulls my underwear to the side. "She gets to have both tonight."

It's so intense, so overwhelming, it's hard to breathe. Every bit of my focus is in that little sensitive bud that Miles is massaging with my toy. When the orgasm hits, I'm gasping, and I couldn't move out of Miles's and Quintin's arms if I even wanted to, which I most certainly don't. I've used that toy on myself, but it's never felt like this.

"See, doesn't your boyfriend make you feel so good? Imagine how good he'd make you feel if you had waited like he told you to," whispers Quintin. "But you had to be a naughty girl."

"Don't worry," Miles assures me, "naughty girls still get fucked too. But they don't get to keep their panties on."

His words are so dirty. I shouldn't let a man talk to me this way. But that orgasm he just gave me left me with no strength. All I can do is lie on my side, held up by Quintin's bare chest, as they slowly tug my soaking wet panties down my lethargic legs.

"Are you ready for your first time with your new

boyfriend?" asks Quintin, reaching around my hip to run his fingers through my folds. Feeling how wet I am for the two of them. Turned on by their dirty actions and words.

"Ender said you have a beautiful cunt. Soft and tight." Miles runs the tip of his cock along the seam of my pussy, sliding through the slickness there. He's bigger than Ethan, but nothing like Lionel. "I can't wait to feel you for myself."

Quintin presses closer against my back and raises my thigh again until my knee nearly rests on Miles's hip, and Miles slides in closer as well. I'm sandwiched between two of my gamer roommates and I'm not complaining. This is everything I never even knew I wanted to try, and now that it's happening, I don't want to go back to being alone.

As Miles presses the tip of his cock to my entrance, anxiety breaks through the haze of my previous orgasm. Growing up, I'd always been told to worry about my body count, and here I am adding another name to the list. The shame I'm supposed to feel wars with worry about if Miles will think I'm good in bed.

His cock slowly slides into my pussy, and my nerves start to slither away. The stretch feels so good, and he's not being rough with me. If anything, being bracketed by two men is comforting, even if they are doing dirty things to me.

"Tell me how it feels," says Quintin, holding my leg up so that Miles can pull out and slide home again. He's developing a steady rhythm, stirring the embers of my last orgasm.

I'm not sure if Quintin is talking to me or to Miles. My hands creep up to wrap around Miles's waist as his hips thrust in and out, pressing me back against Quintin's bare body with each movement.

"So good." They're the only words my mouth can form as I struggle to process the pleasure of Miles's cock fucking me and Quintin's equally hard cock pressing against my ass.

My tight forbidden hole. I can't help but shift my hips a little in his hold so that he's seated right against it. He could press in at any moment, and the terrifying possibility ratchets up my pleasure even more.

Quintin chuckles in my ear and presses even closer, wedging his cock between my ass cheeks.

"Our Clarissa is a very dirty, daring girl it seems," says Quintin. "So eager to have both of us impaling her at the same time. She wants all of her holes filled at once. Can you imagine what that will be like? For me to fuck your tight, pert little ass while Thrower pounds your beautiful pink pussy?"

It's getting harder to breathe with every second I imagine that scenario. To be so full, and although I'm already the center of attention for two men, it'd be even more intense. I want that so much.

I push my ass back a little more against Quintin's cock.

"Soon, Clarissa." Quintin chuckles. "We'll have to train your ass before you'll be able to take one of our cocks up there. But don't worry, we can make your training sessions very fun."

Miles groans, pistoning faster, gliding easier with each thrust as I imagine the dirty forbidden things these two men want to do to me.

"Fuck, I can't wait. She's so tight. Even better than Ender described. Play with her clit. I want to feel her come on my cock."

Quintin's hand slides from my hip to right above where Miles's cock is filling me. It only takes a couple swipes with his wicked, fast fingers before I'm exploding between them.

Miles freezes, clutching me close as he groans his orgasm into my neck. "Such a beautiful pussy. Thank you."

My body doesn't even feel like it exists. I feel like I'm

floating through the most beautiful part of space. Like I'm one with everything around me.

"Then if it's okay with you, I'll take my turn with our girl," says Quintin.

"Of course." Miles rolls onto his back and my body naturally follows, unwilling to give up the cozy snuggles of post-coital bliss, so I'm splayed out on his chest.

It's cold, but Miles is warm.

The blanket is a tangled mess at the bottom of the bed, but the chill on my skin is forgotten as Quintin moves to kneel behind me. He's a dark shadow in the room, and I wish the light was on so I could see him. Although then he would see me completely too, and I'm not sure I'm ready for someone else to see how I look right now. Miles's softening cock is still in my pussy and my juices are running down the inside of my thighs. Not to mention that my ass is probably spread with my legs on either side of Miles's hips, displaying the tight little crinkle of my asshole.

Quintin reaches out to shift my hips and Miles's cock slips out. There's something so sad about no longer being filled, no longer being connected in such an intimate way. At least until the head of Quintin's hard cock notches at my pussy and he eases right in, not even seeming to care that his friend was just in the same hole, or that said friend is still right there beneath us, his dick only an inch or so away.

"Fuck, you're right. The perfect pussy," groans Quintin, bottoming out in one smooth motion. "I'll never use my hand again now that we have a girlfriend."

"She's perfect," agrees Miles, turning my head to capture my lips in a kiss.

It's sweet and soft, which is a contradiction to the rough way Quintin is holding my hips and fucking me from behind with a single-minded determination. This is a new position for me, and the way the tip of his cock brushes against the front wall of my pussy with each thrust is absolutely delicious. Everything is more sensitive after two orgasms so close together, nearly in succession.

I lift myself off of Miles slightly, my nipples brushing against his bare chest as I push back a little, pressing myself onto Quintin's cock even as he thrusts forward to impale me. This is what I wanted. To participate, to enjoy Quintin's roughness against Miles's softness. And the added tease of bare skin against my nipples is tantalizing.

Breaking our kiss, Miles reaches up with a lazy smirk and pinches one of my nipples. It hurts and I can't stop the squeal that rushes out of me, but as soon as he releases, pleasure floods where there was pain only a moment ago and it sends me over the edge. I collapse on top of Miles's chest as my body writhes with waves of pleasure. Quintin leans over the both of us, thrusting into my pussy a couple more times before collapsing as well in a heap of pleasure.

Chapter Nine

I'm absolutely starving, and there are no snacks in my room. Which means I need to go downstairs and face my roommates.

They're the reason I'm so hungry, I'm certain of it, but the idea of facing them after last night has me blushing furiously and wanting to hide my face under my pillow. It's embarrassing enough to know that I masturbated to the thought of them, but for Quintin and Miles to come upstairs and call me out on it after their game is positively humiliating, and what we did after that ...

My inner thighs are sticky from my own wetness where it dried, and the memory of the things they did to my body while talking so dirty has me flushed and fanning myself for a whole separate reason from embarrassment. I'm not sure when they left my room because I'd fallen asleep quickly after so many blissful orgasms.

And now I may have to face them when I go down to find some breakfast.

I scrub off the smell of sex in the shower and try to turn on my author brain without getting worked up again. If I loved it this much in real life, my critique partners and readers will hopefully love it too.

When I step into the kitchen, fresh and clean from my shower, Quintin and Helix are sitting right there at the table eating cereal. They stop talking as soon as they see me freeze in the doorway, which probably means they were talking about me. Quintin was probably filling Helix in on all the dirty details of last night's encounter, and giving Helix ideas of his own.

I shove down the urge to go hide back upstairs, but I'm hungry, and this is my house too. Practicing the confidence that I've been faking since my first day here, I walk right past my gamer roommates and head to the cupboards to pour myself some cereal.

Joining the guys at the table, I keep my eyes focused on my food and take slow, methodical bites, waiting for them to start talking again.

Helix is the first to break the silence. "I heard you were naughty last night."

I look up sharply and catch the amused glint in his eye. *How much did Quintin tell him?*

"Who was naughty?" asks Lionel, breezing into the kitchen and grabbing a protein bar out of the cupboard and an energy drink from the fridge.

"Clarissa masturbated last night when Miles had specifically told her not to," says Quintin over my head, as if I'm not sitting right here between the three of them.

I blush, but keep eating my breakfast. So I was right—they had been talking about me. I know I'm sharing the details of our sex life in my writing, but no one will know it's based on them. Knowing they're discussing *me* is humiliating.

Lionel tucks his food and drink into the pockets of his sweatpants before coming up behind me and placing his hands on my shoulders. I can feel the chill on his hands from the cold energy drink through my t-shirt.

He begins to rub my shoulders, but my body refuses to relax.

"Did Clarissa get her punishment?" asks Lionel, leaning down to whisper the words in my ear.

"Well, we did give her pussy a pretty good pounding last night." Quintin laughs. "But I'm sure she would be up for more, the way she was pushing her ass against my hard cock."

"Good," says Lionel, "because we need to take care of our girl *and* our needs."

"I'm hoping to have our needs met so often it will help release some tension and we'll be able to play better," says Helix.

"I hope so," Quintin agrees. "We all saw your gray screen the other day."

Helix flips Quintin the bird before scooping up more cereal.

"I'm just saying, I definitely feel better after coming in Clarissa's pretty pussy last night, so I'm ready for our game today and I'm going to kill it," says Quintin.

I'm trying to listen as a dispassionate observer so I can note down the way they're talking to each other for later, but how can I ignore the way their words flying by my head are making me feel?

I want to remind them that I'm a living, breathing woman and not an inanimate receptacle for their cum. But if I open my mouth I'm afraid it won't be to chastise them, but to ask for a kiss. Maybe more.

Before I can decide what to say, my roommates are already piling their dishes in the sink.

Finally I manage to unlock my jaw and speak. "The dishwasher is empty, put them in there."

The gamers look at me questioningly before easing open the dishwasher a crack as if they're nervous what they're going to find inside. Granted, it had looked pretty nasty in there before I ran the dishwasher. So nasty, in fact, that I had to run it twice.

"Thanks," says Quintin, his voice tipping up at the end of the word and making it sound more like a question.

I shrug my shoulders. "I live here too, right?"

"Very true," says Lionel with a smirk as he walks out of the kitchen.

"Don't worry." Helix leans down to whisper in my ear. "I'll come find you later."

It'd been a struggle to keep my body from squirming from their dirty talk, but Helix's words—both a promise and a threat—send a shiver through me. I'm not sure if I should be excited or scared.

I'm both.

I'm also no longer hungry, so I empty out my bowl and put it in the dishwasher beside theirs.

My phone pings with a text from Sasha.

Write in day? The Giraffe in twenty minutes. Save me a seat near an outlet.

Okay, so I guess I'm not going to go upstairs to write in my normal, comfortable solitude. I'm going to write in public, on display to an entire café and Sasha. I'll have to dim my screen a lot so no one can read the dirty things I'll be writing. Although I doubt that will work with Sasha.

See you there, I text back as I head to my room to collect my things.

Packing up my computer bag, I consider texting her back again saying something has come up, but decide that would be a stupid thing to do. I should take this opportunity to really learn from her since I'm trying to shift my career path like she did.

Plus, we're friends. We should hang out. Even if I've been feeling self-conscious around her lately, and even if I'm scared she'll try to pry information I don't want to share out of me.

I'll have to be brave. I've done things in the last twenty-four hours I never thought I'd do. I can go see my friend and hide all my secrets from her. How hard can it be?

Turns out, it's harder than Miles's and Quintin's cocks last night.

Sasha breezes into The Giraffe at least ten minutes late, looking around for me in the crowd. As soon as she sees where I've chosen to sit, she frowns. But all the other tables are full, so if she's so unhappy with my choice, she should have gotten here on time. Or better yet, early.

I'm super lucky to have Sasha as a friend, not only because she's so successful and can help guide me, but because she forces me to get out and be part of the city by coming to writing sessions like this, or attending book launches by other local authors.

It's just that sometimes she annoys me.

"Good morning!" I say, light and friendly. "Thanks for inviting me to come out for a writing session."

Or ordering me to, I think, since that's really what she did. But I was going to write today anyway, so I might as well put a positive spin on this and keep an ear out for any good advice Sasha may impart in passing today.

"Of course," says Sasha breezily as she pulls out her laptop and adjusts where her coffee sits on the table.

"What are your goals for today?" Whenever we meet to

write together, we always try to set out goals so that we know what we're working toward. Normally they're a specific word count.

"You can show me what method you use to outline your books. Everyone thought it was so good last night, and so different from your normal work, I figured you could show me how you do it."

"Oh, I don't think I'm really doing anything different than before," I hedge.

"You must be doing something different for your writing to improve this much," she insists. "Besides adding in spice, of course."

"Not really," I lie. "I guess I ... jot down some basic stage direction notes for my characters, and make lists of all the emotions they could be feeling during each scene, and then once both of those things are done, I go back and write out the entire scene."

"And you've always done this, or it's new?" she asks, sipping her coffee.

"I've always done it this way." I try to match her feigned nonchalance, sipping my own coffee and glancing at my screen, which has gone black because I haven't typed anything in a few minutes. "How do you begin your story process? I'd love to learn from you."

And I really would, because Sasha has done so much research to change her genre and is doing so well as an author. I would love to be like her one day. I'm not ready to do anything so drastic as change genres yet, but adding in the sex scenes should help. Especially with my new hands-on research method.

"I set out each beat and then thread them together for the story." Sasha frowns, setting down her coffee and abruptly changing the subject. "Tell me about your new roommates. You never did tell me how you found them."

"Oh. I just answered an ad." I laugh it off even as I'm panicking inside about how to get the conversation back to writing—or literally anything other than my living situation. "I met them, and they seemed nice enough and like they weren't going to kill me, so I decided to go for it."

This is basically the truth. A flyer is a type of ad, and they are nice enough. Giving me orgasms is nice. Fantastic, even. Mind-melting. And they definitely don't give off murder vibes. More like slightly-awkward-but-ready-to-fuck-me-at-any-moment vibes.

"Hmm, it just seems like your writing changed as soon as you moved in with them." Sasha boots up her computer, and I hope that means she's ready to get to work and we can stop talking about this.

"Maybe a new view out my window from my desk changed my view on writing." I wake my own computer back up and find the spot I was working on, double-checking that my screen is as dim as it can go.

"Maybe," she agrees. "Okay, let's write for twenty-five minutes and then we'll get a five-minute break. We should be able to get in three of those sessions before I need to leave."

"Sure, that sounds good." I really don't care what our method is for today so long as Sasha stops asking questions about my roommates. I'll have to say more about them at some point, but this is not that time.

Besides, how do I explain that I'm using the guys to further my career? I'm a nice person and I don't like using people, even if it is a fair exchange and they're getting plenty out of it too? I mean, it's not like they were going to get a girlfriend by meeting her in person. I haven't seen them leave the house once since I've moved in although I suppose Helix did have to leave the house to put the flyer up.

Closing my eyes, I focus on the way I felt this morning when Helix whispered dirty things in my ear, the pleasant shivers of anticipation that ran up my spine. And on the way it felt to be sandwiched between Miles and Quintin last night in bed. To be cocooned in the safety of their arms while they did filthy things to my body. My readers will absolutely adore their over-the-top sexy-time tactics, if how well my pages went over at critique group this week was any indication.

My fingers fly over the keyboard as I let all of the feelings from last night and this morning loose onto the page, building out one scene after another. Even during our short breaks, I'm finding the threads of scenes and planning how my FMC will move from one to another, building a relationship with the MMC.

So much of myself is going into this book, but my characters are going to fall for each other. With my roommates, we're going to end at some point—probably when I can afford to live on my own again. But I'll need at least a couple of new books out before that will happen, so I've no idea how long our lives will be interconnected.

At least I'm getting a lot of material out of them so even when I do move again, I'll still have research notes to go back to for future books. After all, at the rate things are going, I'll be gathering material faster than I can use it.

"All right, looks like we're done for the day. Not bad overall," says Sasha, closing her laptop and looking at me expectantly. "Let's walk to the train together."

"Oh, uh." I've written a lot more than I thought I would, but there are still so many notes I could jot down to build out my MMC. Still, if Sasha is ready to leave, it's probably best to call it a day. I can always keep writing once I get home. "Sure, let me pack up my stuff."

"We'll have to hurry though, I don't want to miss my train," says Sasha, all of her things already gathered.

"Not a problem." I haphazardly shove everything into my backpack. I can organize it on the train, or not even bother since I'll pull everything out again at home anyway.

"So when do we get to meet these new roommates?" asks Sasha, striding out the front door of the café ahead of me.

"Uh, well, they work a lot of weird hours and don't get out much." All of this is true. Their scrimmages are sometimes at weird hours because of the time differences, and they *don't* get out much. Or ever.

"You should have them come by a critique group sometime for a drink after." Sasha weaves through other pedestrians on the sidewalk as we head to The El.

"Hmm, we're not really friends," I say, hurrying to keep up. "I just moved in and we're still getting to know each other."

"This will be a perfect way to get to know them," she says, checking down the tracks for the train. "By introducing them to our critique group so we can help you vet them."

"I'm already living with them." *And sleeping with them.* We might not have had any real getting-to-know-each-other conversations, but we have for sure been spending time together. Naked. I let out a nervous laugh. "So I think that time has passed."

"Either way, you should invite them." Sasha's train arrives and she moves to get on. "I'll text about another writing session soon."

Left on the platform alone, I watch the train disappear. The announcement board says I still have fifteen minutes before my own train arrives. I probably just missed one. *Oh, well.* I reach into my overstuffed bag for a book. May as well use the extra time to do some of the reading that I claimed I was already doing.

Chapter Ten

When I arrive back at the house, there's a delivery package addressed to Helix resting against our door. I snag it. My roommates are probably in the middle of a game or a practice or whatever they're doing, and this is the nice thing to do, bringing in their mail.

The note I left them, letting them know I was meeting up with a friend for coffee, is still sitting untouched on the hallway table. They probably don't even know I left. If they're gaming, they're probably locked in and letting the real world fade away around them.

I get it. I've done the same, losing hours without realizing it when I'm in a writing flow. I decide to leave the package in the kitchen, where they'll definitely see it. Who knows if they'll think to check the hall table.

The door to the computer den is open, and as I pass by, I can't help but peek in.

"Clarissa," calls Lionel sharply.

Doubling back, I stop in their doorway, careful not to set foot inside the off-limits room.

"Where were you?" asks Lionel, leaning back in his gaming chair.

"A café with a friend. Did you not see my note?"

"No, but so long as it wasn't a date," says Miles, looking me over. Probably to make sure I'm not dressed in date attire, not that he would know what I'd wear on a date since they've never taken me out. "What's with the package?"

"I found it out on the stoop." I check the label again. "It's for Helix."

"I paid extra for immediate delivery." Helix smiles lazily as he holds out his hand for the package.

I'm not falling for it. My roommates were very clear about not stepping into their gaming room. I stay where I am.

"Bring it here," says Helix. "You can come in. Just this one time."

"What did you order?" asks Quintin as I drop my bag to the floor and cross the room to Helix.

"I can show you," says Helix. "If Clarissa is up for assisting."

"You need my help to show us what you ordered?" It can't be that hard to open the package and pull whatever it is out.

"Yeah. If you're up for it." Helix shakes the box at me. "I ordered it right after breakfast."

"After breakfast." I don't know exactly what Helix ordered, but I definitely remember the conversation he and Quintin had at the table. Glancing at Quintin, who is biting his lip, I bet he's remembering the exact same thing.

"Are you up for it?" asks Helix. "You're allowed to say no, but I'd love you to show my teammates what I ordered because some of them weren't there for this morning's debriefing."

The other gamers move in a little closer on their rolling computer chairs, tension filling the room.

I could say no and head upstairs to continue what I was

working on at the café. But then I'd miss out on what is in the box, and it'll only be brought up later, either in conversation or to my room. Besides, isn't this part of the experience I've signed up for? Helix is offering me something new right now, right here.

"Okay."

"Okay what?" Helix fingers the tape holding the box closed.

"Okay, I'll help you show everyone what you ordered," I say in a small voice, my stomach churning with anticipation and nerves ... and excitement. These guys haven't hurt me once. Even if I was nervous about trying something, they've always made me feel good in the end. And throughout.

"Awesome." An excited, megawatt smile lights up his face, and he turns off his computer screen. "Come lean over onto my desk."

I move between Helix and the Ethan's empty chair to the desk. I'm not sure exactly what Helix wants me to do, so I half sit, half lean on the desk, still facing the group.

Where is Ethan? Should we wait for him?

Helix opens the box. I want to peek, but Quintin is already there looking over Helix's shoulder. And his grin makes me nervous.

"Maybe it would be better if Clarissa was actually leaning over more?" suggests Quintin. "She'd have to get her shoulders onto the desk for the best view and there's not enough space with the computers."

My shoulders onto the desk? Best view? I don't understand what they're talking about, but they're looking more excited by the moment.

"Clarissa, why don't you come over here instead," says Lionel, patting his lap. "You can put your hands on my thighs. That will get you in the best position."

"Are you sure?" asks Helix. "You won't have a good view."

"I can look after," says Lionel. "Besides, this way I get Clarissa touching me."

They all look at me, waiting. My stomach flutters as I realize I have to move, bend over, and look Lionel in the eye while touching him in front of all of my other boyfriends.

Well, I did agree to this. Slowly, I straighten and shuffle over to stand in front of Lionel.

"Put your hands on his lap," says Quintin.

"Right here." Lionel points to the top of his thighs. Very close to the growing bulge in his sweatpants.

My mouth suddenly feels dry, and I lick my lips. Lionel watches the small motion very closely.

Then I place my hands just shy of where Lionel pointed. If I put my hands there, my thumbs will brush the still-growing bulge. I'm also very conscious of the fact that my ass is now pointed at the rest of the group, and that if I lift my eyes, I'll be staring at Lionel's lips. I'd only have to lean forward the tiniest bit and we could kiss.

"We forgot to have to drop your pants first," says Helix over the rustling of the packaging paper in the box.

"Fail," chuckles Quintin.

I start to stand, but Lionel covers my hands on his thighs with his own.

"Arrow, why don't you help Clarissa out?" says Lionel.

There's movement behind me as Quintin moves to stand directly behind me, so close as he wraps his hand around my hips to unbutton and unzip my jeans. I can't tell if he pulls me back so my ass hits against his cock hardening in his sweatpants, or if I'm so on edge being on display like this in front of my roommates that I press back into him, seeking comfort.

Quintin takes a moment to grind against my ass so I can feel just how much he wants me. And I can't help but remember the way he did this exact same move last night in my bed before sliding his hard cock inside my tight, wet pussy. *Is he going to do that same thing again?*

Glancing up into Lionel's eyes, I wonder if Lionel is hoping he does. Would he want to watch his teammate fuck me? All of them are here. Would they take turns? Could I manage to take them all, one right after the other? My panties dampen at the thought. And as soon as Quintin pulls down my jeans, they'll all see how wet and ready I am.

It's not them getting me wet, though. It's the idea of what could happen. Am I about to take five big, hard cocks in my pussy for my future readers? Yes, definitely. It's absolutely not because I want to feel all of my boyfriends inside me. One after the other.

Quintin hooks his thumbs into the waistband of my jeans and drags them down over my hips. The backs of his thumbs draw a line of heat down my thighs as he bares me not only to himself, but to his friends.

I shiver as he steps away, letting his teammates get a good look at the wet spot forming on my panties. Blatant and embarrassing evidence of how glad I am to help Helix show our roommates whatever he ordered.

I wait for any of them to say something about how turned on I am, but it doesn't happen.

"Pull down her panties too," says Helix.

I can't tell if the churning in my stomach is from nerves or excitement, but when Quintin runs a finger over the wet spot and up the crack between my ass cheeks, I'm blushing and biting my lower lip in an effort to keep silent. *He definitely knows now.*

Quintin drags my panties to the floor, where they stretch between my ankles along with my jeans. If I tried to run, I'd trip and fall over. But as I flex my fingers on Lionel's thighs, I know I'm not going anywhere. I want to experience this fully.

For my readers, obviously. They'd be so disappointed if I walked away right now.

A little voice in my head says, *So would I.* But that voice is stupid. This is just research, nothing more.

"Are you ready to show everyone what I ordered?" asks Helix, his lips near my ear.

When did he move so close?

"Yes," I whisper, my gaze fixed on Lionel's hard cock tenting his sweatpants so I don't have to look any of them in the eye.

"Good girl," murmurs Helix. A thrill runs through me at the words, just like when Lionel said them in the kitchen.

"Let me help you," offers Quintin, shifting to stand at my side, his stiff cock pressed against my bare hip through his sweatpants. Then his hands are on my ass. And he spreads my cheeks.

My eyes go wide. All of them are now staring down at my most forbidden hole. I'm not sure what to do except hold still. Sure, I'd pressed my ass back against Quintin last night, but I was sleepy and horny, I didn't actually *mean* it.

Did I?

Lionel's cock twitches as something prods at my back entrance. I clutch his thighs harder. It's a weird sensation, but ... I think I might like it.

"You're being such a good girl," says Helix, gently pressing whatever it is against my asshole just a little bit harder—not hard enough to slip inside, but enough to make my think about what it would feel like if it did. "You want us to fuck your ass, and this will help prepare you for our cocks."

"Isn't this so nice of Helix to buy you this toy?" says

Quintin, dragging his erection across my hip as he holds my ass open for his friend. "Do you want to say thank you to him?"

"Thank you, Helix," I whimper. Helix pulls the toy away and squirts a cool liquid over my hole.

"Now relax," says Lionel, pulling my chin up so I have to look him in the eyes, "so your boyfriend can put your new butt plug all the way in."

My eyes go wide. Is that what Helix has back there? I never got a chance to see what was in the box. I'd thought maybe it was his finger, but an actual toy? I've never even seen one before, and now I'm about to have a guy I barely know shove one in my ass.

Lionel leans forward and captures my lips in a kiss. It's dominating and fierce, and he's completely in charge. It's different from when Miles or Ethan kissed me. But it's the distraction I need as Helix moves the butt plug back to my rear entrance, swirling it in the lube he coated my hole with, then pressing it against my asshole again. Only this time, he presses harder, just a little, and I feel the pressure of the toy as it begins to open me up.

When Lionel moves my hand from his thigh to his cock, I nearly fall forward, losing my balance from surprise and from the pressure coming from behind me. Quintin's hands are still spreading my ass wide open, and his grip helps steady me from toppling into Lionel's lap.

I grip Lionel through his sweatpants. He's so hard. Is it just because I'm here in front of him? Or is the fact that I'm completely on display in front of his friends making him so excited?

Helix eases the toy back slightly before pressing it in again, sliding it further into my ass, little by little.

Lionel places his hand over mine again and moves my hand up and down his length. I wish there wasn't the fabric of his sweatpants between us. His cock had been so firm and soft like velvet in my hands before, when I'd taken him in my mouth. Now, Lionel's tongue fucks my mouth just like his cock had in the kitchen, and Helix continues to fuck my asshole with the toy, pulling back before pressing it in a little more each time.

It's overwhelming. Being so exposed to my roommates, and having my ass played with for the first time. Kissing Lionel for the first time and feeling how turned on he is. All of it adds to my own arousal. I've never thought of myself as a particularly sexual person, and the few guys I've dated never made me feel anything close to this. Now I completely understand why people love sex so much.

There's a more intense press of the toy and my asshole stretches more than it has yet, just bordering on painful, and then the pressure disappears.

"There," says Helix. "All the way in."

"It's absolutely gorgeous," murmurs Quintin, rubbing his thumb around the toy.

"It's like it's winking at me," says Miles.

Lionel breaks off our kiss, leaving me dazed. "Turn around and let me see."

I'm confused. I thought Lionel would want me to blow him again, yet here he is telling me to stop touching him.

Quintin releases my ass and guides me to stand up straight. It feels weird, having my hole so full. The hole where nothing is supposed to go. I can't say I dislike it though.

Lionel helps me turn around so I don't trip on the jeans still around my ankles, and then he spreads my cheeks with his thumbs. "That is gorgeous."

"What's everyone doing?"

Ethan stands in the doorway, holding an energy drink.

"Helix gave Clarissa her first butt plug," says Miles.

"She wanted Arrow to fuck her ass last night, so we figured we'd stretch that hole out a bit so we could make that happen," says Helix.

The way they describe buying this toy for me is way different than I would have described it. I'd have said that *they* want to fuck me in the ass so they are starting with this. But I guess I had been the one to press back against Quintin in bed last night. And I had been the one to wonder what it would be like to be fucked by two of my new boyfriends at once.

Unfazed, Ethan walks up to us and reaches out a hand. I expect him to spread my ass cheeks just like Lionel to look at the toy, but instead he reaches around and runs his forefinger through the seam of my pussy.

"Hmm." Ethan dips the tip of his finger slightly into my entrance. It's embarrassing how wet he finds me, but then again, I have been kissing Lionel and playing with his cock while the other guys played with my ass, so it's hardly surprising.

I bite my lip to keep from moaning as Ethan dips back in again, just up to the first knuckle. I'd love for him to slide in a little more. I'm on edge and want to fall over. I want to fly. This has all been a tease. Not one of my boyfriends has bothered to give me an orgasm yet.

Pulling back, Ethan circles my clit once. "Feels like Clarissa enjoys it too. Interesting."

"Don't worry, we'll make sure to stretch you out enough to prepare for us, then we'll make you feel even better." Helix steps in and plants a soft kiss on the corner of my lips.

"But right now, we have to finish training." Quintin bends down and tugs my jeans and panties back up my legs.

"And this time, no vibrator." Miles sits back in his chair and tucks himself under his computer desk. "We'll find you when we're done."

"Wait, what?" I hold on to Quintin's shoulders as he buttons and zips my jeans. "But you left this toy inside me."

"It'll give you something to think about until we're done here," says Helix. "Don't worry, a couple of hours will pass by in no time."

Chapter Eleven

The time does not pass quickly.

My whole body buzzes with the unreleased tension of our encounter in the computer den. These are so similar to the feelings I had last night when Miles and Quintin joined me in bed, but at least then I knew I was going to get the release of an orgasm. Now I know I have to wait. Potentially hours. All while this toy shifts and teases inside me with each move I make.

I could go upstairs and take care of this myself with my vibrator. They haven't taken it away, even after I used it when they told me not to. And I did very much enjoy their punishment for having taken care of myself without them ... but I'm so curious to see what will happen if I do as they say. If their punishment was that good, just how delicious will a reward be?

Opening up my laptop, I attempt to sit down to write out everything that just happened in the computer den and what I'm feeling right now with the toy still in my ass, but there is absolutely no way I'll be able to sit down with the plug there and still resist pulling out my vibrator.

What I need is a distraction. Anything to keep me from

focusing on what's happening right now in my body and what will be happening after my roommates finish whatever they're doing right now.

I pick up my room, but it's quick and easy. I should learn how to be messier.

How long has it been? I slip downstairs and slowly walk past the computer den, but the door is shut and I can hear them talking strategy.

But it is a mess down here. I wander over to the table in the front hall, thinking it's no wonder they didn't see my note here. It's practically overflowing with mail and pieces of computers and who knows what else.

I grab one of the smaller boxes from my room that I haven't broken down yet and throw everything in there that doesn't belong on the hall table. The only thing interesting on here is the mail, which I keep out. Checking who it's all addressed to, I'm a little surprised to see that my roommates have given me their real names. If I want to google who I'm living with, I can.

If I'm going to keep sleeping with them, and I am because that's what the research requires, maybe I should vet them a little more, like Sasha had suggested. Not that I'm going to tell her she'd made a good point.

I throw out the junk mail and leave just the envelopes that look important, or at least legit. I move through the hallway collecting and throwing things into the box for my roommates to go through after their game. If I'm not allowed to masturbate and I can't write, I might as well make this place more habitable. I'm not sure how long it will take to publish enough books to earn enough to afford my own place again, and I don't want to spend that time living in a hovel.

It feels good to be productive and make this place feel ... if not homey, then at least not dirty. I even discover some dusting supplies under the kitchen sink and make the front hallway shine. The only real challenge is all this movement, all the stretching and bending, keeps me hyperaware of the butt plug. So while the cleaning keeps me occupied, it definitely fails at distracting me.

In fact, if I sequence my movements just right, I could probably give myself an orgasm right here with only the toy. Would Helix consider that breaking the rule about not masturbating though? I technically wouldn't have *masturbated*, but I would have given myself an orgasm on purpose, and then I might not get my reward. Which I really want.

Right as I'm reaching up into the ceiling corner with the broom, the computer den door opens and Ethan's head pops out for a moment before disappearing again.

"Am I being too loud?" I call. If I was, they should have said something when I started, not when I'm almost done.

All five of the gamers trickle out into the hallway to stare at me still fighting this cobweb.

"Maybe you should order Clarissa one of those sexy maid costumes next, Hel," says Lionel, crossing his arms and looking me up and down.

"Only if you get one for yourselves too." There is no way I'm doing all of the housework around this big house. They said they would pay room and board for being their girlfriend, not for being their girlfriend and their housekeeper.

"What's with the boxes?" asks Ethan. "I thought you'd already moved everything into your room."

"Wait, you're not moving out, are you?" asks Miles, a hint of panic in his voice. "Is this because we gave you a butt plug?"

Setting the broom back in the corner, I notice how they shuffle nervously in place, waiting for an answer. I could mess with them, but I'm not sure they'd find it funny. Or I could negotiate with them. In exchange for my not moving out, I could ask for things to be more defined between us. But they look so nervous, I'm not sure I have the heart to do that to them.

Besides, everything in these boxes belongs to them, and I really would like it put anywhere other than the public areas. Though if how they maintain the public spaces is any indication, I'm almost afraid to see what their bedrooms look like. Maybe there's a reason they come to my bedroom instead of inviting me into theirs.

"No, these are all of the things that don't belong down here." I point to the boxes. "I'm not sure what belongs to who, so you'll have to each dig through to find your stuff to put it away."

"Oh." Lionel wanders over to the piles of junk haphazardly tossed into the boxes. "Maybe we could do that. We'll see."

"But first, are we done with this butt plug?" I shift a little to look at my ass, but you can't see or even tell that the toy is in there with my jeans on. "I couldn't sit down at my desk to work."

"It's late. You should tell your boss not to work you so hard." Lionel moves behind me and undoes my jeans.

Slipping his hand inside, instead of pushing my jeans down past my thighs, he moves straight to my pussy. My embarrassingly wet pussy. I've wanted to touch my clit myself since they closed the door to the computer den, so I'm too relieved to really be embarrassed.

However, Lionel zips right past my desperate clit, sliding through my seam and dipping a finger into my entrance.

"Are you sure you want us to take out your toy? You're soaked." Lionel pumps his finger twice and then adds a second. The pressure, combined with the fullness from the toy, is unbelievable. "Maybe instead you want your toy left in while you get fucked?"

Lionel's finger finally brushes against my clit and it's hard for me to think, let alone stand. I lean back against him for support as I enjoy this little reward. I'd hoped it would be worth it, and he's not disappointing.

"Let me help you," says Miles, coming to kneel in front of me as he reaches for the waist of my jeans.

The rough fabric scrapes my legs as Miles tugs them down and off, but I can barely keep my eyes open. Lionel's finger applies just the right amount of pressure as he rolls tight circles around my sensitive bud. The cool air is a shock as my jeans disappear, leaving my bare pussy suddenly on display right there in our front hall. If Lionel's ministrations didn't feel so amazing, maybe I would be embarrassed and try to cover myself up, but right now I'm too turned on to care.

Miles's hands trail up the inside of my thighs, gently spreading them to give him a better view of how wet his teammate's finger work has made me.

"Such a beautiful sight," says Miles. "I bet it tastes just as good as it looks."

"Give it a go and let us know," says Lionel, pulling his hand away.

I whimper a little as my hips try to follow. I'm not ready for him to stop, not when he was leading me right where I wanted to go. Where I've wanted to go since Helix stuck this toy in my ass.

But I nearly topple over when Miles picks up my leg and drapes it over his shoulder before diving face-first right into where Lionel's hand was a moment again. And it turns out that Miles is as talented with his tongue as Lionel is with his fingers.

As soon as Miles latches on to my clit and sucks, I'm lost. Thank fuck he and Lionel are holding me up, because otherwise I would fall over right here onto the dirty floor. Especially because he's also using the fingers of his free hand to fill the hole Lionel has so recently abandoned.

There are so many sensations running through my body, but the overwhelming feeling is one of fullness. Miles is building a fire inside my body, and with both of my holes filled to the brim and my clit being played with, fast and hard, there's no way I won't come any moment now.

My head falls back onto Lionel's shoulder. One of his fingers hooks around my chin and pulls my lips over to his in a slow, passionate kiss. The languidness of his kiss emphasizes the speed and roughness of Miles's touch. I only break the kiss as Miles pushes me over the edge and my entire body flutters with tiny but intense spasms.

When Miles steps back to admire his handiwork, Ethan steps up.

"Can you take one more tonight?"

Ethan's voice is soft and sweet as if he's waiting for me to say no, but my body feels pliable and there are no thoughts in my head right now. I'm still riding the wave of pleasure and Lionel is the only reason I'm still upright.

"One more," I whisper against Lionel's lips. "I think I can do it."

"Of course you can," says Lionel, deepening our kiss as Ethan drops his pants before lifting my leg again and placing it around his waist.

Ethan slides on a condom and slips in smoothly, my juices already flowing from the first orgasm. Last time Ethan fucked me it was soft and quick. This time is the same, except that one of the guys, I'm not sure if it's Ethan or Lionel, reaches around to my ass and tugs a little on the butt plug.

Now not only are both of my holes filled, but the pacing of Ethan's cock and the press and release of the butt plug are too much. I'm not sure I can handle it even though it feels so good.

"You can do it. Be our good girl and come for Ender," says Lionel, silencing my whimpers with a kiss.

Ethan brushes his thumb over my clit, and my eyes roll back in my head as stars explode behind my eyelids as the most intense orgasm of my life rolls through me. I'm dimly aware of the sound of liquid hitting the tile beneath us, and my body goes limp as the pleasure coursing through my system robs me of my ability to stand. Thankfully Lionel continues to support me as Ethan speeds up, fucking me fast and hard until he comes himself.

"Did you see that?" whispers Quintin.

"Fucking sexy," says Helix. "That's what that was."

I have no idea what they're talking about, and after that last orgasm all I want is to roll over in Lionel's arms and sleep. I may fall asleep right here in the front hall, half-standing as he holds me up.

"All right, time for bed." Lionel sweeps me up into his arms and carries me up the stairs. "One of you mop the floor," he calls over his shoulder.

He's so sweet, almost like a real boyfriend instead of ... whatever he is. I'd expected these guys to fuck me whenever they wanted and then have nothing to do with me otherwise, but carrying me to bed is such a kind gesture. And asked the others to finish cleaning the hall for me. I would have gotten to mopping tomorrow, but it's sweet that they want to help out too.

I really did get lucky to find these guys, for them to help me with my research and for them to not be terrible people.

"Are you going to fuck me now?" I whisper into my pillow as Lionel tucks me in.

"No," says Lionel, reaching beneath the covers and spreading my cheeks to slowly remove the butt plug.

Even though I'm exhausted from two orgasms, there is still a shiver of pleasure as the toy slides out of my tight hole, stretching me to that almost-painful point again before slipping out completely.

"Are you going to sleep next to me?" I whisper, on the edge of sleep.

"You want to cuddle?" asks Lionel, sounding shocked.

"Mmm." My whole body feels soft. I don't think I can move.

There are footsteps, then Lionel calls out to the others downstairs, but I can't make out what he's saying.

As sleep takes me, someone slides into bed behind me and pulls me back against their chest. It's warm and cozy, and maybe there are definite perks to not living alone.

The door to the computer den is already closed when I go down for breakfast the next morning. The hallway really does look better now. The guys did a halfway decent job mopping the floors last night. I'm not sure who did it, or if they all pitched in, but I appreciate it regardless. I'm also not sure who I snuggled last night. I half remember someone joining me in bed, but they were gone when I woke up this morning.

Still, the entire time I'm eating breakfast, I keep glancing over to the door. If my roommates are gaming, they probably won't be out for hours, but I keep checking to see if one of them is about to join me at the table. But they never show up.

It's weird. I almost feel ... disappointed, but that can't be it. I don't care if they eat breakfast with me or not. This is my job, nothing more. If it is disappointment, it's merely that I won't be getting any more material for my book. *But that's okay*, I remind myself. *I have all of last night still to make notes on.* That should fill my entire day.

In fact, if my roommates are gaming, I should take advantage of the fact that they'll be occupied for a few hours at least so I can write uninterrupted. I'd fully intended to write more after my meeting with Sasha yesterday, but of course, as soon as I brought that package to my boyfriends nothing remotely close to work got done.

At least one small portion of the house got cleaned. As I head upstairs, I note the banister and the upstairs hall need the same level of deep cleaning, but that will be for another day. Right now, it's spicy pages time.

I can actually sit down at my desk now that I don't have the butt plug in, and I let myself fall into the work of setting up a scene and fleshing out the characters and then letting them discover where they want to go for themselves.

After a while, I'm vaguely aware of a ringing emanating from the other side of my room. It's not until the third ring that I'm pulled out of my manuscript to search for the source.

Dad's name flashes across the screen of my phone, and I fumble to answer his call before it goes to voicemail.

"Hi, Dad."

"Everything okay, hun?" he asks. "You sound a little breathless there."

"Oh, I'm just writing. Got a little distracted, that's all."

Dad chuckles. "You always have been one to get lost in a task and forget about the world around you."

"What can I say?" I laugh a little, even as my eyes want

to shift back to my computer screen. "I'm enjoying my work."

"Well then, I don't want to keep you long, but I wanted to check in and see how you're doing. Ask how the new place is," says Dad. "Your mom and I weren't super impressed by the state of the house when we moved you in, and we never did get to meet your roommates."

"Hey, Clarissa," says Quintin, walking into my bedroom without knocking. "Oh, you're on the phone."

Quintin doesn't leave though, he just stands there in the middle of my room, waiting. Like he plans on just listening to my side of the conversation.

"One second, Dad." I close my laptop with my free hand as I say to Quintin, "What can I do for you?"

Silently, I beg Quintin not to say anything sexual. It'd be just my luck that he'd have come in to ask for a fuck when I'm on the phone with my dad.

"We're ordering pizza," says Quintin. "Anything a no go for you?"

The tension rolls out of my shoulders. This is a fine, perfectly ordinary question, and one I don't even have to think about before answering.

"Anchovies, pineapple, olives."

"Olives? Seriously?" Quintin shakes his head. "You're missing out. We'll be downstairs."

I return my attention to my phone. "Sorry about that."

"Not a problem. I'm just glad you're eating regularly. You used to forget to eat all the time when you'd be working," says Dad. "And it sounds like you need to get going. Maybe your mom and I could come up sometime soon and take you out to lunch. We'd love to hear all about how your writing career is going."

"That sounds great. Definitely. Name a day and I'll put it in my planner."

"Your mom would love to meet your new roommates too," adds Dad. "You know how she worries about your safety."

"Um, I'll have to see, with their work schedule. Like I said, they tend to work crazy hours. Not just long, but all over the place too."

"At least they have a good work ethic. Probably how they can afford such a house. Helps with so many of you living there too," says Dad.

"That's life in the big city." I force a laugh, looking around the room for an escape before our conversation veers off into territory I'd rather not talk to my dad about. "Well, I should probably get going. Five guy roommates, I'll need to be there right when the pizza arrives."

Dad chuckles. "Probably. All right, talk soon. We love you."

"I love you too, Dad."

Running my fingers through my hair, I blow out a deep breath to calm myself. That went surprisingly well. My dad didn't seem suspicious, and Quintin didn't give us away. And we're getting pizza, which I love, so I'm just going to put my parents out of my head, because I do *not* want to think about them as I spend time with my boyfriends. That would be too weird.

Figuring I still have some time before the pizza arrives, I reopen my laptop to finish the scene I was working on when my dad called. Once I get to a good stopping point, I close the computer and head downstairs.

They aren't in the kitchen or their computer room, so there's only one other likely place for them to be.

I open the door and make my way to the basement.

Chapter Twelve

The guys are sitting around on the sofa again, and for a moment it feels like the last time I came down here and Miles sat me on his lap. My stomach flips at the memory as I weave through the darkness to sit on the empty spot they left for me. This time, though, it smells like fresh warm pizza and there's a stack of boxes on the coffee table.

"What's the occasion?" I ask, as Ethan passes me a doubled up plate and opens a few boxes for me to pick out which kind I want.

"We won today," says Lionel, snagging two big slices weighted down with olives for himself and sitting back to lounge on the sofa.

"Is that rare?" I still haven't researched my roommates. I should have done that today since I found their names last night, but after all the ...activity ... yesterday, all I wanted to do was write down all the sensations and emotions before I forgot any of them.

Not that I think that's about to happen any time soon. Those orgasms were *memorable*.

"No, but they're a high-ranked team, so we figured we'd take tonight off," says Helix.

"So what are we watching then?" I get as comfortable as I can on the sofa, highly aware that as soon as we're done eating, they may decide that part of their winning celebration includes fucking their girlfriend.

"Oh, this show is awesome. You're going to love it," says Miles. "It's about a guy who flies through time and space in a police box."

"I've never heard of anything like that." Living here is apparently going to broaden more than just my sexual horizons.

Miles presses play and we all sit back to watch the show, casually munching on pizza. My roommates are especially hungry, grabbing seconds before we even fully know what the problem is that the travelers are supposed to be solving on this planet. Not that I blame them. I'm hungrier than normal myself after last night, and they did most of the work.

It's not long before all the pizza is polished off and the boxes have been moved to a corner so they can prop their stocking feet on the edge of the table. Half of me immediately thinks that we need to give this entire basement a solid once-over with some cleaner, and the other half is jealous that they get to stretch out and I'm stuck curled up in the corner.

As the second episode starts up, and my roommates make no attempts to move from the sofa, I begin to shift more in my seat. Not only from feeling cooped up in the corner, but because I'm wondering if and when they are going to flip the mood down here from "hang out" to "horny". I mean, this is nice, just relaxing together, but it's not how things have historically gone for us, and it's weirding me out.

"Stick your legs out straight," says Helix on my left.

This is it. The moment things turn from friendly to sexy.

"No, across my lap." Helix grabs my knees and turns me slightly so my legs drape across his lap and my feet end up in Miles's lap next to him.

But no one reaches for the zipper on my jeans to pull them down. Instead, Helix simply holds my legs as Miles massages my socked feet. It is not sexy, but it is relaxing. Having Miles rub my feet is the most pampered I've ever felt, which is both a little sad and also weird given that these guys aren't my real boyfriends. I've had actual boyfriends before, sort of, but they never just casually touched me like this. My roommates haven't taken me out on dates or anything, but here they are, making me feel almost cared for.

Ethan hooks his arm around my shoulders and turns me slightly, tucking me against his side so I can watch the show without getting a crick in my neck. The touch is so nonsexual, I'm not sure what to do with myself. I lay against him, waiting for something to change and for one of them to make a move, but nothing happens.

Eventually, I give in to the cozy vibe they've created and drape my arm low across Ethan's stomach, allowing the soothing touch of my roommates to help me sink into a sweet sleep.

I'm cozy and warm, snuggled into a soft pillow and hugged by blankets. I should still be solidly asleep. Why am I awake?

A hand snakes around my waist and pulls me back against a hard chest, shifting me to lay completely on my side as something firm nudges its way between my thighs.

I'm groggy, my throat dry from sleep and my thoughts muddled. Is this a dream?

The firm thing slides between my thighs, and a male voice groans behind me. Then the thing—a cock?—hits my clit on the next stroke before pulling back. A hand moves down my thigh, pushing it forward until my knee lays on the bed, giving whoever is behind me better access to my pussy. On the next stroke, the cock presses against my entrance and then shoves homes.

There's no foreplay, no slow stoking of the embers. No, he starts at full inferno, pumping hard and fast in short strokes. It takes my body a moment to catch up, but the fact that one of them snuck into my bed in the middle of the night for a quick fuck is a turn-on in and of itself.

Especially not knowing which one he is.

"I want you to squirt again," he groans in my ear, distorting his voice. "This time for me."

His words are dirty, if indecipherable. My entire focus is on the way our bodies are hooked together.

Still inside of me, my mystery boyfriend rolls me onto my stomach and begins pounding me into the mattress, his hips slamming into my ass with each powerful stroke. My fingers search for purchase, clawing into the pillow as my boyfriend drives this rollercoaster I'm on. It's so good, rough and wild and so different from the other experiences with these gamers. Pulling my pillow closer, I moan into it as an orgasm explodes through my body.

My boyfriend pounds into me twice more, and I'm sure I'm going to have bruises on my ass in the morning from his hipbones. Then he drops onto my back, pressing me down into the mattress as he groans into the crook of my neck. He's heavy on top of me, but my whole body feels so languid that it's like having a weighted blanket. Perfect for sleeping beneath.

My sleep shirt is rucked up beneath my arms. It's uncomfortable and bulky, but the weirdest part is that my body is warm. And getting warmer by the second. My head is still fuzzy from sleep and it feels so good, I never want to wake up from this dream.

"Good morning, sleeping beauty," whispers Helix, laving one of my nipples with the flat of his tongue. "Did you sleep well?"

"Mmmm." I can't even think of any words right now, let alone form any. Not with the way Helix's fingers are walking their way over my hip and down between my thighs.

My legs fall open of their own accord and let him in. I stretch my arms above my head, waking up quickly as he stretches my pussy open with two fingers. There's next to no resistance on my body's part, which makes me wonder how long Helix has been warming me up before I actually woke up. What a nice way to ease into the morning.

"Are you ready to take on the day?" Helix shifts until he's kneeling between my legs instead of lying next to me. "And my cock as well?"

Helix replaces his fingers with his cock, teasing the head along my seam before sliding the length of between my folds, hitting my clit and waking me up faster than any other method he's used so far.

"Yes." My body is ready. Helix might be a little cheesy in his own domineering way, but it's completely him, and most people aren't very authentic so the fact that he's not changing for anyone is special.

Without another word, Helix slams into me in one long stroke.

"Fuck!" My arms fly up to press my palms to the headboard so my head doesn't hit the hard wood. Helix touching me—fucking me—is the perfect way to begin the day, and a concussion would ruin it.

"That's the idea." Helix grins as he grips my hips and starts pounding into me with determination, slamming his hips into mine with each panting breath. "We have a ranked game today"—*slam*—"and I'm going to dominate."—*slam* —"I'm going to deal so much damage"—*slam*—"they'll be running back to their base"—*slam*.

Is Helix setting his intentions for the day while he fucks me? Or is he making a wish on this fuck?

Should I make a wish too? I wish first that he keeps fucking me and then, second, for my new book to be a bestseller.

Wait, no, those should be the other way around. Helix's thick cock driving into my wet, needy pussy is making me feel amazing, but I still need to remember my purpose here.

My thoughts are derailed as Helix reaches down to play with my nipples, swiping his thumb over them until they're standing tall and eager for attention. He's still whispering his mantra as he begins alternating pinches on my eager nipples. It hurts a bit, but when he lets go and the blood flows back, the pleasure is a high in and of itself.

"I'm so close to coming," says Helix, abandoning my breasts and lifting my hips to fuck me even faster. "Come so I can."

Helix flicks his thumb over my clit and stars burst behind my eyes. He fucks into me like I'm a toy until he's groaning out his own release. I should be memorizing the expression on Helix's face as he orgasms for my book, but I can't focus on anything but the pleasure coursing through my veins, both from my own slowly receding orgasm and from the knowledge that I did that to him. My body pushed him over the edge just as much as his did to me.

"Fuck, I needed that." Helix pulls out and gently sets my hips back on my bed as he rolls off the mattress. He leans over to plant a quick kiss on my lips, then heads out the door, still completely nude, his cock jutting out in front of him, slick with both of our cum.

"Good luck on your game," I call as he closes the door behind him.

Staring up at the ceiling, I let my breath regulate again and my heartbeat to slow back down to its normal rate. Thank god I'm on the pill because I hadn't even thought of a condom until now. Every so often, I glance over to the closed door, expecting it to open and any one of my other roommates to come in to fuck me also.

When I'm calm and my cooling sweat has me feeling a little chilly, I head into the shower. Helix didn't say anything about my being fucked by one of the other guys in the middle of the night. It almost feels like I'm sneaking around, but they all know about each other. And I assume they're all telling each other just about everything. We have a text thread between all six of us, but they probably have one between just them where they share who knows what.

The hot water from my shower eases my muscles from the multiple hard fucks I've had in the last twenty-four hours. I wouldn't change it for anything though. Not only because my body feels amazing, but because I now have so much material for my new books.

Drying off, I run through the list of things I should accomplish today. Number one on the list is sending out the new chapter for my critique group so they have enough time to read over it before we meet again. Looking up the term "squirting" so I understand what my mystery boyfriend said to me last night in bed. And I really need to do some actual research on my roommates. I'd thought they were nerdy, shy gamers, but based on their fucking styles, I'm beginning to wonder if there's much more to them than I realized. I really should find out more about them.

Not only for my safety, but because it seems they're going to end up being such a large part of my new books.

Chapter Thirteen

My face is beat red and I'm glad none of my boyfriends are in the room. I looked up the term I didn't know and now I almost wished I hadn't. Even more, I wish my body hadn't done it, let alone squirted in front of my boyfriends. I don't know how I'm going to look them in the eye again.

The only solution is to throw myself into my work and my research. The research that doesn't involve my boyfriends fucking me. At least right now.

I comb through my latest chapter that I wrote at the cafe with Sasha before uploading it onto our shared file folder. I'd thought I was on top of things, but Maddie and Angela have already uploaded their next chapters. Are they writing that far ahead? Now I feel like I'm behind. Maddie and Angela are both so confident and calm with the way they approach their businesses and writing. That's why I'm critiquing with them, to learn their ways and improve my own process.

I print off both of their chapters, and I really should dive in to the first read-through. Usually, I read through it once to see where things are going, and then go through the chapters again for actual edits and notes. Not that Angela and Maddie really need my input. They're both so talented, and their careers are proof of this.

It feels pointless to read their chapters. They probably throw my edits in the recycle bin as soon as they get home, never once looking at them.

My door is still closed. I wonder if any of my supposed boyfriends came in while I was in the shower, but didn't stick around. Although honestly, I'd be surprised if they showed up and didn't come to join me in the shower.

Helix had said they have a ranked game today, so maybe they've already started and I won't see them for hours. If that's the case, maybe now is the best time to research them. Still, I turn down the brightness on my screen in case one of them shows up for a last-minute fuck before their game.

Then I put the names of my roommates in the search bar and sit back, stunned, as millions of hits populate on the screen all the link descriptions them to each other and to other names I don't recognize.

Most of the links looks like they're videos, but if my roommates come upstairs they might be able to hear what I'm doing through the walls. I click on the ones that aren't videos. They're mostly press releases announcing either wins or that the guys are competing in different competitions.

The closer I read, though, I start noticing that the random names I occasionally hear my roommates call each other are also listed, and I realize that those are their gamer names. Their having gamer names isn't so different than authors having pen names, and a flutter runs through me at the thought. Could we have actual things in common other than our sexual needs?

I need to watch the videos. I grab my headphones and click on the first video that pops up. It's some guy talking about my roommates, complimenting them on the way they strategize and work together. There is some game-playing in the background, and the commentator seems to break down exactly what the team is doing, using phrases I don't understand, like "wombo combo" and "dunking". If he thinks they work together well in the computer world, he would be doubly impressed with how well they work together in real life.

Although I've only really seen partnerships so far, not the entire group involved at once.

Yet.

I'm sure they will want it to happen at some point. And if I'm honest with myself, as great as they've been so far I'll probably want that too.

I click through a couple of other similar videos until I come to one with some familiar voices.

A game is playing in the background, and the characters and imagery look similar to the game in the other videos. But there are five little boxes along the top of the screen, each one containing one of my roommates. They're strategizing what they're going to do next and telling each other where to go on the map, talking each other through the game and into a win.

I can see similarities between this version of the group and the men I know. They like to be in control in the game so they always come out on top, and they're just as bossy in the bedroom, ensuring they always get their way.

Not that I don't enjoy it.

Jumping ahead through the video, I watch them go through different scenarios, none of which make much sense to me. All I really understand is that they're trying to win, and they're working together to do it. And so far, they haven't really said anything about themselves. Everything is about their game.

I scroll down the page and my eye immediately catches

on the comments. Most of them are complimentary, commenting on my roommates' strategies and saying how much they like the game. Some are about the commentator's own struggles with the game.

When I jump back up toward the video, I spot that the description box right under the video has a "read more" dropdown arrow. I'd been so interested to see what everyone else thought of my guys that I'd completely skipped over it before.

The description is pretty basic, and none of the words besides "win" mean much to me. But at the bottom are links to watch live.

I glance over at the door again. It would be so embarrassing if they caught me researching them. I mean, I've been using them for research ever since I moved in, but they don't know that, and there's a difference between using them to help me research and actually researching them.

Clicking on the link, I see that my roommates are running a live stream.

That answers the question of whether or not they're about to barge in on me researching them. Though it's more like borderline stalking them at this point, since I'm literally watching them through a camera right now. But to be fair, they're the ones streaming the video for the whole world to see.

Listening to my boyfriends confidently order each other into different battle strategies, I try to read the chats and comments from other people watching them play, but it's all going so fast. How many people are even here watching them play this game in the middle of the day?

The view counter is on the left side bar, and if I were drinking anything, I'd probably choke. Over thirty thousand people are watching this live stream right now? How is that even possible? Don't they have to go to work?

No wonder there is so much happening in the chat that I can't follow along.

Giving up on that, I scroll down a little farther, and right below the list of the team members' names is the most shocking thing of all: the guys have over *two million* subscribers to their feed. How is that even possible? I don't think any of the romance authors I've checked out while debating whether or not to make the move to writing higher heat levels even have close to that many followers.

My mind can't even wrap around the fact that these five gamers, who had to put up a flyer around town to *hire a girlfriend*, are actually that well-known and have that many followers. It can't be real. My head is reeling as their voices chatter in my headphones without me paying attention to what they're saying.

On their site, I can see their whole streaming schedule. That could be helpful, so I can know when I might be interrupted in my work and when I'll have ensured solitude. But they also seem to have a private, paid-subscription chat where followers can have even more access to my roommates and actually talk to them.

Should I do it? I'm so curious what my roommates talk about in the private chats that no one else can see. Are they talking about me? Telling their followers all about the live-in girlfriend they hired, whom they can share whenever and wherever in their house?

I have to know. I don't know what I'll do if I don't like what I see, but if it's really upsetting I want to know so I can leave this situation and go ... I don't know where. That's a bridge I'll cross if and when I get there.

It's pretty cheap to subscribe, and although I'm not making much right now off the few sweet romance books I have published, I'm also not spending money on rent or food, so I can swing the cost. Besides, I don't have to subscribe forever. I can subscribe for a month just to look around and see what my boyfriends are like when I'm not around, and then bail. This could help me get to know—and my current situation—better.

Obviously, I don't want them to know it's me, so I need a fake name to join under. I'm not sure any of the guys even knows my last name though, to be honest. I've never told them and they've never asked. Still, it's better to be safe than sorry, and luckily, I already have a fake name I'm planning on using for my upcoming spicy romance books.

As I'm putting in my credit card details though, I start doing the math. If this is how much they charge to be their follower, and they have over two million followers, then they're making intense amounts of money each month. I can't wrap my mind around such a figure. The platform probably takes a portion, and then taxes, but still. So much money! No wonder they can afford such a big house here in Chicago.

And they should also be able to afford a cleaner to come in regularly so this place isn't so dirty.

Although I'm not sure how I'll approach that conversation. It's not like I can go up to them and say that I've stalked them online and now I know they're loaded so they need to hire a housekeeper so the house isn't so gross all the time.

Once I hit the button to submit my payment and I'm officially a follower, I check out their private chatting platform. It's both overwhelming and quiet. There are tons of chats I could go back through and read, but the latest update is just a post from Helix that they're starting a live stream and everyone should jump in to watch.

No sense in reading the whole backlog right now, though, with my roommates playing an actual game I can watch.

I pull out the chapters I need to critique for this week and turn down the volume a little on my headset so I can focus while still listening to the commanding voices of my boyfriends. I'm not really following along with their game, but it doesn't matter since I couldn't really follow along when I was paying attention, either. Besides, while yes, it is soothing to listen to their voices, listening to the stream will also let me know when they're finishing up with their work so I won't be caught by surprise if they come straight upstairs to find me.

I'm definitely not listening mostly because their voices are comforting. Nope. Not at all.

Chapter Fourteen

Fuck, I'm running late. I'd been so distracted with listening to yet another of my roommates' live streams—it's become a bit of an obsession since I joined their subscription platform a week ago—that I lost track of the time. Now I need to shower and dress for lunch with my parents as fast as possible. Hopefully they'll also be running behind due to traffic.

The front doorbell rings and I freeze in the middle of brushing my hair. I'd been planning to pull it back in a braid, but now there's absolutely no time. *They're here.* I yank the brush through my hair to make sure there aren't tangles before throwing down my brush and grabbing my purse.

Please let my boyfriends still be playing their game.

Racing down the stairs, I nearly trip as I spot Miles opening the door. *Fuck.*

I practically crash into Miles as I attempt to shove my body between him and my parents to usher them back out the front door. For being a gamer, he's pretty solid though, and doesn't budge. Just stands there holding the door open as my parents stand, confused, on the front stoop.

"Ready to go?" I duck under Miles's arm to grab my jacket. I can put it on outside in the cold so long as I get my parents away from Miles and all the potential for this to become very awkward, very fast.

"What's the rush, honey?" asks Mom. "It's almost as if you don't want us to come in and meet your roommates."

"Yeah, Clarissa," says Miles. "Do you not want your parents to meet all of us?"

He smiles, and there's a teasing aspect to the way he lifts the corner of his mouth. Of course he had to call me out in front of my parents. It's either admit to them all that I don't want them to meet, or let them talk and potentially tell each other my secrets.

"No, that's not it at all." I attempt to wave way Miles's question as if it's not a big deal. "I just figured my parents are hungry, and I don't want to make them stand around on the front stoop for ages. Better to head out to lunch someplace warm."

"You make a very good point," says Miles, his grin turning Cheshire. "Why don't you two come on in where it's warm, and you can meet everyone else."

Miles forces the door open even farther, practically yanking it out of my hand as I attempt to hold it in a way to block their view of the inside. I still remember all the negative comments my parents made about the state of the house last time they were inside, and I fear they're going to make the same types of comments again, but this time in front of the people who pay for everything. As if the stress of them finding out the reality of my living situation isn't enough.

"Oh, that sounds wonderful, thank you," says Mom, immediately stepping inside and looking around as if inspecting the space to catalogue the differences.

"I wouldn't mind meeting these fellas also, Clarissa,"

says Dad, joining us in the hallway. "Would be nice to know who you're living with in case something goes wrong, and to make sure you're being safe and taken care of."

Miles chokes on a laugh that he hastily turns into a cough as my face goes beet red. There's absolutely no way my dad can know just how well my roommates have been *taking care* of me. This is already so embarrassing, and we've only all been together for a minute. And without the other four guys.

"I can take care of myself, Dad," I insist, avoiding Miles's eye.

"Yeah, you can," chokes out Miles, still hiding his laugh.

I shoot him a glare, my face heating at the memory of Miles discovering that I'd fallen asleep in my bed after masturbating to thoughts of him.

Which my parents do *not* need to know about.

"Well, I will say that this hall looks much better than when we helped you move in," says Mom, looking up into each corner to search out any missed cobwebs.

"We did recently mop due to a"—Miles glances at me —"a spill."

This man is determined to embarrass me in front of my parents, and I hate that it's working.

"... because your roommates couldn't be bothered to help," says Mom, continuing on as if Miles hadn't said anything.

My cheeks heat again, but this time it's my mother who's embarrassing me. I really don't want my parents to insult my roommates the entire time they're here.

"I told you, Mom, they were working." I don't want to look at Miles because I don't want to embarrass him, either. They'd been very clear about needing to work and now that I've seen the intensity of their streaming schedule, I don't know how they handle working so much. And that's coming from me, someone who really likes to work a lot.

"And no one could take a day off work?" asks Mom. "Your father did."

"Their work is a little bit different than Dad's," I say, although I'm not going to go into details about how different. Mostly because I still don't fully understand their job, and I'm sure neither of my parents will either.

"I'm just complimenting them on cleaning up this front hallway," my mom argues. "It was a mess, and now it looks better."

"No, you were complaining that my roommates work a lot."

"I agree that the front hall looks fantastic," says Miles, jumping in before Mom and I can get into a fight. "Clarissa has definitely been a big help around the house. She's quick to jump in and take care of things we may have let slide as we get distracted by our gaming."

I glance to my mom to see if she's actually listening because if she heard Miles say "distracted by our gaming" she's going to have a fit about what is proper behavior for someone our age.

"I wouldn't say fantastic," counters Mom. At least she is focusing on the wrong part of the conversation.

Miles's eyes dart to the box filled with all the junk that I'd declared doesn't belong in this room, still sitting in the corner waiting to be moved to a proper place.

"Well, at least you're making progress," says Mom, as Dad links her arm through his. This silences her, but she still gives me a look that makes my stomach sink.

It's the same disapproving-yet-resigned look she gives Dad whenever I mention my author career, and for some reason I don't want my parents to feel that way about my roommates. I still want to hide that there's more of a relationship between us than I've let on, but I don't want my parents to think badly of them.

"Maybe we should get going." If my parents keep looking, they'll definitely find more things to disapprove of and complain about, and then they'll spend lunch pressuring me to move back home. "We don't want to be late for our reservation."

"We didn't make one," says Dad. "We wanted to see where you recommend we go, since you know the city better than us."

"Oh, if you have time then, I can show you the rest of the house if you like," offers Miles. "Admittedly, we haven't gotten to cleaning the other rooms yet, but like you said, we're making progress."

"He means *Clarissa* is making progress," Mom whispers to Dad, but we all hear her.

Dad pats her hand, resting in the crook of his elbow, and we trudge behind Miles deeper into the house. Miles stops right outside the computer den and throws open the doors for my parents to look inside.

Admittedly, this is the one room the gamers maintain fairly well, probably because they care so much about their computers and need the videos to look good for their streams.

"What all is it that you all do again?" asks Dad. "I'm not sure Clarissa ever told us."

"We're gamers," says Miles as if that's a perfectly ordinary job and my Dad won't have a hundred more questions.

"All of you?" asks Dad, not sure how to process such a career. "Doesn't sound much like a job, more like a fun hobby."

If Dad knew what I recently discovered about their finances, he wouldn't say that. And definitely not to Miles's face.

"Oh, we do okay," says Miles, glancing over at me. I keep my face neutral.

"I suppose you're young yet, but you'll want to start thinking about your future at some point and what you're going to do long-term." Dad lifts his hand in acknowledgment that he's giving unsolicited advice before adding, "But I'm sure your parents have already had that discussion with you."

This is so embarrassing. My boyfriends are all my age and based on my math, they're earning more in a month than my parents could dream of making in their lifetimes. But of course, I can't say anything because then I'll give myself away as having looked into them.

"Who was at the door?" asks Lionel, coming around the corner from the kitchen with a bag of chips in one hand and an energy drink in the other.

"Clarissa's parents," says Miles over his shoulder.

"Oh, hello Clarissa's parents," says Lionel, shooting me a smile that gives me the sinking feeling that I'm about to regret everything that has led me to this moment.

My other boyfriends trail in from the kitchen behind Lionel. They must have taken a break from their gaming for snacks or lunch. *Great, now my parents can judge the way they eat as well as their career choices.* At least Miles takes over the task of introducing everyone so I don't have to, allowing me to fully wallow in my embarrassment and anxiety that my roommates are going to let something slip about our unconventional relationship.

It doesn't help that they all look like cats who caught the canary.

"Now that you've met everyone, we should probably leave for lunch. I'm sure you're both hungry." I step between my parents and my boyfriends in hopes that I can herd my mom and dad back toward the front door.

"Since you don't have reservations already, maybe you want to check out the Thai place down the block. We get it sometimes for takeout," suggests Miles, holding my parents' attention.

"That's a good idea," says Mom. "I love Thai food."

"We wouldn't lose our parking spot and have to find a new one somewhere else," Dad muses. Of course he's thinking about the practical logistics instead of what he's actually hungry for.

"Since you know where it is, would you like to join us?" asks Mom, as if I can't get us there myself.

Although to be fair, I don't know exactly where this place is since I've never been there, but Mom doesn't know that. Besides, how hard can it really be to find a Thai takeout place that's just down the block?

"We can continue to discuss your future career options too," says Dad, finally heading toward the door and apparently having forgotten that he isn't supposed to be offering unasked for career advice.

"And how it's going with all of you living together," adds Mom, completely committed to the idea of interrogating my roommates.

"I'm sure they have to work, and we don't want to intrude on their plans," I say weakly. I have to stop this potential disaster forming right before my eyes.

"Not a problem," says Miles. "The benefit of working for yourself is that you get to pick when you take breaks. You all don't mind pushing back practice a little bit do you?" he asks the others. "For our Clarissa."

I didn't think I could blush any harder than I already

am, but apparently my embarrassment knows no limits today and my face heats even more. My parents cannot learn how much I really am *their* Clarissa. *This is not going to end well.*

"Thai sounds better than chips. I'm in," says Lionel, and the other gamers quickly agree.

"Wonderful," says Mom, pausing beside the front door. "We can wait here while you get ready to go."

"Oh, we're ready now," says Helix, dropping his snacks on the hall table.

Mom glances down at their sweatpants, horror clear on her face. For a woman who can't imagine leaving the house without a full face of makeup, the idea of going out in public with five gamers in sweatpants and T-shirts is making her eye twitch.

"Let's go upstairs and you can all change into jeans instead." I herd my roommates up the stairs even as they grumble about preferring their sweatpants. "Do you even own jeans? All you ever wear are sweatpants."

"Are you at least going to help us take off our pants, then?" teases Helix as soon as we hit the upstairs landing. At least he has the decency to keep his voice low enough that my parents won't hear him from downstairs.

"No," I answer immediately, but at his pouting look, I relent a little. "Maybe after my parents leave, but only if you all agree to be on your best behavior during lunch."

"We're always good," says Ethan.

"Especially based on all of your moans," agrees Quintin. "I'd say we're very good."

"That's not what I mean, and you know it." I cover my face with my hands and fight to regain my composure. If my parents weren't here, I would probably give in to their flirtatious banter. It's been less than twenty-four hours since I've gotten any new research material, and while I'd never admit it to anyone, I've kind of missed their attention. But my parents are downstairs and I don't want to keep them waiting because if they're left unsupervised for too long, they'll snoop around. All in the spirit of taking care of me, but still. It's better to get them out of the house as soon as possible.

"I still don't understand why we have to wear jeans to leave the house since we've never had to before," says Ethan, pouting.

"My parents are ..." I hesitate, struggling with how to describe my parents in a way that won't reflect too negatively on them. "... strict about what they think is appropriate."

Really, my parents just have strict beliefs about how lives should be lived, and they involve dressing a certain way, ticking off certain life achievements in a certain order, and never discussing certain topics, such as sexuality. Which is a big part of why I initially decided to keep the romance in my books closed-door. That way I could write the genre that I love without them disapproving of my career choice.

They're also big on monogamy, so they will *not* be pleased if they find out I have five boyfriends.

"Parents love us," says Ethan, looking around at his teammates. "At least, they love me."

"Not my parents," I shoot back.

"But we're your boyfriends," says Lionel, crossing his arms as if he's ready to take a stand against my parents and force them to like him.

"Yeah, well, they don't know about that part." I scrub my hands over my eyes because this conversation shouldn't even be happening. I mentally kick myself for being so behind in getting ready for lunch. "They'll like you fine enough as my roommates even though they definitely disapprove of your career choices, but they don't know about the whole supposed-dating aspect of our living together."

"Just so we're clear," says Lionel, stepping closer until I back up into Quintin, "there's no supposed about it. You're our girlfriend, all the benefits included, end of discussion."

"Not end of discussion where my parents are concerned," I shoot back.

"So we're your dirty little secret?" Ethan looks so hurt, and I cringe a little, hating that I put him in that position.

They're not just a secret from my parents, they're a secret from everyone.

"Fine," grunts Quintin, wrapping his hands around my waist from behind and pulling me tight against his body. "What do we get for keeping your secret?"

"Any ideas?" adds Lionel, steeping closer until I'm pressed between their two bodies.

Oh, I have a lot of ideas. One of them being to hook my leg up over Lionel's waist and let him fuck me right here against Quintin's body.

But my parents are downstairs. Waiting for us. So we can go to lunch.

"You'll wear normal jeans and be nice to my parents and keep my secrets?" I glance at the stairwell, praying my parents haven't overheard this entire conversation.

"If the conditions are right for us," agrees Miles, eyes dark as he takes in the way I'm pinned between two of his teammates.

"What do you want in exchange?" I bite my lip. All of my ideas might be dirty, but I'm sure anything they come up with will be dirtier. And way more enticing than going out lunch with my parents.

"Maybe we could watch something together," suggests

Helix, looking around to his teammates to gauge their reactions.

The slow smirks that unfold across their faces tell me they're not suggesting just any old movie. My heart races, eager to follow them down whatever dirty path they lead me.

After lunch with my parents, that is.

Chapter Fifteen

"Fine, deal." We don't have time to sort out details right now because we've already been up here a suspiciously long time and I really don't want my parents coming up to check on us.

As soon as the words are out of my mouth, Quintin drops his hands and they all disperse into their rooms. I kind of want to peek inside their rooms since they've all seen the inside of mine, but now isn't the time.

Maybe I can get them to invite me into their personal spaces at some point. If I suggest a little sexy time on their beds, would they really say no?

As my boyfriends come out of their rooms still zipping their jeans, I realize I've watched them pull down their sweatpants, but I've always been so wrapped up in my post-orgasm haze I haven't paid attention to the part where they get dressed again after.

Maybe we do have an extra couple of minutes to spare. If we're quick. And extra quiet.

I shake my head to dislodge the thought. I'd rather have enough time to really enjoy myself. Plus, we really *have* been up here a lot longer than we should have been.

I lead the group of them back downstairs. There's a shuffling sound and when they come into view, my parents are standing weirdly straight and stiffly, and I'm certain they were snooping through the box of random stuff I'd cleared off the front hall table. I hope they haven't found anything embarrassing. I don't think there were any sex toys in there. Pretty sure I'd remember if I threw any in.

Yikes, we need to leave now.

"Ready?" I ask, my voice coming out higher than normal. I open the door for everyone to file out quickly, and hope any awkwardness stays behind and we can get through lunch without any trouble.

My parents hurry outside. I'm not sure if they're also feeling the tension, or if they're just hungry and ready for lunch.

"Yeah," my boyfriends grumble as they troupe out the door behind my parents.

Moving to the front of the pack, I lead my parents down the street in what I'm pretty sure is the direction of the restaurant. I keep the conversation light, hoping they forget about how they disapprove of my roommates' careers, and focus on things they actually want to talk about. Such as their drive in today, and all their neighborhood gossip.

I'm not ignoring the guys, or punishing them for tagging along on our little lunch outing. I'm just distracting my parents from asking about how our living together is going. They might have agreed to keep the fact that we're sleeping together a secret, but that's not to say they won't accidentally let something slip and end up with my parents shifting from conversation to interrogation.

We file into the restaurant and suddenly I get the overwhelming feeling that this whole thing is about to become even more of a disaster.

"Table for eight," I tell the host. Hopefully they have

enough space to push a few tables together for us without too much of a wait. Otherwise, we'll have to choose a different place to go, and probably will have to drive there since my parents claim public transport makes them nervous.

"Actually we have a reservation under Miles," says Miles, stepping around us.

"Of course," says the host, "right this way." They weave through the tables to the back of the restaurant, stack of menus in hand.

My parents follow immediately, but I grab Miles' arm and slow him down, bottlenecking the rest of our roommates behind us.

"You called ahead?" I'm shocked that he thought ahead and I hadn't. I'd been so preoccupied with ensuring my parents don't learn my secret, I hadn't even considered how hard it could be for the restaurant to seat eight people.

"It's lunchtime," points out Miles, looking back at our roommates. "And there are kind of a lot of us."

I want to say more, to thank him and tell him what he did was thoughtful, but we've arrived at a large round table and now I'm distracted worrying about the seating arrangement. It will be hard to keep my parents separated from the guys with this too cozy layout.

It's not that I don't trust my roommates. It's just that aside from their live streams, I've only heard them talk about fucking me, so the options for conversation seem to be gaming—which my parents wouldn't enjoy—or fucking—which neither my parents nor I would enjoy at this moment. Well, my parents wouldn't enjoy it at any moment, and while I've recently been coming around to the topic, it's not on my list of things I want to talk about in a restaurant with my parents.

As soon as we've ordered, the interrogation I feared

begins. Although at least I'm their first victim, not my roommates.

"How's the writing going, honey?" asks Dad, trying to sound supportive in spite of the fact that I know he wishes I would give up my dream of writing full-time.

All five of my roommates' heads turn in my direction, and they sit up straighter, leaning in for details of this part of my life that they're not aware of.

"Good." I want so much to look over at them, but I resist. Instead, I take a quick sip of my water as I brace myself to brush off something I would normally love to talk about. "My critique partners are really enjoying my new chapters, so I'm quite pleased."

"That's good news," says Dad, oblivious to my desire to change the subject to almost literally anything else. "And they're being helpful with advice?"

It's so generic and unspecific, I can't help but smile. At least Dad's trying to be involved in my writing career, even though he would rather I pick a "normal" job, something that he'd actually understand. He wants me to have consistency in my life. A regular paycheck. Clear, easily defined achievements. Working for someone else and barely getting by is something he understands. Deciding to be an author, especially a romance author, not so much. But at least he's still showing me he cares by trying to be supportive.

"Very," I assure him.

Dad drums his fingers on the table. "And you're still meeting regularly?"

"Every week in the same place," I add, treating the conversation as seriously as possible given how vague and boring his questions are. He doesn't know what to ask me because he doesn't really want full details. "It's good to have that consistency to hold us accountable and ensure we hit our goals. Breaking them down so they're manageable."

"Good, good." Dad nods and sips his water. "Consistency is key."

Mom shifts in her seat, turning toward me as if about to ask a question. I steel myself for her to shift the topic away from my writing to god knows what. Maybe which of my old classmates are engaged, or which of them just got promoted. She seems to think I should be jealous of them or feel bad that we're living life so differently. I don't want what they have. I don't want to get engaged to some guy I had barely interacted with in high school, or to be the manager of a team of people I used to ride the bus with. I want to be a successful author, living in the city, having experiences I couldn't find in my small hometown.

Like living and sleeping with five famous gamers I met through a flyer.

But before Mom can say whatever she was planning to say, Miles speaks up.

"You never told us you're a writer," he says, almost accusingly.

I lick my lips nervously. This was part of what I'd wanted to avoid.

"You never asked." I don't entirely blame them, but there's a power difference between us in the house, and even if I wanted to tell them what I do—which I really didn't—there hasn't exactly been an opportunity, on account of almost all of our interactions being exclusively sexual in nature.

"If you're so ashamed of what you're writing that you don't want to tell anyone," says Mom, "maybe you shouldn't be writing it."

I sigh deeply. *This old argument.* "I'm not ashamed of

writing romance. I merely don't want to make others uncomfortable with it."

Because I'm more than aware of how uncomfortable it makes my parents. Dad tells people I write sweet romance books, even though my next book will be super spicy. Mom, on the other hand, doesn't tell anyone what I do for a living here, just that I'm "chasing my dreams"

"Isn't the fact that it makes others uncomfortable a sign that you should pursue a different career?" says Mom. "Jodie down the street was just saying the other day that the real estate company she does accounting for is looking for a new receptionist. You'd be great at something like that."

"I don't want to be a receptionist. I'm an author," I repeat for at least the hundredth time. I am a little impressed at their ability to suggest a different job each time, I have to admit. Very creative of them.

"You didn't even tell your roommates what you do for a living," argues Mom. "Didn't you have to disclose your job to them when you applied for the room so they'd know if you could cover your share of the rent? Are you just making up jobs now so you don't have to tell people what you're really doing?"

Yikes. How am I supposed to respond to that?

"I tell people I work from home, and most people are so blasé about jobs they don't really ask for any of the details." All of this is true. Like my stories, the fibs I've been telling lately are always a little bit based on real life.

Our food arrives and I'm crossing my fingers that it brings a change in conversation, but as soon as the waiter steps away, my roommates are right back on the subject. They've chosen the worst possible time to take an interest in my life for the first time ever. If we were at home alone, I could use sex to distract them, but that's not an option in the middle of a restaurant with my parents right here.

"What type of romance do you write?" asks Ethan, cutting his noodles into small bites with a knife and fork instead of using the chopsticks.

The others all look at him in surprise. I'm not sure if it's because of the question itself, or because he asks it so nonchalantly.

He looks up from his food and shrugs. "I have two sisters. They're always talking about the book club they're in, and apparently it's a smutty one."

"Our Clarissa writes sweet, heart-warming love stories that involve a lot of feelings and emotions," says Dad.

I nearly choke on my tofu. "How do you—have you, uh, have you read them?"

Please, please, please say no. I wouldn't be able to look him in the eye ever again. Even though the ones that have already been published don't have an ounce of spice.

"Uh, no." Dad's cheeks redden a bit. "I read the reviews."

"Oh, okay." I didn't want him to say he had read them, but at the same time, I'm disappointed that he hasn't. I'm not sure if it's because he didn't read my books to support me, or because if he read my reviews, he probably knows how few of them there are.

A tiny part of me debates telling them my next book will be straight up smutty, but I shove that though as far down as it will go. I'm not remotely ready to open that can of worms. Especially in public when we're trying to have a nice lunch.

At least if we're talking about my writing, there's a lot less chance of someone slipping up and clueing my parents in to what the guys and I have been getting up to around the house.

"Even if it's not smutty, you'll have to tell me the name later so I can recommend it to my sisters," says Ethan.

"They'd love to read it. Even more so since I know the author."

All I can do is sit here in shock, fighting back the tingle of tears. I barely know these men. I've all but lied to them about what I do for a living and I'm using them to further my career without their knowledge, yet Ethan is being casually supportive as if it's the most natural thing in the world.

"That's very kind," I manage to squeak out, dropping my eyes to my plate to pretend that didn't just happen. If I can ignore it, I won't have to unpack the swirl of emotions I'm feeling at this unexpected act of kindness and can focus on surviving this lunch.

Everyone is silent for a few awkward beats, until Helix launches into a story about how once when he was a kid, he'd found a romance novel his mom had left in the living room and he'd been traumatized. The others tease him about maybe having read it in private at some point, alluding to him masturbating to the story, but Helix vehemently denies this, aghast at the thought.

"My *mom* read that book," he reminds them. "And probably enjoyed it. Even back then, I knew what a lot of romance novels have in them. No way was I opening it up. I don't need to know what sorts of stuff my mom was reading in there." He shivers, accenting his disgust at the suggestion.

It's not the story I would have chosen for Helix to tell in front of my parents, but at least it carries us through to the end of the meal when we can finally leave. Next time my parents visit, I'm setting multiple alarms so there is absolutely no way I'm not the first one to the door.

Dad signals for the check, and the waiter comes over to inform him that the bill has already been taken care of. His eyebrows lift in surprise, and he looks to Mom, silently asking if she'd already paid. She looks just as confused as he does.

My roommates aren't surprised at all though, and are standing to leave. They've got a schedule to stick to not only for their gaming, but for their fans too. All two million of them. Including me now.

"Thank you for lunch," I tell them, because if my parents didn't pay the bill, and it wasn't me, it has to have been them.

"Yes, that was very kind of you," says Mom, clearly skeptical about how they can afford it.

"You let us pick the place, so treating was the least we could do," says Quintin.

"Besides," Lionel says, looking at me. "We're just glad we were able to all meet."

Well, they definitely know I'd been trying to avoid them meeting my parents today. As soon as we get home, they'll say something about it, and it'll be a whole thing. I'm not even sure why they wanted to be here, since they're missing out on time they could be working, and it's not like we're actually in a relationship. They're not really my boyfriends. More like my bosses, and roommates.

"Us too," says Dad. "It's good to know who Clarissa is living with since we just want to make sure our little girl is safe, and happy."

"Next time we go out, it can be our treat," suggests Mom.

I doubt she actually wants to have lunch with my roommates again, but her Midwest compass is strong. Besides, she probably thinks they're like me, young adults struggling to get by in jobs they love and are passionate about, but aren't necessarily big money makers.

How wrong she is.

We return to the house and I pay special attention to

my parents the whole way, avoiding the upcoming difficult and awkward conversation with my roommates and ensuring my parents' feathers aren't too ruffled from all the talk about romance books at lunch. They've always had a strong sense of propriety and what is and isn't appropriate conversation, especially in public and in front of strangers.

Besides, I need distance from my boyfriends right now because their automatically paying for our lunch is unsettling, and my thoughts about it are all over the place. It makes sense, since they can afford it while my parents would have blown their whole monthly budget to pay for all of us to eat at that restaurant. But was it more than that? Were they trying to make a good impression on my parents? Or is it because they're just nice guys? I had intended to keep things strictly business between us so I can easily move out once I'm earning enough money to afford my own place.

Even if that business includes getting fucked frequently and in all sorts of ways.

Outside our house, the gamers lead the way up the steps to unlock the front door. I have a key, but they're always home so I never use it.

"Do you want to come inside for coffee?" asks Ethan, making no move to approach the door.

My other roommates pause on the stairs, and I groan internally. It's sweet of Ethan to offer, and he's definitely impressing my parents with his manners, but there is no way in hell that I'm letting him drag this out any longer.

Mom and Dad are probably more impressed than me because they're not also juxtaposing this kind thoughtfulness with the way he fucked me against Lionel's chest the other night in the front hallway.

"Thank you," says Mom hesitantly, glancing at Dad. "But we can't."

"Traffic, you know," says Dad, jumping in to help Mom.

"We don't want to get caught in any rush hour traffic on our way home."

"Of course," says Ethan, as if he ever even leaves the house, let alone drives.

Every single one of my roommates jogs back down the stairs and shakes hands with both of my parents, murmuring that it was nice to meet them before heading inside.

Left alone with my parents on the sidewalk, I'm intensely aware of all the unsaid things between us. I'd like to ask what they think of my roommates, but that might give away that there's more between us than just platonically living together. They can't find out they're my boyfriends. Especially if Dad is reading the reviews of all my books.

"Well, we have to head out, but it was good to see you," says Dad, pulling me in for a bear hug goodbye.

"Just consider Jodie's offer." Mom leans in to give me the quickest of hugs and a kiss on the cheek. "It'd give you a chance to move back home and be among family again."

"Thanks, but I'm happy here." When her face falls a little, I rush to add, "But if that changes, I'll be sure to let you know."

She nods and takes my dad's hand. I watch as they walk over to their car, their shoulders brushing gently until Dad opens the car door and helps her inside. It's always been that way, his acting like a gentleman. He's part of the reason I started writing sweet romance. So I could show people the true love I witnessed every day growing up.

But that's not what sells, and it's not what everyone gets in real life. So as soon as they pull into traffic, I head up the stairs to my own much more precarious and naughty reality.

I'd expected to find my boyfriends waiting in the hallway, determined to have a postmortem of our lunch. They probably have more invasive questions about my romance writing that they didn't want to bring up in front of my parents. Not to mention, I owe them a thank you for being on such good behavior, and they will probably want a reward.

Honestly, after how sweet they were and having seen them looking ... well, not dressed up, exactly, but maybe more presentable, in jeans, I'm not opposed to giving them all some sort of treat. I could use an orgasm or two myself to relieve the tension from all the stilted conversation.

But the front hall is empty, and they're not in the computer room or kitchen, either. Very weird. They're almost always in one of those two places, and now I'm not quite sure what to do with myself.

Work, I guess. Work is always the answer in the face of uncertainty. Besides I'm not caught up on my notes about my last encounter, with Helix. Then there's turning those notes into actual chapters. In fact, they've been giving me so much material, I'll have enough to either write multiple books, or—and the idea makes my thighs clench—I could release some erotica shorts. I've heard of other authors doing that under other pen names, just dirty scenes with little to no plot.

That's actually not a bad idea. It's another way I could earn money so I'm not completely dependent on my roommates to pay for everything. It'd also supplement my income in between my full-length novels, since those take longer than I'd like to write.

Heading up the stairs, I nearly run into Lionel coming down, still tying his sweatpants.

"Don't forget about our deal," says Lionel.

"I won't." I swallow hard, my eyes focused on the way his hands are so close to his cock.

It'd be easy for Lionel to hook his thumbs into the waistband and push them down just enough for his hard cock to pop out. I had a big meal at the restaurant, but I could make enough room for a bit of cock.

Quintin nearly runs into us in the middle of the stairs, adjusting his own sweatpants. Clearly they all rushed up to their rooms to change so they didn't have to spend a minute longer than necessary in jeans.

"Did you remind Clarissa about our deal?" asks Quintin. "Because we all wore jeans like she asked."

"Lionel did. And you were all very nice to my parents, which I appreciate." It wasn't an experience I want to repeat, but they weren't as terrible as they could have been. At least they didn't mention that I'm sleeping with all of them.

"We're going to work for a bit, and then you'll fulfill your end of the bargain, Clarissa?" asks Miles, joining us on the stairs.

There isn't much room here on the stairs. We could have moved this conversation anywhere else, yet here we are, all shoved together in this tight space.

"Sure." I nod. A movie might actually be a nice, relaxing way to finish off a stressful day.

They slide past me and make their way downstairs while I continue heading up. I meet Ethan closing the door to his bedroom behind him as he steps into the hall.

"Thank you again for being so nice at lunch." I go up on tiptoe to kiss his cheek. "I appreciate your offer to tell your sisters about my books, but I won't hold you to it."

"Why not?" asks Ethan.

"Because it was just something nice you said in front of my parents to get them to like you, and it might be weird for you to suggest my books to them," I explain. "Especially because my next one will be more, uh, spicy."

His sisters won't want to read spice inspired by their brother. Or, in some cases, lifted almost completely from his actions. Not that they'll know it's inspired by him and his teammates, but still.

"If you're writing a spicy romance, that's all the better because they'll love it even more," says Ethan, setting his hands on my shoulders to keep me facing him. "Look, you're our girlfriend. That means we're here to support you, and not just financially."

"I know, you're supporting me sexually too." It's a bad joke, but I feel like I need to make light of this situation. I don't want Ethan to know how much his words mean to me right now, after my parents' lack of support for my dreams.

"Yeah, that too." Ethan chuckles good-naturally. "I have practice, but we'll see you after, okay?"

I nod, and he leans down to kiss me once more. "Oh yeah, and the guys texted—they don't want you to masturbate while we're downstairs working."

"Okay." I turn my face away so he doesn't see how embarrassed I am. They probably all noticed how I was checking the front of their sweatpants to see if their cocks were hard as they went past me on the stairs. *How did I become this thirsty woman?*

Ethan jogs downstairs to catch up with his teammates, and I glance around the upstairs hall. If they're down in their computer room, I have at least an hour or two alone when they won't come looking for me. There'd be no way for them to find out if I peeked inside their rooms. I wouldn't even need to go inside, just open the doors and take a look. See what they look like. It's not really snooping if it's just a quick glimpse, right?

I put my hand on Ethan's doorknob because it's the closest. All I have to do is turn the handle. It'd be so easy. But I can't bring myself to do it. This isn't like researching my roommates online. That's all available information they put out there for the public and their fans to know, but this feels personal and invasive in an icky way. I'd never want them to do it to me.

Dropping my hand, I cross the hall to my own bedroom. I have new chapters to write.

Instead of pulling up my document though, my mouse is already clicking on the bookmarked link to their subscription channel. I might not be willing to invade their privacy by going into their rooms, but if they're online for everyone to watch, I may as well keep an eye on when they're finishing work so I can be prepared for them to come looking for me. It's not like there's any other reason that I'd sit and listen to them talk about gaming all afternoon.

Except they're not streaming, and my stomach sinks. If they're downstairs, they should be online, and the fact that they aren't is more than disconcerting. That's probably why I feel funny—I'm anxious about what they're up to. Not disappointed that I can't watch them.

Grumbling to myself, I click on my manuscript, but I left off in the middle of a sex scene and I don't want to write this right now. The blinking cursor taunts me, reminding me that every minute I don't spend writing is a minute farther away from making money off this book. But I just can't make myself put my fingers on the keyboard.

I'm out of sorts after seeing my parents and distracted with wondering what the guys are up to. *That must be it.*

I click on my critique group's shared folder to check if Sasha has uploaded her new chapter yet. If I can edit her work, I'll successfully avoid my own work and take my mind off of my roommates not streaming, but still be doing something productive.

But there's nothing new yet. *Why is the world not letting me procrastinate the way I want to?*

My body feels fuzzy, like I can't quite settle, like I have this crackling energy waiting to come out and be used, and normally I would put that energy to use writing. But right now, I want to do anything else.

This is the job you dream about, I tell myself. If I force myself to sit down and write a couple of sentences, maybe I'll get into the flow.

So I do. I open a new document and write about my boyfriends' sweatpants and their jeans and all of the other depraved thoughts that have crossed my mind since I dragged them upstairs to change their clothes.

Chapter Sixteen

As soon as my bedroom door opens, I slam my laptop closed. I respected their privacy earlier by not snooping in their bedrooms, and there is absolutely no way I'm letting any of my roommates look over my shoulder at what I'm working on. Not if I can help it.

"Writing?" Lionel flops onto my bed.

"Books don't write themselves." I turn in my desk chair, wishing I'd had more notice that he was coming in. My head is still wrapped up in my characters and needs to be eased back into the real world, not flung into it without warning.

"Why did you let us believe you just worked from home?"

"I do work from home most of the time." It's not my fault they never asked any follow-up questions. "Except when I write in cafés with other authors."

"And you write romance?" I nod, and Lionel looks around my room as if he's looking for clues about my profession that he may have missed when he was in here before. A big sign above my desk that says, "I Write About Getting Railed", maybe.

Although to be fair, I think the only time he's been in

here was to put me to bed the night they used the butt plug on me, so maybe he's just taking in the space.

"What kind of romance?"

"Um ... sports romance." Shit. Why did I say that? I don't write sports romances. Although I guess they are inspired by athletes in a way. Esports are, after all, sports, according to Helix. And come to think of it, even though my boyfriends don't really fit the mold for the book boyfriends usually seen in sports romances, but they're certainly athletic enough in bed to qualify.

"Can we read it?"

A bolt of panic shoots through me at the idea. "It's not done. I don't like to share rough drafts outside of my critique group."

He tilts his head, confused. "Didn't your parents say you had other books published?"

I don't want the guys I'm fucking to know anything about my writing. Even my already-published stuff.

"Those are sweet romances," I explain. "Very different from what I'm writing about now."

He grins. "You're writing dirty sex."

I can feel the blush creeping up my face, so I change the subject. "Was there a reason you came up here?"

"Yeah." Lionel stands and walks toward the door. "We're ready to watch something." He pauses halfway and looks back. "If you're done with work for today."

I'm shocked. Lionel cares about my work schedule? None of them have ever seemed to pay attention before. With their weird schedule, I'm not sure they ever considered that most people work a normal nine-to-five even if they work from home. I can't help but mentally give him brownie points for being considerate.

"Yeah, I'm done. Let's go." I push in my computer chair and follow Lionel down to the basement.

The other guys are already splayed out on the sofa, but the projector screen is dark and they're just sitting here, waiting. I'm mildly annoyed. Our agreement was to watch something, but they don't have it ready. I could have snuck in at least another paragraph while they're setting this up.

"What are we watching?" I move to sit between Ethan and Helix.

"Actually, you're going to sit right here." Lionel points to the coffee table, and I notice that for some reason it's covered with a blanket.

"On the table?" At his nod, I perch on the edge and I look around at all of them. They're completely focused on me. "What's going on? I thought we were going to watch a movie."

It feels more like we're going to have an intense talk. Like the world's most bizarre family meeting. *Oh, no. Maybe they're disappointed in me as a live-in girlfriend. Are they kicking me out?*

My chest rises and falls quicker as panic and uncertainty set in. I don't like this situation at all.

"No, the deal was that we'd get to watch *something*, and we didn't pick a movie," explains Helix.

"I don't understand." I fidget on the table, the blanket shifting slightly beneath me.

"What we want to watch," says Miles, leaning forward and balancing his elbows on his knees as he focuses on me, "is you touch yourself."

"Excuse me?" I'm shocked. This is outrageous. I should walk right back up to my room. "You didn't say that in our deal, so it shouldn't count. You need to be clearer."

"We asked you if you worked from home and you said yes," says Quintin. "You didn't tell us that you write romance."

"Smutty romance," says Ethan.

"Exactly," agrees Lionel. "*You* should have been clearer."

"So you're going to sit there on the table and masturbate for us," explains Quintin.

"You want me to masturbate in front of all of you, right now." My mouth is dry, and my hands are shaking. With nerves, anger, or a touch of excitement, I can't say.

"Yes." Lionel scooches lower on the sofa, spreading his knees to display his growing cock inside his sweatpants.

The other gamers do the same, watching me with hungry eyes. All except Miles, who's still leaning forward, intent.

I'm not sure I can do this. I've had sex of some sort with all of them, but they've always been the instigators, and have more or less just fucked me without me having to do much. Now they're asking me to be an exhibitionist. I've taken the initiative with them a few times—that first night with Ethan, calling Lionel's bluff in the kitchen when he asked for a blow job—but showing them how I enjoy touching myself is something else entirely.

"Go on," commands Lionel.

I spread my legs a little and run my sweating hands down my thighs from my hip to my knees, gearing myself up for this. It only feels invasive and personal because I'm making it this way. This is business, part of the job they hired me for. I can catalogue each emotion for my notes so I can use these feelings for my heroine. She could masturbate for her book boyfriend. She'd have no problem with it. Probably she'd have fun doing it.

I can do this.

My fingers move closer to the seam of my leggings, but then I glance up and make eye contact with Ethan and I drop my hands, the panic creeping back in.

I can't do this.

"Nope, I can't." I stand up and shake my hands out, trying to release the unsettled tension inside me.

"It was the deal," says Lionel, annoyed.

"Maybe you need a little help getting warmed up," offers Ethan, spreading his hands.

Is he offering to help me warm up himself? He's fucked me in front of all of them before, so it wouldn't be anything I haven't already tried. And I enjoyed being watched much more than I thought I would. Plus, this way he'd make the decisions for me for a while. It's nice to be taken care of once in a while instead of always being responsible all the time.

"We can do that," says Helix with a grin, getting off the sofa and messing with the projector.

I let out a breath, some of the tension leaving my body. Good, we can watch a movie and relax and then if something happens, it happens. No pressure.

Helix flips through a few options and as soon as the movie begins, he sits back on the sofa.

"Clarissa, why don't you sit here with us for a bit. Then you can sit on the table when you're ready." Miles pats a small space on the sofa between him and Quintin.

He doesn't need to ask me twice. I tuck my legs up under me and wrap my hands deeper into my sweater for maximum coziness.

The movie isn't anything I've ever seen before. Or even anything I recognize. The acting is terrible.

And they're half naked.

Nope, now they're completely naked. And fucking each other.

I've never seen pornography despite all of Angela's suggestions that I try it. I was expecting a normal movie, and I'm not sure how to feel about this. I peek at my roommates to gauge their reactions.

They slouch more on the sofa to get comfortable.

Quintin's cock is twitching in his sweatpants. *Fuck, this is really happening. I'm watching porn with my roommates and they're getting aroused.* I have so many questions I want to ask, like do they do this often? Sit around watching porn together? But now is not the time. Mostly because I don't want to draw more attention to myself and remind them that they put this on to "warm me up" so I can eventually masturbate in front of them.

We sit in silence, watching a female pirate get fucked from behind while she's blowing another pirate. I hate to admit it, but it is kind of hot. Especially the way she's pushed onto each of the cocks by the other. It's almost like the guys are pleasuring each other, in a way. My panties are definitely dampening.

Quintin is already rubbing his cock through his sweatpants, his eyes intent on the fucking pirates.

Watching him touch himself, even if he is still wearing pants, is hotter than the display on the screen. Maybe that's how they'd feel about watching me touch myself. Like they enjoy watching porn, but it's not nearly as good as watching the real thing happening right before their eyes. Knowing they could reach out at any moment and be a part of it too.

"If you take off your leggings, you'd enjoy this movie even more," says Quintin.

There's a glint in his eye as he waits for me to take him up on his challenge.

"It'd probably help you uphold your end of the deal we made too," adds Miles.

I did promise them, and it's my fault for not clarifying. And I did come here for new experiences that I wouldn't normally do in real life. This is my research life, where choices don't count.

So I tug down my leggings to drop them in a heap on the floor by my feet. It's not quite the teasing strip my boyfriends probably hoped they'd get, but it did the job. And it's exciting, but it's also a bit chilly down here. They probably didn't think about the fact that we're in a basement, and didn't turn the heat up a little bit more.

No one pressures me to do anything more though as we watch. My boyfriends obviously don't need any encouragement other than the movie though, because they're all scrunching down the front of their sweatpants just enough to pull out their stiff cocks.

They aren't nervous or ashamed to jerk off in front of each other. That confidence is attractive. It also makes me wonder how often they do this, or did this before I moved in.

I cross my legs to stay warm and to clench my thighs together because watching the five of them touch themselves is very sexy. I understand now why they want to watch me touch myself. I'm just not sure I'm ready for that.

Quintin and Miles have other ideas though. They pry my legs apart and each hook one over one of their knees. They don't do anything else, just continue watching, mostly ignoring me. I'm on display, but at least I'm not out in front of them and the sole focus of their attention.

The porno does a little bit for me, but watching my boyfriends touch themselves is turning me on even more than the video. As soon as one of them looks over between my splayed legs, they'll know it too. The damp spot on my panties is spreading. Proof that I'm as naughty and dirty as my boyfriends.

I want to get more comfortable, but Quintin and Miles are holding my knees so when I shift, I slide down on the sofa, spreading my legs even more until I'm practically on my back with my pussy lined up with the edge of the sofa. This is absolutely not what I'd intended. I'm even more on display than I was before.

From the sidelong glances my boyfriends send me, they've noticed as well. Now they're half watching me and half watching the video.

This will continue until I give in. And the longer I watch them touch themselves, the more I want to do the same.

Slowly, my fingers inch over my hip and walk down to the damp gusset of my panties. I trace the edges, then run my fingers through the center, warming my pussy even more. It feels good to be touched there even if it's through the fabric, and only by my own fingers. It'd be nicer if it were their fingers, and they were taking control. Or if I had the little vibrator that's upstairs in my bedside drawer.

My boyfriends seem to have enough of their own toys though, so they could produce one at any moment. The idea is exciting, and has me reaching beneath my panties to my bare pussy. They can't see my fingers now and the freedom of doing something secret and hidden from my boyfriends even as I'm on display is invigorating.

The female pirate on the screen is now being held in another pirate's arms as he stands and fucks her. His friend stands behind her and fucks her ass, bouncing her on both of their cocks at the same time.

"Do you want to try that?" whispers Quintin in my ear.

"Do you think you're ready to take us both as the same time?" Miles asks, his voice rough.

"I'm not sure I can wait," says Helix. "I need your ass so bad, Clarissa."

He pulls a bottle out of the side table and stands up, dropping his sweatpants completely. He positions himself between me and the projector screen, his hard cock jutting out proudly, begging to be licked.

"Stand up and drop your panties," orders Helix.

I look to the other gamers for confirmation, but they're

all just staring, waiting to see what I'm going to do. Miles and Quintin release their hold on my knees, allowing me to pull my legs from their laps. It sounds like Helix is about to help me make decisions, which was what I'd wanted. I'm definitely interested in whatever he's planning. Especially if it involves that thick cock of his.

As I stand, Helix's cock bumps against my sweater, leaving a small drip of pre-cum on the fabric. I've barely let my panties fall to the floor before Helix spins around me and plops us both back on the sofa so I land on his lap, his hard cock pinned beneath my ass.

"Are you going to be our good little girlfriend and let me fuck your ass?" Helix slides his hands up under the front of my sweater, cupping my tits and pinching my nipples with his dexterous gamer fingers.

"Yes." The moan is practically pulled from my throat under Helix's skilled touch.

"Good girl," says Helix against my ear. My pussy clenches.

"Let me help you take off your sweater," offers Lionel. "You promised us we could watch. We don't want to miss anything."

My sweater had been baggy and bulky, so I hadn't needed a bra. When Lionel tugs it over my head, I'm laid completely bare before my boyfriends. And based on how stiff their cocks are, they're loving it.

I am too.

The bottle in Helix's hand opens and closes behind me, but my eyes are locked on Lionel's.

Helix lifts my hips, then pulls me back farther on his lap. His cock doesn't line up with my wet pussy, though. No, he's pressing it against my puckered back entrance.

My eye go wide. I'd figured Helix's words were just

dirty talk to get me wet. But this is really happening, right now.

Helix reaches around me, past my needy, aching pussy, and slips a lube-covered finger over my asshole. His wrist brushes against my clit and my hips buck, seeking more contact, but his other arm snakes across my waist and holds me still against him. The finger skating over my hole presses inside slowly, pushing and pulling just like Helix did with the plug at first. I suck in a breath when he adds a second finger, slowly working me open, preparing me to take his thick cock up my ass.

Finally, he must decide I'm ready, because he pulls his fingers out and squirts more lube onto my hole. He scoops some of it up and rubs it over the length of his cock before pressing the tip of it against my tight, slippery asshole.

The head of Helix's cock is bigger than the butt plug they used on me the other night, and it's stretching me as he attempts to press his cock inside a hole where things aren't supposed to go. I tense up, whimpering at the assault on my forbidden hole.

"Relax, Clarissa, let me in," says Helix, laying my back against his chest and slowly pressing my hips down so my own body weight eases me on to his cock. There's a moment of pain as the head slips inside, followed by the sensation of being stretched and filled in a way I could never have imagined. "There's a good girl. You're doing so well. This is the same thing as that butt plug you liked. You enjoyed being so full, didn't you?"

"Mm-hmm." My body slowly adjusts to the big, warm-blooded cock penetrating me. Helix's body heat warms me as he runs his hands up and down my sides, nothing between our bodies, just skin to skin. I begin to relax, giving myself over to the warmth and stretch.

This is even better than the toy was.

Miles and Quintin each take one of my legs again and hang them over their own as they stroke their own cocks, rubbing them along the outsides of my thighs.

My boyfriends aren't shy about showing how much they want me and enjoy my body. Especially Lionel, as he lowers himself to his knees before my pussy, leaning in to worship me with his tongue and fingers. The pressure of his mouth eases me another inch onto his teammates cock, and I let my head fall back onto Helix's shoulder as I appreciate the full feeling in my ass and the teasing tongue on my clit.

My eyes flick up to the projector screen, where the first mate is riding the captain's dick as I sink ever further down onto Helix's. There are so many stimulations at once, I'm not sure my body can handle it.

But I'm doing it, and I'm so close. My hips buck again, trying to get Lionel's tongue to apply more pressure on my clit. Helix hasn't even moved yet beneath me, but my own little movements are sliding him deeper into my ass in a way the toy never did. I roll my hips forward against Lionel's tongue and back onto Helix's cock.

Reaching out, I grip Lionel's hair and hold him right where I want him. Where I need him. He sucks on my clit as he spears two fingers into my pussy, rubbing against the inside wall until I'm bucking faster and coming hard, not even caring how loud I'm being as I cry out my release.

I release my grip on Lionel's hair as I come down from the orgasm, and moan a weak protest when he sits back, withdrawing his fingers from my body and wiping the back of his other hand over the moisture glistening on his lips and chin.

"Did our girlfriend enjoy riding Lionel's face?" asks Quintin, stroking his cock with one hand and massaging the inside of my thigh with the other.

"Mm-hmm." My pussy feels empty without Lionel's

fingers. It's unbalanced with my ass still so full of Helix's cock.

"If you loved my tongue, you'll enjoy my cock even more." Lionel has shucked his sweatpants and moves back into position between my legs, lining up his hips with mine.

This is really happening. Never in a million years would I have thought I'd find myself spread wide on a sofa, surrounded by five men watching me and stroking themselves, but there's absolutely nowhere else I'd rather be in this moment than about to be pierced by one of my boyfriends' cocks as another fills my ass with his.

"Fuck, your pussy feels so good," groans Lionel against my neck as he sheaths himself. "You're so tight with Helix stretching your ass. I don't think I can last."

I'm so full, and I'm not sure what to do with my hands, so I reach up and pinch my nipples, rolling them between my fingers like Helix had done. All I can focus on is the fact that I'm sandwiched between two of my boyfriends as they use me exactly how they want. This is what I wanted, what I needed—for them to take over and show me what's possible. Nothing exists but this moment between all of us.

"Then finish quick and let me step in to take care of our girl properly." Stroking himself, Miles moves to get into position as Ethan slides into his now empty spot, draping my leg over his knee to keep my pussy spread wide for his teammate.

Lionel pistons his hips even faster, causing Helix to groan behind me and tighten his grip around my hips, holding me in place.

"Fuck, you feel so good when you're getting fucked hard," says Helix. "Are you going to come on his cock? I want to be fucking soaked when he pulls out of you."

Lionel leans back enough to swipe his thumb across my sensitive clit and my hips buck once, hard, as stars explode behind my eyes for the second time tonight. My arms drop to my sides and Lionel groans his own release, pressing his pulsing cock hard into me as he comes. He's gorgeous like this, confident and with a little bit of a smirk as he withdraws from my body and admires the way I'm splayed out across his teammate, his own cum leaking from my pussy and trickling down onto the cock that's still filling my ass.

"Let me show you how it's really done," says Miles, taking Lionel's place between my legs.

I'm so wet, Miles slides in in a single stroke. He's a little girthier than Lionel, and my hips have to shift to adjust to his size. Needing more stability, I reach my hands out to the side, but instead of landing on the sofa, they land in the laps of Quintin and Ethan. I grip their hard cocks, squeezing and stroking. Normally I wouldn't be so daring, but right now all bets are off. And my hands are right there so I might as well. It's not like they're going to stop me.

"Are you ready for this, Hel?" asks Miles once he's fully seated in my pussy.

"Let's do this." Helix kisses my neck. "You're going to love this, Clarissa."

Miles sets his hands right below Helix's on my waist as he leans down to capture one of my tits in his mouth. He flicks his tongue over the nipple as he starts to slowly rut in my pussy. The slow drag of his cock against Helix's in a separate entrance is tantalizing.

When Helix starts to move, thrusting beneath me in a shared pace, my eyes roll back in my head. My whole body is focused on the slide and play of their cocks, moving in and out of me at the same time. There's not even enough strength in my hands to keep stroking Quintin and Ethan properly. All I can do his hold their hard cocks as Helix and

Miles keep the same pace, pounding into me harder with each determined thrust.

"Is this what you wanted when you moved in here?" Helix growls in my ear. "Is this why you were so desperate to move in with us? To be used whenever and however we want you? To be our dirty, slutty girlfriend?"

"Yes," I whimper. Miles bites down on my nipple and then flattens his tongue against it in a slow lick, chasing away the pain.

"Are you going to let us take your ass whenever we want?" asks Helix.

"Yes." I want to wrap my legs around Miles's waist, but Quintin and Ethan are still holding them wide.

"Keep your legs open," Quintin orders.

"Your pussy looks beautiful stretched around our teammate's cock," says Ethan.

Their filthy words only drive my need for release higher. I should be cataloging each sensation and phrase, but there's no way I can think about my writing right now. All I can do is hold on as Helix and Miles fuck me in tandem, building up the embers of my third orgasm into a blazing fire which finally bursts, carrying me along on the tumultuous waves of pleasure.

When Helix lifts me off his cock after coming in my ass, all I can do is lean forward, nearly falling to the floor. Quintin and Ethan move the coffee table toward the wall right beneath the screen, which is still playing the pirate porn. I dimly register that the pirates are fucking in a burning building, and wonder how they got there, but my mind is fuzzy from having taken three of my boyfriends already and the thought slips from my head as quickly as it appeared. With the table out of the way, I crumple to all fours.

"Look how beautiful your holes are all stretched out by

our cocks," says Lionel, pulling apart first my ass cheeks and then the seams of my pussy to get a better view.

"And your thighs are glistening with how wet you are," says Quintin, running a finger up the inside of my thigh to collect my juices, then licking it off.

"Did you like having your ass fucked by Helix?" asks Ethan, positioning himself beneath me and spreading my legs so my knees are on either side of his hips.

"Mm-hmm." I'm so low on energy, I can't even find words. My body is humming with the pleasure of being thoroughly and completely fucked in a way I'd never dreamed of before.

"Did you like being filled and used by two cocks at the same time?" asks Quintin from behind me, massaging my ass. "Are you feeling well taken care of?"

"Mm-hmm," I murmur as Ethan puts a hand on the back of my neck and tugs my head down to capture my lips in a soft, reassuring kiss. It's slow and sweet and irresistible, so I lean into it, reveling in the pleasure a simple kiss can bring when we're both naked and being watched by all of our roommates.

Ethan's hands trail up and down my spine before pressing down at the base, lowering me onto his waiting cock. I'm still so wet from his friends that I glide down easily, letting him feel me envelop him in one smooth motion. I'm so stretched out from Lionel and Miles that it's more pleasurable than rough.

"Ride me," whispers Ethan against my lips, letting his tongue fuck my mouth while his cock fucks my pussy.

He's asking me to take control, and while I couldn't earlier, it's easier now. I'm so sated with pleasure that it's not so daunting to raise my hips that little bit and slide back down onto him. Feeling Ethan's smile through our kiss, and the way he clearly wants me, gives me confidence that I'm doing this right. That I'm not terrible at this.

So I raise my hips again, looking to find my own rhythm of what I enjoy, and hoping Ethan enjoys it too.

"Such a good girlfriend, riding your boyfriend while all of his friends watch," says Quintin behind me, his fingers still massaging and spreading my ass for his viewing enjoyment.

Quintin's compliment makes me feel so good, warm and wanted and admired. It makes me want to keep going, to make Ethan come so they all know how amazing I am.

There's the click of a bottle opening and warm liquid drizzles against my asshole before Quintin's cock presses against it.

"You can do this, just one more cock," says Quintin as I tense up. "You're going to feel so good and full with both of us inside you at once. Five cocks isn't too much. Not when we're your boyfriends."

Quintin eases in, finding little resistance between the lube and Helix having stretched me out already. As he bottoms out in my ass, I'm pressed down onto Ethan's cock and chest, sandwiched between the two men.

"Now move your hips, baby girl," says Quintin. "Fuck us at the same time."

"I'm not sure I can," I groan. I'm so full, and my body is exhausted. I want them to bring me to orgasm again, then let me sleep for a hundred years.

"You got this, Clarissa," says Ethan. "Romance writers know all about fucking, right?"

Hesitantly, I roll my hips back so I'm taking more of Ethan, and his groan of satisfaction helps bolster my confidence. When I roll forward again, it feels as if both Ethan and Quintin are stroking my holes in an opposite rhythm. But I'm the one with all the power. I can make it as hard and fast or slow and teasing as I want. They're completely at my mercy.

I sit up and press my back against Quintin. If I'm completely in charge, I want their hands everywhere. I don't want to know where I end and they begin. Grabbing Ethan's hands, I use them to cup my tits, encouraging him to play with them. I move Quintin's hands down to my clit, letting him play with my sensitive nub, even as his friend fills my pussy with his cock. My own hands come up to wrap around Quintin's neck, helping me to stay upright for them to see the way they're making my body feel, and to give me enough leverage to tilt my hips exactly how I want.

So much foreplay and stimulation. So many eyes on me. Appreciating me. It's fantastic and exhausting and so perfect, it's not long before all three of us are coming. As the tremors ripple through my body all I can do is collapse on top of Ethan, enjoying the completeness of this moment. Is this how all of my heroines feel each time with their love interests? I hope so.

As he slips his softening cock out of my sore, stretched-out asshole, Quintin says, "If this is the reward for wearing jeans, I might switch to wearing them all the time."

His teammates all chuckle, the sound of Ethan's soft laugh reverberating through his chest beneath my ear. I can't help a little giggle myself, but I hope they don't. Rewarding them was great, but I love the way they look in their sweatpants. There's just something so sexy about my nerdy boyfriends in them.

Chapter Seventeen

I reach for my phone as soon as I wake up to check my overnight notifications. My business always comes first. Except the first app I open is the gamer subscription chat. If my boyfriends are already awake, they'll have posted.

There's a new pinned post in the thread and I drop my phone, smacking myself in the face. *What the hell?*

Sitting up, I read the post again. "Going on vacation. See you in a week."

They can't be serious. They can't take a whole week off of work, ignoring their subscribers and fans. They could lose their momentum and success. And also, when the hell were they going to tell me?

I don't bother getting dressed, I march right downstairs in my sleep shorts and tank. If they're leaving, they should at least have the decency to tell me in person. Because as far as they know, I haven't been informed. They don't know I'm a subscriber.

"Morning." Lionel brushes past me, rushing into his room before I can stop him.

At the bottom of the stairs, a row of suitcases block most

of the hallway. I edge past them and make my way toward the voices in the kitchen.

"Van comes in fifteen minutes," says Miles. "If you're not ready, we're leaving without you."

"I'll be ready," mumbles Ethan, sitting at the table with his cereal.

"Morning." I hover in the doorway, not sure what to do or how to confront my boyfriends.

"Ugh, really?" says Quintin. "We're getting ready for our flights and you come in looking this fuckable?"

"Where's Lionel?" asks Helix. "He was so panicked about us being on time, but he's not down here yet?"

"I saw him head into his room as I was coming down." Hopefully by butting into their conversation, they'll remember they haven't actually informed me that they're leaving. Or where they're going.

"Do we have time for a quick fuck?" Quintin hooks his thumb under my chin and brushes a kiss across my lips.

I'm annoyed and confused, yet my lips automatically tilt up to keep kissing Quintin. With all of the uncertainty happening around me, this I understand. The passion, desire, and need to connect to another human being is high. And if I'm not going to see them for a whole week, I'm not sure what I'll do without them around.

I realize with a start that I'm actually going to miss them. *When did I get attached enough for that?*

Quintin lifts me onto the kitchen table as he kisses me deeper, distracting me from my realization and the chaos around us. The way his tongue seeks permission to cross my lips and explore has me lifting my arms up around his neck to hold him close. To put off their departure for a few minutes more.

Miles brushes past us to step out into the hall, calling up the stairs, "Faker! Hurry the fuck up! You're making us late."

The middle of my shorts is tugged aside and Quintin runs his finger through my seam, warming me up. Not that he has to do much after all the dreams I had about them. I dream and think about my boyfriends so often for my books, making up scenarios with them, that sometimes I'm not sure what's real and what's fake. But the way my pussy is already juicing for Quintin is very real.

"Such a good girl," says Quintin, easing first one and then two fingers inside me until I'm tilting my hips to help him find the perfect spot.

A phone beeps. "Van is here. We need to load the luggage."

"See, I told you I'm ready," says Ethan, drinking the last of the milk from his bowl as Quintin replaces his fingers with his cock.

"Fuck," I whimper as he pounds into me. One hand falls back to the table to hold me upright as my other holds Quintin close.

"Almost ready," grunts Quintin as he pounds into me over and over, the table moving an inch each time.

We're slowly sliding across the kitchen floor, but Quintin doesn't stop until we're banging into the cabinets. The other gamers move in and out of the room as they pack up the van, but Quintin's eyes are focused on me. Our world right now is just the two of us and the magical rhythm he's created. It's almost as if my heartbeat is shifting to match the rhythm of the table banging against the cupboards. Quick and hard.

"Come on my cock," he grunts. "I can't leave until you come."

I fight off the impending orgasm. If I can draw this out, I can make them stay. I'm not going to think about why I want them here. I hold my breath, keeping the pleasure at bay.

"Arrow, we're waiting on you," says Helix.

"Clarissa needs to come first," pants Quintin, railing me harder.

"I left you a little toy on your pillow," says Helix, coming over to stand next to us. He reaches out and rubs tight little circles on my clit as his friend fucks me. "But don't open it until I call you because I want to see your reaction."

Helix gives my clit a little pinch and my hips buck as I come, my pussy clenching down on Quintin's cock.

"Fuck, yes, there it is," groans Quintin as he allows himself to orgasm too.

"The driver says he can't wait much longer," complains an exasperated Miles from the doorway.

"I'm ready." Quintin pulls out and tucks his cock back into his sweatpants.

"Good." Miles hurries over to where I'm still panting on the table to kiss me quick on the lips. "We'll see you in a week."

The others all follow suit, a quick kiss and then calling out their goodbyes as they hurry out of the house.

I'm left on the kitchen table, my shorts and panties still pushed to the side, coming down from a fast and hard orgasm. I can't believe they've done this to me. Sure, this is technically a business agreement, but if they want to call themselves my boyfriends they should have at least told me a couple days in advance that they were leaving for a vacation without me. I shouldn't have had to find out the same way the rest of their subscribers did.

Sliding off the table, I look around the kitchen, feeling as if I haven't truly seen it before. It's big. And I'm going to be here alone for the next week. I'd love a little privacy sometimes since the guys are always popping into my room for a quick fuck, but now I'm a nervous about staying in this big house alone.

I straighten my sleep clothes and shove the table back to

the middle of the room. One inch at a time, the same way Quintin had fucked it over. Ethan left his bowl in the sink, so I put that in the dishwasher. I wander around first the kitchen and then the hallway, putting things away, and it almost feels like I'm erasing them from the house. From my life.

Shaking my head, I clear the thought. *This is a business arrangement, nothing more.* At some point I'll earn enough money to move out on my own again. I've lived on my own since I got to the city. I'll get used to it again. By this time tomorrow I'll be completely comfortable and have forgotten all about my five gamer boyfriends who use words I don't understand and fuck me at all hours of the day, based around their schedule and not mine.

On the second day they're gone, I have to admit that I miss my boyfriends. Their subscription chat is silent. The house is silent. And I can't bring myself to open my laptop. I'd thought I'd be able to get loads of writing done, but instead I'm staring up at my ceiling as I listen to a recording of one of their old games just to hear their voices and make the house feel less empty.

I'm completely alone and I could do whatever I want. Except open the little present I'd found on my pillow from Helix. He hasn't called or texted yet to say I'm allowed to open it.

I should do something besides lay here and be unproductive.

I shoot off a quick text to Sasha. *Movie night?*

I can't tonight. Let's do tomorrow night instead. There's a new romance movie that just came out I want to analyze. 7 pm at yours? Can't wait to meet your roommates.

Well, that's not was I was hoping for. *They're out of town and I feel like getting out of the house. Can we do yours instead?*

Sasha replies, *Yes, we can do yours next time when they're back then. See you tomorrow at 7.*

Well, I have something to do now, but not until tomorrow. *Damn.*

I don't know why Sasha wants to meet my roommates so badly. They're nerdy, and not great conversationalists. All they do is talk about their game and fucking me. And I'd rather Sasha not find out about that last bit.

Hopefully getting out of the house and having a bit of girl time will get me out of this funk. In the meantime, though, I need something to do.

I glance at my closed door. I'm alone in the house and my roommates won't be home for days. Based on how they left the kitchen before their flight, I wouldn't be surprised if they left snacks out in their bedrooms. A good girlfriend—a good roommate even—would check to make sure there isn't anything that could attract bugs or mice or anything of that nature.

Slowly stepping out into the hallway, confirming that it's empty even though I know it is, I step over to the first closed door. *I'm not snooping. I'm being helpful.* I open the door to Ethan's room and stick my head inside.

The bed is haphazardly made, but everything else around the room looks fairly orderly. There are little action figure toys on some of the shelves and posters of cartoon characters on the wall, but otherwise nothing incriminating.

The next room is similar, if a little more messy. I open each door and pop my head in, but they're all fairly the same: action figures, cartoon posters, computer equipment, and Legos are in every room. In fact, even knowing my roommates, it's hard to tell whose room is whose.

Aside from Ethan's, which I can only identify because I've seen him go through that door, the only bedroom I can easily pick out is Helix's. Mostly because delivery boxes are scattered around the room and since I've moved in, he's received at least three or four packages each week.

A fair number of them being toys for me—dildos, nipple clamps, and a variety of butt plugs that all of us had a lot of fun with one day.

I wonder if that's what he left on my bed. I'm even more curious now and want to open it.

Pulling out my phone, I message our group chat. *When am I allowed to open my present?*

I hope they haven't forgotten about me. They hadn't said they would check in or anything before they left. I mean, they hadn't even told me they were leaving. If I hadn't gotten up and caught them in the act, I would have woken up to an empty house.

They clearly only think of me when they want to fuck, and the rest of the time I'm absent from their minds. Yet here I am snooping in their rooms because I miss them. Which is ridiculous. We're roommates and fuck buddies, nothing more.

So why am I climbing into Helix's bed and staring at my phone as I wait for them to respond?

His bed is actually comfy. Almost like a cloud. Way better than mine. And the pillow smells like him. When was the last time he washed these sheets?

Nope, I'm not going to focus on that right now. I'm just going to lie here where he sleeps and enjoy being wrapped in his scent.

Chapter Eighteen

My phone ringing wakes me up. It's dark, and I reach out to turn on my light but it's not there.

I'm still in Helix's bed. I must have fallen asleep and taken a longer nap than I should have. Instead of a normal lamp, he has a salt lamp on the bedside, so I follow the cord to the switch to let its soft glow light the room.

I reach for my phone. The screen is lit up with Helix's name and a little video icon.

Fuck. It's been ringing for so long if I don't answer now, I'll miss the call, and there's not enough time to run back to my room. *Maybe he won't notice.*

Cringing, I swipe up to answer his video call as I scoot down into the bed to only show me and the pillow.

"Miss me already?" asks Helix, also laying back on a pillow. But he's showing more of the room he's in, mostly a twin bed headboard and the bottom of some posters.

"Where are you?" I ask. "Is that—are you in your childhood bedroom?" They'd never told me where they were going. And I don't want him to know I'm missing them. They hired me to do a job. Emotions aren't supposed to be involved.

Helix flips the camera to pan around the room. It's not all that different from the room I'm lying in. More action figures and posters on the walls, though, covering up the bright, cheery blue paint.

"I'm visiting my parents, which means I'm trapped in this bedroom again," says Helix, flipping the camera back to him.

"You were really into posters it looks like." I glance past my phone at the posters dotting his walls.

Helix gives a choking laugh. "My mom wouldn't let me paint the room black, so I was determined to cover as much of this blue as possible."

"I've never heard you talk about your parents or family before," I say, pulling up the blanket to just under my chin to get extra cozy.

"It's never come up," says Helix, tilting his head in confusion.

"You could offer information, you know," I tell him. "I hardly know anything about any of you."

"You know a lot about us," says Helix, his eyes focused on the screen, but not on me.

"Your dick size and favorite sex position doesn't count," I counter. Now that we're on the topic, I want to know more about the gamers I'm dating. I mean, sleeping with. Or whatever.

"Where are you?" asks Helix.

"At home." I blush and glance around the room, anywhere but at the camera.

"Your comforter is pink. Where are you?"

"Tell me one fact about your family first," I bargain, pulling the black comforter up over my face to hide my embarrassment. This is so awkward and he's going to make fun of me or use this to get something.

"I have two brothers and one sister," says Helix. "Where are you?"

"That's barely an answer, and not even really personal," I complain, peeking my head out from under the blanket. My hair looks wild in the little box where I can see myself in our video call.

"You said one fact and I gave you three, now answer my question." Helix's voice is gruff as he slides down more into his childhood bed.

"I'm in your bed," I whisper.

Helix's responding grin says it all, and I hide my own smile in his pillow. Of all the beds I could have been in when he called, it had to be his. If he'd have texted, I could have had a heads up and moved anywhere else. Yet the way it makes him clearly happy for me to be in here sends a flutter into my heart. I fist my empty hand in his comforter and hold it close.

"What are you doing in my bed?" Helix sets down the phone so I only see the ceiling for a moment.

"Taking a nap." I am not about to tell him I was snooping in all of their rooms. Or that I'd climbed into his bed to feel closer to them and less alone in this big house.

Helix picks his phone back up, and now he's shirtless.

"Nothing else?" He raises an eyebrow and holds the phone at arm's length so I can see as his free hand slips beneath his covers.

Of course Helix's mind dives straight to the gutter. I'm not *not* tempted, but it's different when they're not here. They can't walk in to join me or turn me on. This distance feels too far.

"I'll tell you exactly what else if you tell me another fact," I tease. Our past deals have worked out fairly well so far. Maybe I can convince Helix to open up with the promise of dirty things.

I have no desire to analyze why I want to learn more about him. Perhaps my book boyfriends need to have more depth, and not just be great in bed.

"What do you want to know?" Helix groans, pulling his hand out from under the covers.

"Everything." I grin. This feels a lot like winning.

"Fine, but for every fact, you have to take off a piece of clothing."

"Deal." I'm not feeling spicy right now, but I don't put it past Helix to get me there at some point in this conversation. "But the facts better be good."

"I make everything good." He gives me a stern look, and I laugh. "My family lives on a cattle farm, and my siblings still live in this small town."

"Yet you moved to Chicago and got into gaming." I unhook my bra and slip it off through one of my sleeves, holding it up to show him before dropping it on the floor next to the bed.

"I got into computers in middle school and gaming in junior high. Which was a challenge, because the internet connection out here isn't great."

"That's when you joined the team and started taking gaming seriously?" I hold up my shorts, then drop them over the side of the bed too.

"There were a couple of kids at school who played, but not nearly as much as me." Helix's hand slips below his blanket again. "I didn't hook up with our team until halfway through high school. We'd met through the chat and played together well."

They still play together well from all the commentary I've listened to on their games. In the bedroom too, from my own personal experience.

"When did you decide to all move in together?" I drop

the phone to yank off my t-shirt and pull the covers up to my shoulders again before picking it up again.

"I saved up all of my money and our senior year, we met up for a competition." Helix bites his lip and there's a slow rhythmic movement under his blanket. The tendons in his arm flex, emphasizing his veins. "We used all of the winnings to move to the city after we graduated."

"When did you start sharing your girlfriends?" I drop my panties on the floor so I'm completely naked in Helix's bed. I wish he were here. Or that any of my boyfriends was.

"You're our first," says Helix. "Now throw off those blankets so I can see you naked and spread out on my sheets."

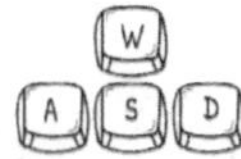

Sleeping in Helix's bed last night and talking to him was exactly what I needed. I'd been so used to living alone before this, but it's nice to have others around. It's clearly doing great things for my writing. Yesterday I couldn't write at all and today I've already completed two chapters.

Hearing about Helix growing up in a rural town and how he met his teammates makes me feel closer to him. Not necessarily in a physical way, but a mental one. I'm not the only one who grew up in a small town and dreamed of moving to a big city to be around people who share my own artistic values.

We'd gotten so distracted once I threw off the comforter though, and then Helix told me more about visiting his family, and I'd fallen asleep without asking again if I'm allowed to open his present.

My phone rings and it's a group video call.

I answer right away, glad I'm not in an embarrassing situation this time.

"You're finally out of bed," teases Helix.

"I've been writing all morning." I roll my eyes as Helix tells the others about our escapades last night in his bed.

"Did you give her your present, Hel?" asks Miles.

"Yeah, I want to see what it is," says Lionel.

The gamers are all sitting against different colored walls. Lionel and Miles are both dressed and look wide awake, but Ethan and Quintin both look like they just woke up. If they're all at home, the time difference probably makes it harder for them to call me as a group. But they're used to keeping odd hours for work.

"Clarissa," says Helix, "why don't you open the box so they can see?"

I'd been excited, but now I'm nervous. I have a vague idea of what it could be, but it feels more serious with all of them watching me. There are random voices far away in the background and I wonder if one of them doesn't have complete privacy for this call.

A wash of jealousy rips through my stomach, and I squash it down. I'm just curious about who my boyfriends are spending time with after hearing about Helix's family last night, that's all. Taking deep breaths as I grab the present off my bed, I remind myself that they're visiting their families, so realistically, it's a family member they're staying with. They're not cheating on me. It's not actually jealousy that I'm feeling.

"Clarissa, use your phone holder so you can use both hands to open the gift," says Quintin.

"I don't have one." What would I need a phone holder for?

"I don't want her to move any ours because our positioning is perfect," says Lionel.

"Set your phone against a stack of books," says Ethan. "It's not ideal, but should work for this short call."

My shoulders slump a little as I prop up my phone. Of course they're not calling to spend real time with me. They just want me to open the gift and then they'll move on with their day and spend quality non-gaming time with other people who aren't me. And I'll go back to sitting here all alone.

"I'll add getting Clarissa a phone stand to my list," says Helix. "Now open your gift. You're going to love it."

Lifting off the lid, there's a small pink egg lying on a bed of tissue paper.

"Thank you?" I lift it up and show it to the camera. "I've always wanted an egg?"

They chuckle a little, which is nerve-wracking because it means they know something I don't. And I'm probably not going to like it when I find out.

"Stick that up your pussy," says Helix, "It'll let you know when we're thinking about you."

"You can't be serious." They're all hundreds of miles away, yet they still want to play with me using one of their toys. They wouldn't even be able to enjoy it. Unless ... are they wanting me to masturbate for them right now on camera using the toy?

"Of course we're serious," says Lionel, shocked that I could believe otherwise.

"Should I put it in right now?" I'm sure they want to watch, and not so sure I want them to.

"Miles, your grandparents are here," says a woman's voice off camera. "You can't spend your whole visit in your bedroom."

"I'll be out in a second, Mom," groans Miles.

"Well, hurry up, they're waiting," his mom tells him.

"I gotta get going," says Miles. "If I don't come out immediately, she's just going to come back in."

"I need to run here quick too," says Lionel.

"Same," says Ethan.

"Just put it in, Clarissa, and you'll know we're thinking about you even when we're so far away," says Quintin. "Talk soon."

"Bye," chorus the others, and the screen goes black.

I still don't understand why they left me this toy as a present if they weren't going to watch me play with it. This whole situation is so frustrating. Not to mention, if they knew they were leaving well enough in advance to order the toy, they could have also told me about their trip.

Even now, they call, but don't really talk to me. Not like Helix did last night. *Why do I even care?* They're not really my boyfriends. They're roommates who pay my room and board so they can have me on standby anytime they want a fuck.

I put the egg back in its box and toss it on my bed so I can keep working. I don't want their stupid present anymore. I'm going to write out my annoyance in this manuscript. My heroine is about to tell off her boyfriend so he can shape up and get his act together. Then I'll make him suffer. A lot. And finally, he'll grovel and come crawling back. It's so satisfying because when my heroine does it, I can ensure that everything goes exactly her way and her boyfriend doesn't say anything that throws a wrench into her plans.

If only real life worked the same way.

Being pissed off apparently inspires my writing as much as blissful orgasms, because when I check my word count, it's higher than it's been in ages. Took me most of the day, but it's worth it.

As I'm getting ready for movie night at Sasha's, I check

my messages to see if there's anything last-minute she's asked me to bring. The only text, though, is in our house chat.

Did you put the egg in? asks Helix.

Taking several deep breaths, I remind myself that when they piss me off, they're still helping me write the book. In fact, just today they've helped me nearly finish the first draft. Besides, when I check for the anger, it's mostly gone. Displaced into my heroine instead.

I open the box again. The egg is smooth, and doesn't seem sinister. Maybe it's supposed to help my pussy stay stretched out enough to take their cocks again when they come home. Lifting one foot up onto my bed, I pull aside my panties and start to insert the egg, but I'm annoyed and completely dry.

Lube, that's what I need. I'm nearly positive Quintin'll have some. I go into his room and open his bedside drawer, and sure enough, among all the detritus in there is a bottle of lube.

I coat the egg with a little and press it again to the lips of my pussy, slowly easing it inside. It's a definite stretch, but once it's in it's not so noticeable. I'm aware of it, but it's not the worst. And now I can tell my roommates I'm still playing by the rules.

It's in, I text the group. *Heading out to a friend's for a movie night. Talk tomorrow.*

There. Now they know I'm not here pathetically waiting for them to spend time with me or talk to me. I have friends and plans and a life. *Take that, boys.* Although a little part of me wonders if I'd told them I'd talk to them tomorrow so I wouldn't have to deal with the disappointment of them not messaging me again tonight.

Their lack of immediate response says it all.

Chapter Nineteen

The movie is fine. It's typical in the most commercial way, but that's what sells these days. They have to make it palatable for everyone so it can be successful. I'm practically looking at my own future since I'm doing the same thing. Changing what I'd normally write to be more commercial and successful.

"So your roommates are gone?" says Sasha, casually eating popcorn as we stretch out on her sofa.

"Yeah, they left two days ago." I don't know why Sasha cares.

"Check it out, the asshole hero is helping our heroine recover from a cold even though they're rivals. We've reached the shift in feelings moment," she points out. "How long are they gone for?"

"Uh, a week, I think, but they didn't really share their plans with me." I try not to sound too bitter. "We're not that close." *Apparently*.

"Overall, the structure of this rivalry is quite well done," says Sasha, switching topics seamlessly again and nearly giving me mental whiplash. "The author is setting clear boundaries for her characters to push while also propping up the entire story."

"I like the banter." I snag a handful of popcorn.

"We're supposed to be analyzing the breakdown of the story points," says Sasha, giving me a look.

"Banter can help support a storyline by displaying their rivalry and how well they can break down each other's barriers by pushing the right buttons." But really, I just enjoy it. The story is cute and fun, and I've been rooting for the characters to get together from the beginning. Not that I had any doubt they wouldn't, since this is a romance and a happy ending for the main characters is required.

"Are they dating anyone?"

"No, she used that guy at the beginning to make the hero jealous because she wasn't dating anyone, remember?"

"I'm not talking about the movie," clarifies Sasha. "I mean your roommates. Are any of them dating anyone?"

Is she asking because she wants me to hook up with my roommates? Have my very own little romance story where I fall for one of them? Because that's not happening. I have a very solid working arrangement with them, nothing more. But there's no way I can tell her about this.

"Why do you ask?" I say slowly. I'm not sure where this conversation is headed.

"They never bring any girls home?" asks Sasha, still not looking at me.

"They don't actually leave the house very often so they'd have a hard time bringing a girl home." And also that would be against our agreement. I think. I'm really not sure, but now I'm definitely going to ask.

Sasha doesn't say anything else, just keeps slowly eating popcorn and watching the movie. I'm not paying any attention to the screen now, though. She's not *interested* in my roommates, is she? She's never even seen them before, let alone met them. No, it's much more likely that she's working up some scheme to hook me up with one of them.

If she only knew.

There's a sudden flutter in my pussy, and I nearly jump off the sofa. *What the fuck was that?*

Then there's another. Two little separate flutters, and finally I remember that stupid egg Helix gifted me. I'd completely forgotten it's still inside me. If I'd known the egg would vibrate all of a sudden, I wouldn't have left the house wearing it. What the hell could have set it off?

It buzzes again, and I freeze, realization dawning.

They wouldn't. No, my roommates wouldn't have *remotes* for this toy. And even if they did, it wouldn't work across such long distances. The idea is ridiculous.

Still, as discretely as possible so as not to draw Sasha's attention, I slip my phone out of my purse and text the group chat.

What type of toy did you say this egg was again?

Helix responds instantly. *Is the toy inside you right now?*

Yes! And it did something. Could it be broken? How concerned should I be?

Like this? texts Lionel. The message is immediately followed by another quick buzz that has me drawing up my legs so I don't react too much. I can't believe Sasha isn't noticing any of this.

What the hell are you doing? I text. *I'm out at my friend's house right now. She's sitting right next to me.*

Lol. That's not a good place for you to be right now. Helix is laughing at me. I can practically picture his expression, and I want to reach through the phone and smack him. This is *not* funny.

There's more buzzing, and I have to bite my lip to keep from crying out.

I can't leave in the middle of a movie.

Sure you can. Lionel again. *You stand up and walk out the door to head home.*

No.

Suit yourself, texts Helix. And this time the buzzing is so intense I do cry out. I try to stifle it with a cough, but Sasha finally looks over, frowning.

"Are you okay?" she asks. "Why are you on your phone? We're supposed to be analyzing the story points in this movie."

"Actually, something came up. A family thing." I hold up my phone as if it's my excuse but am careful not to show her the screen. Just in case. "We can do a full analyzing session next time, but I really have to go now."

"Fine," says Sasha, sitting back. "At your place, though."

"Sure, not a problem, bye." I don't even care what I'm agreeing to. That's a problem for later. Right now, I need to get out of this apartment before my legs refuse to move and I completely embarrass myself.

The now nonstop vibrations in my pussy are so intense I need to hold on to the railing in the elevator. Thank god there's no one else in there.

I'm leaving now, I text. *I'll let you know when I'm home.*

Hopefully they stop with the egg in the meantime, because I'm not sure how I'll hold myself up enough to walk to the train station if they don't. I could take it out, but I'm not quite desperate enough to yank down my jeans and stick my fingers inside myself in public. While some people here in the city do that, I definitely don't.

Thankfully this ridiculous egg stopped vibrating long enough for me to get home, but I was on edge the entire train ride, waiting for it to start up again at the most inconvenient time.

Are you home yet? texts Miles just as I'm dropping my purse on my desk.

Just got upstairs, I text back.

Ender wants you in his room tonight, Helix types.

I freeze. Do I pretend I don't know who he's talking about? My roommates have called each other by their gamer names a few times in my presence and I've never really asked them about it before so maybe it would be weird to do so now. But I also don't want to give myself away that I've been watching their live streams.

Where is Ender? texts Quintin. *Why is he not here?*

The phone starts ringing with an incoming video call before there's a response. I answer it, and everyone but Ethan looks out at me from my phone screen.

"He was being dodgy earlier when I talked to him," says Helix, picking up the conversation right where it left off. "All he'd say was that if Clarissa was going to start sleeping in our beds, then he wanted her in his tonight."

"Wait, we get to have Clarissa in our beds now?" asks Lionel. "When did we decide this?"

"We didn't. Clarissa did," says Helix.

"You never told me this," Miles complains. "What happened?"

Helix grins. "Clarissa was missing me yesterday so she climbed into my bed and asked me to help her with her needs."

"Juke! I call juke," says Quintin.

"No, seriously. It happened. She looked sexy as fuck naked on my sheets," Helix announces, still grinning ear to ear.

"Do you need me here for this conversation?" I roll my
eyes as I move from my bedroom to Ethan's. They're so
caught up in their fight they won't even notice that I know
who Ender is. Besides, even if they do, he's the only one of
our group who isn't here so it's fairly obvious.

"Of course we do," says Lionel, surprised. "Since you're
moving beds now. Which day can I get you in mine?"

Miles taps a finger against his chin. "We can create a
rotating schedule when we get back."

"Fine, but I'm holding you to that," Lionel retorts.

"Right now, we have a better plan than making a
schedule," says Miles, smirking.

"That's very true," says Quintin. "Let me get comfortable
here."

I notice that they're all in or on their beds as they
adjust pillows and blankets. I slide into Ethan's bed. Like
Helix's, it's super comfy. They definitely sprang for the
good mattresses. Lucky me, now I get to reap the
enjoyment.

"Okay, what's happening exactly?" I ask once I'm
situated.

There's another flutter of the egg in my pussy and I can't
help but arch my back a little.

"That's what's happening," says Helix, wearing the same
wolfish grin that he had on last night when he realized
where I was sleeping.

"We figured you'd be lonely without us, and we know
how much you love your vibrator," says Quintin.

"But this way we get to be part of it." Miles smiles as his
hand slips beneath his blankets. "Right there with you."

"So you're controlling this?" I cross my legs, twisting
under the covers as the flutters change rhythm.

"Not just me," says Miles. "We're taking turns."

"Tell us what you usually like when you touch yourself,"

says Helix, laying on top of his blankets as his hand snakes out of view below the camera.

I'm not sure how to fully describe what I enjoy. When I'm alone, I usually focus on direct continual stimulation to my clit until I come, but I suspect that's not going to be exciting enough for them. I try to think of other things I can say. I've loved everything my roommates have done when they've touched me. And I love watching them touch themselves. Maybe I can use some of that to spin a sexy enough story for them.

"We never really did get to see much during our deal," Quintin points out.

"Although we're not complaining about what happened," says Lionel. "Just to be clear."

"That whole evening was bomba," agrees Quintin.

"Take off your shirt, Clarissa," Miles says. "We want to see all of your pleasure."

"Yeah, don't hide from us," says Lionel.

Biting my lip, I shift a little as a wave of pleasure flutters through me, courtesy of the egg and ... whichever one of them is currently in control of it. It's kind of hot, not knowing who it is. Like that night one of them woke me up by fucking me from behind, never letting me see his face.

"Same rules as last night?" asks Helix, sighing.

"Wait, what's this?" asks Quintin.

"Yes, please." I can't help but smile. My unintentional pause has had a positive outcome. "But if I take it off, you have to too."

If they want to see me, I deserve to see them too.

"Fine," agrees Helix. "We have to tell something personal, then Clarissa will take off a piece of clothing," He explains to his teammates.

Lionel and Quintin both raise their eyebrows, their hands still out of the frame.

"How personal?" asks Miles. "Like, could I say I'm six foot, two and Clarissa would have to take off her shirt?"

"No, that doesn't count. It has to be something I don't already know," I say. "Besides, you're five-nine, tops."

"Ope!" says Lionel, raising a fist to his mouth, but he's barely hiding his smile. "Clarissa is flaming!"

"I love it," says Quintin, settling in more. "She's not a noob anymore, and she's not going to let you backseat game her."

"Fine," says Miles, and while he's not actually pouting, he sure sounds like he is. "Show us how it's done then, Hel."

"I do a little mantra before our bigger games to get hyped and focused," says Helix.

"Really?" asks Miles. I'm surprised he didn't know this. I assumed they all knew everything about each other.

"Yeah." Helix looks a little sheepish.

"That doesn't count, I already knew that." Helix had been repeating his mantra while fucking me once before one of his games.

"But we didn't know that, so it still counts," argues Miles.

I'm not sure I agree with that argument, but I hadn't specified that the facts need to be new to me. I set down my phone to take off my sweater and throw it over the side of the bed.

"Ugh, no fair, you have way more clothing on tonight," groans Helix.

"But this time there are four of you and only one of me," I point out.

"True," Helix reluctantly agrees. "Your turn."

"What?" It's barely out of my mouth when the vibrations' rhythm switches from pointed intermittent buzzing to two short pulses followed by one long one, causing me to hook one leg over my other, trying to keep my mind on the conversation.

"If you want us to take off our clothes too, you have to tell us a personal fact," explains Helix.

I didn't realize that's what I was agreeing to. I just figured they'd strip every time they got to make the egg vibrate inside me. Now I'm going to have to think of something personal that I'm okay with them still knowing when I walk away at the end of our little agreement.

"I grew up in a small town," I say.

"Not enough," says Quintin, and none of the gamers moves to take off an item of clothing.

Pursing my lips, I try again, "My mom and I have never really gotten along super well, but I'm close to my dad."

"A daddy's girl." Lionel grins as he shucks off his shirt, flinging it out of view.

"And now you're letting us make you our dirty girl," adds Quintin, pulling his own shirt over his head.

I'm enjoying this. The vibrations are amazing, sure, but seeing four of my guys get shirtless at once and knowing they're as turned on as me right now is what's really getting me where I want to go. And where they want to help me go. The dirty words are the cherry on top of the sundae. I never would have pinned myself for someone who enjoys being spoken to in such an inappropriate way, but there are a lot of things I didn't know about myself before I met these guys.

"We've always had barn cats," says Miles, "but when I was little, I would try to bring them inside because I thought they were too cold in the barn."

"Aww, that's adorable." I can just imagine a young Miles chasing the cats around the yard, trying to love them.

"Every time I snuck one in, it'd claw something to shreds and my parents would get so pissed," rebuts Miles.

"Still adorable." I reach under the back of my shirt to unhook my bra, but Helix stops me.

"Stop, shirt first," he says. "I want to see your tits in a bra."

I set the phone down so I can take off the t-shirt I was wearing under my sweater, then pick it back up, snuggling down into the blankets.

"No, no, no," says Quintin, shaking his head. "It's not fair that you're having the comforter pulled up so high. We can't see what we've earned."

Lionel jumps in. "We aren't covering our chests, so you're getting to see everything." He runs his free hand down his chest until it slips out of view.

Folding down the comforter with my free hand, I let the phone camera pan across my chest.

"Is this better?"

There's a corresponding flutter that again has me arching my back and sticking out my tits to the camera. But it doesn't stop immediately. The vibration continues until I'm squirming on the pillow.

"Since you have so many more layers on, we should take double turns," says Quintin. "The first thing I did once we started earning real money was pay off the mortgage on my mom's house."

"Aww," I say. It's so sweet that Quintin is taking care of his parents, but I don't have time to really enjoy him sharing this secret because I'm already fisting my pillow as an orgasm builds inside me.

"Yes, right there," I moan, reaching beneath the blankets and into my jeans to work my clit as the first orgasm rips through my body.

"Pull back those covers and take off your jeans," says Lionel. "Quintin told you something personal, now we want to see how wet your panties are."

Throwing back Ethan's covers, I shimmy down my jeans, kicking them over the side of the bed. It's a little challenging because my hands feel weaker with the aftershocks of my orgasm, and I need to grip both the phone and my jeans. But they want to see the whole thing, and I did make a deal with them.

"Pan the camera down so we can see the wet spot," groans Helix.

"You pan yours down first." I can see the motion of their arms and the flexing of their tendons but nothing else. If they're touching themselves, I want to see each stroke of their hard cocks and remember the times I've stroked them myself. Or tasted their cocks. Or the times they've suck into my room late at night for a quick fuck or a 69.

"Tell us something about you," counters Lionel.

I'm feeling generous in the wake of my orgasm, so I decide to open up a little more than I'd initially intended to. "My parents think I'm living my dream in the city, but I only have three friends here. I really only hang out with one of them, and I'm not sure she always likes me." Maybe that's a bit too honest, but it's something that's been on my mind lately.

"We're your friends," Miles protests. "We love having you around, and we like you."

I raise an eyebrow. Sure, they love fucking me, but if there's anything else they like about me, I have no idea what it is. And if they do actually like having me around, I don't want to hear it right now. We're having fun, and if they start being sweet, I might start crying. Which would be the exact opposite of fun.

"I told you something, now drop your pants for me," I say instead.

"Yes, ma'am." Helix immediately shimmies down his sweatpants one-handed. He's not even wearing boxers.

In every square on my phone, I'm gifted with the sight of a hard cock being stroked by one of my boyfriends. It's truly a beautiful sight, and they're hard just for me. If they were here, they would take turns fucking me, but right now I get to watch them pleasure themselves to the sight of me.

"Now the wet spot," says Quintin.

Slowly I sit up a bit and spread my thighs so I can pan the camera down over my panties. I'd be embarrassed about how wet they are right now, but they're the ones in charge of the egg's remote and this was their whole goal. Besides, they've already seen me squirt, and they keep coming back for more. I'm beginning to realize that I shouldn't be embarrassed about letting them know how wet they get me.

"That's fucking gorgeous," says Lionel.

"I wish I could taste it right now," says Helix, tugging his cock so hard it almost looks painful.

"Now take them off," says Quintin. "I miss your pink pussy so much."

"You got to fuck her last right before we left," says Miles. "If anything, I miss Clarissa's pussy the most."

Laying back on Ethan's pillow, I can't help but chuckle as my boyfriends argue over who misses my pussy the most. The only thing missing from this moment is Ethan. I'm in his bed and surrounded by his things, but I still wish he were here.

"I used to steal my aunt's sewing pattern magazines and masturbate to them when I was young," announces Lionel. "Now show us your pussy."

Propping the phone up against the folded-over comforter, I hook my thumbs into each side of my panties and slide them down.

"That's fucking gorgeous," repeats Lionel, stroking his cock, then rubbing his palm over the head, spreading the bead of pre-cum down his shaft.

"And you're still wearing your little toy," says Helix, eyes focused on the screen as he continues to jerk himself off.

Using two fingers, I spread my pussy lips a little so they can see the ring of the egg that I'll use later to pull it out.

"I'm not sure I'd call it little," I say, "but compared to your cocks, I suppose you're right."

"Don't worry, we'll give you all of our cocks when we get home," promises Quintin.

"But we can still make you feel good from here," assures Helix.

The egg begins to vibrate again at a constant buzz, and I forget my earlier annoyance at it as I writhe in ecstasy and watch my boyfriends stroke themselves faster at the sight.

Chapter Twenty

It's so cozy in this bed. I can practically feel warm arms wrapped around me, holding me close.

Wait a minute. I *can* feel arms around me. My eyes pop open. My roommates aren't supposed to be home for a few more days. So who the fuck is in bed with me?

Cautiously, I shift enough that I can turn my head and look without waking whoever it is up.

As soon as I see his face, though, I sag back into the mattress with relief.

"You're back early." I roll into Ethan and brush the hair back from his face. He looks exhausted. "We'd wondered where you were last night."

"On a plane," he answers, still half asleep.

"What happened at home?" Something had to have happened for Ethan to change his plans last minute like this. Not that I'm complaining about having him here. It was lonely in this big house by myself, and now he and I will get to have some quality time together.

"Nothing." He pulls me closer until we're wrapped around each other. Less snuggling and more hugging.

"Are you sure?" I stroke his back as I hold him close. If

this is what he needs, this is what I'll give him—that's what girlfriends are for, I think—but he should talk about it if he's upset.

Ethan groans and rolls onto his back, but I'm not letting him off that easy. If he's so upset that he came home from his vacation early, I'm going to be here for him whether he likes it or not.

"You can tell me. I can keep your secret." I follow him across the bed until I'm splayed out across his chest, looking down at him.

"Nothing happened," repeats Ethan. "Nothing ever happens."

"What do you mean?" If nothing happened, why is he home early? Unless he always planned to only go for a couple days and booked a shorter trip without telling his teammates, but that doesn't make sense either.

"I went home to visit, but my parents were still going about their regular life as if I wasn't even there. And they didn't let my sisters come home from school for the week. So I figured if they don't want to spend time with me, I might as well be here." Ethan stares up at the ceiling, his voice so neutral it's heartbreaking.

Turning his face so he meets my eyes, I say, "Well I'm glad you came home, then, because this is where you belong."

If his family can't see how sweet and caring their son is, that's their problem. Ethan might be quiet and shy, but he's thoughtful. He rounds out the atmosphere in the house and he adds to the team. I've watched his games, and even though I don't fully understand what they're doing, I can tell that he's talented. They all are.

"Thank you," says Ethan, and I think I hear a catch in his voice.

"You know, you're still technically on vacation, and I

wrote a bunch yesterday. What do you say we play hooky today?" An idea is forming. Maybe it'll work. It could be fun, if he's interested.

"I'm not sure you fully understand the term hooky." Ethan laughs, his chest bouncing, and I nearly topple off of him.

"Come on, it'll be fun." I push up so I'm hanging over him, looking down into his eyes. He can't avoid me now. "Please?"

It was only a half idea I was throwing out a moment ago, but now that Ethan's uncertain, I'm more committed than ever. We both need to get out of the house and try something new today.

"Okay, let's do it," he says with a sly smile.

"Yay! Let's start with breakfast, because I'm starving." I roll off the bed and walk naked out of his bedroom.

Ethan doesn't stop me. Doesn't demand his benefits as a boyfriend. But I make sure to sway my hips a little so he at least has a good view as I walk away.

I rush through getting ready. I want to look nice for our outing, but I also don't want to take so long that Ethan gets annoyed and decides we shouldn't go out. I'm not sure I've ever seen him leave the house in the entire time I've lived here, except when we went to lunch with my parents and when he left for the airport. And I wouldn't call either of those outings particularly successful.

When I'm ready, I look for Ethan in his room, but he's not there. The bathroom door is open, so he's not still getting ready. Maybe he went downstairs to get a little work done before we leave. People who work a lot are always trying to sneak in a few more minutes.

I hurry down the stairs to roust Ethan out of the den, but find him huddled on the bottom of the stairs. I nearly trip over him.

"Are you okay?" I ask, knowing he's not. Something must be wrong if he's sitting here hunched over.

"I'm fine," says Ethan, slowly standing to his full height. "Lead the way."

Ethan opens the door as I slide on my shoes, but he stays right there holding the door until I step out on the stoop first.

"Where to? This is your idea so you get to make the attack plan," says Ethan, joining me on the sidewalk.

"Breakfast, obviously." I find myself taking Ethan's hand, entwining our fingers. "Then we're going to do what I call an Artist Date."

"Do you want to go to Over Easy? Their reviews list them as having a good brioche French toast," suggests Ethan.

"I didn't know you liked brioche," I tease as we head to the train platform.

"I have no idea if I like it or not." Ethan chuckles. "I didn't have time to google what it is before you came downstairs."

"It'll be a day full of firsts for us then, and I can give you the whole schedule for our Artist Date." One of those firsts is my first date in the city.

Working from home means I don't get out much or meet many people, so I haven't been able to meet potential dates. I'd thought in moving here my life would become glamorous and exciting, but all it's been is work and loneliness. Making friends as an adult is way harder than I thought it would be.

"Good, because I don't know what an Artist Date is either," says Ethan, smiling down at me.

My stomach does a little flip at that smile. At the trust behind it. He's letting me lead him wherever I want, just happy to be here with me.

I'm glad he came back early.

It's more brunch than breakfast, but we split a brioche French toast so we can both try it. We also split an omelet so we have a backup that we know will be delicious. I'm glad we did, too, because I thought the French toast was great, but it was too rich for Ethan.

After breakfast, we go to the aquarium and look at fish. We take turns pointing out our favorites and then making up little stories of their friendships with the other fish in the tanks. And the entire time, Ethan keeps my hand in his, so this feels like a real date.

We even pick up tacos on the way home so all we have to do after all our walking around is flop down on the sofa in the basement. Ethan divvies out the tacos as the projector warms up. I should be helping, but all I can do is sit here and admire him, a warm feeling in my chest as I watch him carefully transfer our food from the to-go container to plates.

"Do I have food on my face?" asks Ethan, not distracted from the taco situation. "You've been staring at me all day. If you've let me walk around with egg on my face this entire time, I'm going to be annoyed."

"No, you're fine." Ethan doesn't say anything. This is the time to say something about how much I enjoyed today, if I don't chicken out. "Thank you for today. For our Artist Date." *There. That wasn't so hard.*

"It was fun." Ethan glances quickly at my face as he passes me a plate, then fiddles with the remote to pull up a movie. "Nice to go out on a date," he adds, very quietly.

My heart swells. I'd been thinking the word *date* all day, and while I'd called it an Artist Date, I'd tiptoed around using the label other than that. Yet he'd paid for everything, which was sweet—and helpful, because my budget is still really tight. He hadn't complained once about what I'd chosen to do, and had readily joined in on my weirdness at the aquarium. I knew we had chemistry in the bedroom, and the connection we're forming in real life is just as special.

"It was a great date." I lean over to kiss him on the cheek before turning to face the screen. "So what are we watching?"

"This one is about an Earthling who befriends an alien, and they end up hitchhiking through the universe," says Ethan. "It's nerdy for me, and there's a little romance for you."

"Sounds perfect." I bite into my taco, thinking the same thing about today.

"Yeah, it is," says Ethan, and I can feel the weight of his gaze on me.

But when I glance over at him, he turns his attention back to the movie.

I smile to myself, settling in next to him with my tacos. Maybe I'm not the only one who needed to play hooky today. Or to go on a date.

"Fuck people." There's the crash of a suitcase tipping over in the hallway, followed by footsteps coming into the kitchen. "Next time I suggest it's a good idea to go out and interact with the world, remind me it's not."

Lionel drops into a chair at the table next to me. There are purple bags beneath his eyes, but he looks more angry than tired.

"You're home early. We weren't expecting you for a few more days," I say, keeping my voice even. If he's pissed, I'm not going to be the one he takes that anger out on. He's always been so in control of his emotions, this side of him is new.

Lionel glares at me for a moment, then glances down to my sandwich. "I was supposed to get in late last night, but my connecting flight got delayed and I had to sleep in the airport."

"That's rough," Ethan says, dropping down across from us with his own plate. "They didn't comp you a room?"

"No." Lionel leans over and picks up my sandwich, taking a big bite of it before getting up to make his own. "And of course, I couldn't get to any of my luggage during that time either, because it was already checked."

"At least you made it home safe." Looking up at Ethan, I smirk and add, "Just in time to join our game too."

"Game?" asks Lionel, perking up a little as he plops back down at the table with his sandwich. He threw it together so fast, it looks more like a pile of lunchmeat and bread and cheese than a proper sandwich, but he doesn't seem to care that half the filling is falling out as he raises it to his mouth. "What kind of game?"

He looks between us as if we might be planning something devious.

Ethan convinced me last night that we should take the rest of the week off and continue our Artist Dates, doing things we wouldn't normally make time for. No work, and all new fun.

"And what are you doing home already, Ender?" asks Lionel, popping a chip in his mouth.

"I wanted to spend some time with Clarissa." Ethan stares at me as he says this, and I feel my cheeks redden.

"Which I appreciate, because I didn't realize how big this house is until I was alone here," I quickly add, changing the subject to protect the secret Ethan entrusted to me.

"Same," agrees Lionel, nodding at Ethan. "That, and I

couldn't take any more of my family constantly talking to me and dragging me around to visit everyone they've ever met in their life. I don't think they have ever heard of personal space or alone time."

"Sounds like they love you and want to be part of your life," I point out.

"They could love me a little less," says Lionel, polishing off his sandwich. "Or at least give me a moment alone sometimes. A guy has needs, after all."

Ethan nearly chokes on his sandwich as he laughs. "Did they walk in on you walking the dog?"

"Twice!" yells Lionel, holding up two fingers for emphasis.

"Wait, what?" Why is it that every time there are more than one of them in the room, they slip into a language I don't understand?

"His family walked in on him masturbating," clarifies Ethan.

Lionel chomps on another chip, still glowering.

Now it's my turn to laugh. It sounds like it's right out of one of my romance books, but it really happened to him.

"If you want to go upstairs and take care of yourself, we promise not to walk in on you or interrupt," I say, attempting to be serious but unable to stifle my giggles.

"Or I could just ..." Lionel reaches for my waist to pull me closer.

"You smell like an airport." I scrunch my nose and scoot farther away.

"Fine," he grumbles, putting his plate in the dishwasher. "I'm going to go shower."

As soon as he's out of the room, Ethan and I double over laughing.

Chapter Twenty-One

"Honey, I'm home!" yells Quintin from the front door.

"We're in here!" I call from the kitchen. I'm in the middle of checking that I have all of the resources I need to upgrade my cities in Settlers, and it's crucial to balance my items perfectly.

Quintin comes to the doorway, but instead of greeting us, he looks at Ethan and Lionel and says, "What are you two doing here?"

"I'm trying to trade some wool for ore," says Lionel. "What does it look like I'm doing?"

"It looks like you're in Chicago when you're supposed to be hundreds of miles away with your family," says Quintin.

"Fuck that," Lionel scoffs.

"Agreed," says Ethan. "Will either of you trade me two bricks for one ore?"

"No, I'm trying to get ore," argues Lionel. "You can't take what I need."

"Of course I can," says Ethan. "Clarissa?"

"I do need bricks to upgrade my city." I reach out and trade resources with Ethan, trying not to giggle at Lionel's look of betrayal.

"You have to know what people want in order to get them to trade." Ethan calmly sets out his resources for his own upgrades.

"You're playing games and don't even care that I'm home?" asks Quintin.

"Of course we care." I smile up at him as I rearrange the cards in my hands so I can better plan my next moves. "Sit down and join us."

"Where did we get a board game?" asks Quintin, plopping down in one of the open chairs.

"I'm not sharing my resources," says Lionel.

"Me either," agrees Ethan.

"We went to a store this morning and picked one out." It was part of our continued Artist Dates.

Ethan and I'd spent the whole morning looking around a comic book store. Normally I wouldn't go in, but Ethan practically lit up as soon as we stepped inside. He showed me around the entire store even though he swore he'd never been there before. He'd been into comic books when he was young before discovering anime, and recognized nearly every poster and explained which shows the action figures were from.

The store had had a full row of games, and we'd decided that learning a new game together would be a fun afternoon date. We hadn't expected two more of our roommates to also come home early, but at least we got a game that works for multiple people.

"Fine," grumbles Quintin. "I'm going to shower and unpack. By the time I'm back, I expect the three of you to be done with this game so we can start a new one and I can join."

"We'd finish sooner if someone would trade me so I can get some ore," complains Lionel.

"I don't have enough points yet to win," says Ethan, "so obviously I'm not going to let you finish the game."

"I can do it without your help," Lionel grumbles.

"We'll see." Ethan lays down more resources for another upgrade.

We go around the table a couple more times. I'm so close to winning.

"Did you finish that game yet?" Quintin steps back into the kitchen smelling fresh from his shower.

"I just need wood and then I'll win!" I nearly jump out of my chair with excitement. These guys are some of the best video gamers in the world, yet I'm winning a simple board game against them. I'm not letting myself consider that they might be letting me win.

"Neither of us have any wood to trade you," says Ethan, grinning as he watches me bounce in my chair. I can't help it.

They win all the time so they're used to it, but this is exciting for me!

"Maybe I can help you out." Quintin shifts me out of my chair and sits down, tugging me down onto his lap. "I definitely have some wood for you."

Lionel and Ethan chuckle, but keep working toward acquiring their resources. I try to do the same, except it's a little challenging with Quintin's hand down the front of my pants, playing with my clit.

It's hard to focus and make the best decisions as my pussy begins to leak for him.

"Keep playing," whispers Quintin as he stands me up and tugs my pants just down my hips.

My jeans are still around my thighs, so they keep my legs pressed together as Quintin pulls me back down onto his lap. Right where his hard cock notches against my entrance. As he lowers me down onto him, his cock stretches my pussy until he's all the way inside me.

When it's my turn, I can barely hold the dice, I'm so focused on the way Quintin fills me. I expect him to move, to fuck me, but he simply keeps himself nestled inside me as I take my turn. I acquire two new bricks, but not the wood I desperately need to win.

"Man, I'm getting so much wood over here now," teases Lionel, fanning his cards in his hand.

"Are you sure you don't want to give me any?" I ask.

"It looks like you're a little full at the moment." Lionel laughs as Quintin wraps his arms around my stomach, holding me still and impaling me on his cock.

I really am, but Quintin isn't doing anything. Just being my chair for this game as his cock twitches inside, holding me against him so I can't move. I need to win this game so he'll fuck me properly. I squeeze my inner muscles around his dick.

"Fuck." Quintin nuzzles into my neck as his hands cup my breasts under my shirt.

"Yeah, that's not distracting to our game play at all," says Lionel.

"Don't be jealous," say Quintin. "I saw an opening and took it."

I can't help but giggle as my boyfriends chuckle, because Quintin literally did exactly that.

It's my turn and I finally draw the wood card I need. I lean forward to lay out my cards, Quintin's cock adjusting inside me and hitting a spot that feels so good I almost gasp.

"And I win." I can't help but grin. Our first game and I actually win. Between that and Quintin's thick cock filling my pussy, I'm feeling pretty good.

"Did you decide whose bed you're sleeping in tonight?"

Quintin rolls his hips, causing the walls of my pussy to flutter.

"She slept in Ethan's bed the last two nights and you're fucking her now," Lionel points out, "so I vote she sleeps in my bed tonight."

"You got to fuck her earlier today because you got home before me. I'm just catching up on our quality time," argues Quintin.

"I haven't fucked Clarissa since getting home," Lionel protests as Ethan begins to clean up the game.

"Seriously? You've been home all day and haven't fucked her?"

"We were busy playing a game," argues Lionel.

"You snooze, you lose," says Quintin.

"I'm not a toy you can fight over." I start to stand because if they're going to be annoying, I'm leaving.

Quintin pulls me back down and his cock slams into my pussy. I let out an involuntary cry of pleasure, swiveling my hips so he hits the good spot again.

"We're not fighting over you, baby. We're just having a conversation." Quintin lifts me up and slams my hips back down into his lap.

"Besides, we just want you to be happy," agrees Lionel. "Let Quintin show you a good time now, and after I'll carry you upstairs to bed."

"I'm off to bed myself," says Ethan, standing from the table. He leans over and captures my lips in a sweet kiss. "Another date day tomorrow?"

"Yes, please. Good night." The last part comes out as a moan as Quintin raises me slightly off his lap and fucks me fast and hard, desperate for me the same way he was before they left for the airport.

My arms come up over my head to hold Quintin close

as he fucks me in the chair. Lionel turns, crossing his ankle over his knee as he watches. Not commenting or saying a word, but his eyes darken in appreciation.

His eyes on me, enjoying the scene playing out before him, turns me on even more. He's probably sitting there watching how his friend fucks me and imagining all of the things he wants to do to me in bed tonight. The thought has me coming fast and hard.

Quintin yanks me down, using my hips to jackhammer my pussy onto his cock until he's coming too.

"I've missed you." Quintin nuzzles into my neck as we enjoy the after-tremors of our orgasms.

"I've missed you too," I whisper back.

"All right, time for bed," announces Lionel, standing up.

I try to join, but my limbs are weak and my jeans are still tight around my thighs. Lionel makes quick work of them, shimmying them to the floor. He leaves them right there in the kitchen as he picks me up, wrapping my legs around his waist.

"Let's go to bed, Clarissa." Lionel walks us out of the kitchen.

"Okay." I rest my cheek on his shoulder as he carries me. "Good night, Quintin."

We decided on the arcade bar for our group Artist Date. Although maybe that's not the right thing to call it anymore, since it's definitely an actual date-date.

Quintin had wanted to go to the zoo, but it's so chilly out that we didn't know how many of the animals we'd actually be able to see. We promised him we'd try again in the spring when the animals are active, and I tried not to wonder if I'll still be here, in their lives.

Maybe they'll get tired of me and ask me to move out so they can hire a new live-in girlfriend. Or maybe I'll have earned enough money that I'll be able to afford living on my own again. Obviously not in as big a house as we live now, because that would be lonely, as I've recently learned. But a small apartment designed just for me.

"How could you fail so hard at pinball?" Lionel asks Ethan now. "The game is like a hundred years old."

"You game for a living," says Quintin, "and that machine only had two buttons."

"You're supposed to be good with your fingers," Lionel teases.

"I told you," Ethan grouses, "the buttons were sticky. It wasn't my fault."

"A likely story." Quintin laughs as he unlocks the front door.

"All of my winning has me starving," says Lionel as we file inside. "What are we thinking for dinner?"

"Noob! Are you angling to get Clarissa to cook us dinner on a date day?" asks Quintin.

"What? No." Lionel looks at me, panicked. "I wasn't. I swear."

"Sorry to break the news to you," I say, stepping in to relieve his worry, "but I can't help cook dinner. I'm heading out to The Moat tonight. I just came home with you to switch bags."

All three of my boyfriends stop their bickering to stare at me as I step onto the stairs, prepared to leave them in the front hallway.

"Where are you going?" asks Lionel.

"It's Thursday," I say, taking the next step. At their blank stares I add, "Critique group?"

"Ah yes, okay." Ethan nods. "We usually have a game or training session about now."

"So, uh." Quintin looks around the hall uncertainly. "What do we do now, then?"

"Cook dinner for ourselves?" asks Lionel.

Ethan rolls his eyes and heads toward the kitchen, so I jog upstairs. Grabbing my cute bird bag, I throw in my planner, highlighters, pens, and the marked-up copies of my partners' chapters. At my bedroom door, I remember my wallet and turn back to my desk to fetch it from my purse. My train card will be helpful. My credit card too.

As soon as I hit the first floor, I can hear arguing from the kitchen. I could sneak out the front door and leave them to their own problems, but my feet have other plans.

"Is there a problem in here?" My boyfriends seem to be having a heated conversation, but I can't tell what about.

"No, not at all," Lionel says, too quickly.

"Yup, no problem here." Quintin wraps his arm around my shoulders and leads me to the front door. "Have a wonderful time at your critique group."

"We'll see you later," says Ethan, following.

Both Quintin and Lionel give him a sharp look.

"When you get home," he adds.

"Have fun." Quintin gives me a kiss on the cheek before opening the door.

Now I'm not sure if it's a good idea to leave. Something is definitely going on, but I don't know what. Or how worried about it I should be.

"Bye." Lionel takes advantage of my pause to kiss me goodbye too.

I've kissed two of them, so it's only fair that I kiss the third. I go up on tiptoe to kiss Ethan goodbye, then head out the door. If they don't want to share their problem, I shouldn't press. Although I'd thought that after the last couple of days, we'd grown closer and they'd start to let me in a little. But I guess we're not there yet. Maybe we never will be.

Chapter Twenty-Two

I'm glowing after the praise Maddie and Angela have lavished on my chapter for this week. I might just be getting the hang of this spicy romance thing after all. Although to be fair, I'd looked over their notes from last week and specifically checked this chapter so see if any of that advice would apply here too, then fixed it.

I did the same with Sasha's notes from last week, but this week's critique has almost as many red marks. A few super helpful, and the rest bordering on nitpicky. It's okay though. *Deep breath.* She's helping me improve, and once we get through my story, it'll be so awesome, my editor will have practically nothing to do.

"How is it going with the new roommates?" Maddie shuffles away the edited copies of her chapter.

"They're actually gone this week, right?" says Sasha, causally sipping her cosmo.

"Yes, well, no. They're technically still on break this week, but a couple of them came home early." And since I need to apologize anyway, I add, "That's why I had to leave early the other night."

"Were they locked out or something? Did you have to go let them in?" Sasha arches an eyebrow.

"No, they asked me to come home and help them with something." I absolutely am not going to tell them what specifically they needed me to help with.

"That's cute though that they wanted you home when they got in," says Angela. "When I lived with friends, we'd get so used to each other being around that when someone was out, the whole vibe in the house felt off."

"It definitely felt that way with them gone." I laugh. "We all work from home so it's weird when the house isn't full."

"What did you say they do again?" Sasha swirls her drink.

"I don't think I did." I know I didn't, and I still sort of don't want to tell them, but I can't really see a way around it. I doubt they'll make anything of it, anyway. "They're gamers."

"As in, they play games all day?" asks Angela.

Sasha frowns as she looks me over, as if she's displeased with my answer. But I can't help what my roommates do for a living.

"And they make a living from this?" asks Maddie, equally skeptical.

"I guess so." I shrug, knowing full well that between their subscribers and their monetization on other platforms, and the fact that they can afford to cover my room and board, they're doing just fine.

"I don't know that I've ever met a professional gamer before, just casual ones," says Maddie, staring off into space for a moment. "Are they super nerdy?"

"Let's just say, I'm watching a lot of new shows I've never heard of before." Police boxes. Hitchhiking aliens. Pirates.

Though that last one wasn't nerdy so much as

instructional, I guess. I like learning new things from my roommates. And I'm pretty sure they enjoy teaching me.

"I had a roommate once who was nerdy. Not a professional gamer, but I think he played some games," says Angela. "We didn't spend much time together, but he had a lot of dolls. He called them action figures though. In general, I'd say he really liked toys."

I nearly choke on my wine. "Yeah, my roommates have some toys too." *And not just the kind Angela is talking about.*

"I'd love to meet them," says Sasha, watching me carefully.

"They work a lot," I remind her. "And at weird times, so that might be difficult."

My parents were easy to fool into believing that we're platonic roommates, but I'm not sure Sasha would believe it as easily. Anything beyond roommates hadn't even occurred to my parents, but she might be looking for it. She had asked if they're dating anyone.

"Roommates who work a lot are the best," says Maddie, "even if they work from home, because they're so busy they're never around and it's almost like living alone. But you don't have to pay all of the bills yourself."

"Yeah, we're in one of those really big old houses because there are so many of us," I concur. "I don't even want to imagine what it costs to heat a place like that."

"You don't see your own utility bills?" Sasha sits up a little straighter.

"Uh, no." I look around at Maddie and Angela. Maybe I just made a huge slip-up. "I just moved in, and we haven't had really cold weather yet. We probably won't have to really turn the heat on fully until it starts snowing."

That sounds plausible. Besides, I could be paying a flat rate each month for my room. I've heard of people doing that, I think. I really hope they buy my explanation and don't ask any more questions.

"Oh my god, don't look now." Sasha's gaze shifts away from me, and she fluffs her hair.

"Oooh, do I have anything in my teeth?" Maddie leans forward and flashes her teeth.

"No?" Next to me, Angela seems just as confused by their weird behavior as I am.

"Good, because two of the sexiest guys I've ever seen have just walked in." Maddie picks up her drink and leans back in her seat.

"They're not buff, but lanky," says Sasha. "They look like I could teach them a thing or two and they'd love it."

"Are you going to go over and hit on them?" I giggle a little as I sip my wine. I've never seen my critique group react like this to anyone, so these guys must be something special.

"They're chatting at the bar," says Maddie. "Maybe I should go up and get another drink."

"Okay, I'm going to turn very slowly and look," says Angela. "At the bar you said?"

Angela twists a little, humming under her breath, before whipping back around in her seat. "They're looking this way. Do you think they saw me?"

"Do you think we could get them to buy us a drink?" asks Sasha.

"I'm not sure about the drink, but they're definitely coming this way." Maddie brushes her hair back over her shoulder and smiles up at whoever is approaching.

I'm super curious who could have my spicy romance author group so excited. These ladies write panty-melting book boyfriends, so it would take a lot for them to notice a guy in real life.

As these apparent hotties approach, my critique

partners sit straighter and smile wider. I'm so curious to turn around and see what they look like, but I stay still in my chair. I already have my hands full with five guys who I admit are pretty hot, and I guess I'll get to see these men my friends are gawking at if they do come over to our table.

Sasha is smiling and looking up through her eyelashes as a presence pauses behind my shoulder.

"Are you ready to go?" asks a disconcertingly familiar voice.

My eyes go wide as I whirl around in my chair, shocked. Yet again, my worlds are colliding and I'm waiting for the floor beneath me to open up and the earth to swallow me whole. Me disappearing would be the best thing that could happen right now.

But nope, I'm still here. Pinned to my seat by Quintin's stare as he and Lionel loom over our table. I'm not sure what to do with myself. I want to hurry them out the door, but that'll be weird. And my critique partners clearly want an introduction, from the way they've been checking my boyfriends out since the moment they stepped into the bar.

"Um, I have to pay my bill." Not original or smooth, but it's the truth.

"Clarissa," says Sasha, a little sharper than usual, pulling my attention away from my roommates, "aren't you going to introduce us to your friends?"

"Yes," I say, drawing out the word and glancing around to my critique partners, then back to my boyfriends. "This is Quintin and Lionel, my ..." I pause, weighing my options. "Roommates."

At my word choice, my boyfriends look sharply at me. I'll definitely pay for this later, but hopefully they'll go along with it for now. It's almost like they keep forgetting that they hired me for this position. Lately, there have been moments where it feels like they want it to be real. But it's not like they're introducing me to their friends and family as their girlfriend. No, it's me out here in public taking such a big step, and when this whole situation ends or falls apart as it inevitably will, I'll be the one left alone and embarrassed.

"Yeah, we're living together." Lionel shoots me a wink, then reaches out to shake Sasha's hand. "I didn't catch your name."

"I'm Sasha." She lets her thumb trail along the back of Lionel's hand, holding on for much longer than is necessary or normal, and there's a look in her eye as if she wants to lean forward and devour Lionel. But he's *my* snack, not hers.

"This is Maddie and Angela." I point to each of the ladies to draw their attention away from Sasha. "This is my critique group."

As soon as Quintin and Lionel move on, my shoulders relax. Although all three of the other ladies are still shamelessly ogling my boyfriends. Since I'd shown up on their front stoop to interview for their girlfriend, I'd known these gamers weren't bad-looking. In fact, I'd readily admit to myself, and absolutely no one else, that they're actually quite attractive. But I'm surprised my girlfriends are checking them out so blatantly.

"It's nice to meet all of you," says Quintin. "Clarissa doesn't talk about her work much at home, so we're glad she has someone to do that with."

Lionel nods. "That's very important."

"So you haven't read her work?" Sasha asks, bringing the group's attention back to her.

"No," says Lionel, "but when she's ready, we'll be here to support her."

Internally, I cringe. If they ever find out how I'm using them, there is absolutely no way they'll be supportive. In fact, I doubt they'll forgive me for violating their privacy this way.

"These are the roommates who made you come home during our movie night?" asks Sasha, turning toward me accusingly.

"Yeah." I cut my eyes over to Quintin, remembering exactly what they made me come home for.

"Were you locked out?" Sasha narrows her eyes on the way Quintin reaches over to squeeze my shoulder. "Why did you need her to come home without any notice?"

"We were supposed to be gone this whole week, and we are off work, but a few of us came home early to spend some quality time together." Quintin drops his hand. "It just kind of happened last minute."

I'm grateful to him for saving me from having to answer such a difficult and pointed question. There's nothing I could have said since I hadn't known ahead of time that my boyfriends were leaving, or even what their plans were for this week. Overall, communication is not one of their top skills, outside of when they're strategizing to take down another team's turrets.

"We have had a few good times this week," I admit, smiling up at Quintin.

We always have a great time together fucking, but it's also been really nice to get to know my boyfriends a little more one-on-one and bond with them outside of the bedroom. Outside of the house too. Between our work schedules and the fact that up until this week, our relationship has been strictly sexual, quality time together hasn't been a priority, or even an afterthought.

Both Quintin and Lionel smile back at me, and it almost feels like we're having a moment together, just us, even here crowded into this tiny bar.

Maddie clears her throat. "Would the two of you like to join us? We could pull up a few chairs?"

"You forgot your receipt." The waitress appears out of nowhere and hands Quintin a slip of paper.

"Oh, thank you." He takes it and folds it up without looking at it.

"You're welcome. Have a good night." The waitress glances once around our table, then hurries away.

"Actually, we've come by to walk Clarissa home." Quintin slips the folded paper half under my empty glass. "Unless you'd rather stay for another drink."

"You should stay," says Sasha. "We'd love to get to know your roommates. Just one more drink."

My boyfriends look at me, waiting, but their faces don't give anything away. I wish I could straight up ask them if they want to stay or if they really did just come to bring me home. They've expressed worry about me walking home from the train alone at night, but if that were their full intention, they could've met me at the station. They wouldn't have come all the way out here to the bar.

"I suppose one more drink wouldn't hurt," I relent, and I'm fairly certain Quintin rewards me with a small almost-smile.

"All right, ladies, what are we all having to drink?" asks Lionel.

My critique group leans forward to give their orders, and only now do I realize how low-cut some of their shirts are, showing off their tits to my boyfriends. Looking down, I ignore the sight as much as possible, but then notice writing on the receipt Quintin put under my glass. Pressing down on the fold, I can just make out a phone number.

Glancing over at the waitress at the bar, I meet her eye, but she immediately looks away. Had she seriously tried to give her number to my boyfriend right in front of me? Very not cool.

"Clarissa," says Lionel, bringing me back to the table, "what would you like?"

"I'll take a house white." I try to smile. It's sweet that they aren't taking the woman's number. That they were going to leave it here. It's a simple thing, but it makes my stomach do a happy little somersault.

"Those are your roommates?" asks Maddie, leaning in to whisper even though the boys are across the room at the bar. "You should have told us they're gorgeous."

"I think they're trying to impress us by coming in here and paying our bill." Angela deftly slips the receipt out from under my wine glass, showing it around to us. Sure enough, they paid our tab.

And right there at the bottom, in black and white, is waitress' phone number.

"You said they're single, right?" Sasha looks past my shoulder to the bar.

"Uh." I didn't say that exactly, I'd said that they weren't dating anyone. But how do I explain that just because they aren't dating anyone doesn't necessarily mean they're single-single?

Luckily, I'm saved from having to answer by my boyfriends' return with our drinks. Maddie and Sasha grab chairs from nearby tables and add them to the head and foot of ours. I'm in too much of a daze about Quintin and Lionel not only showing up, but also subtly turning down the number of the cute waitress, to be thinking clearly about where they'll sit.

If they attract so much attention from women, why did they need to post a flyer in the first place? Unless it's because all of those women want actual dates and conversation, not understanding the rigors of building a successful career and the time it takes, at all hours of the day and night. Maybe it wasn't that they couldn't get dates, it's that they didn't want the pressure of an actual relationship.

I'm more confused than ever as Lionel hands me my glass of wine. "Thank you."

The guys glance at the two empty chairs and then at me. If I ask Angela to move over, I'm making a statement about wanting to sit by my roommates. Would that imply that there is something more between us? Would normal roommates insist on being next to each other?

When I don't say or do anything, my boyfriends come to some type of silent agreement because Quintin moves to sit on the end by Angela and Maddie while Lionel claims the chair closer to me and Sasha.

"Yes, thank you." Maddie rests her hand on Quintin's forearm.

"Of course." Quintin takes a sip of his own drink, letting Maddie's hand fall away.

"So. Tell us about yourselves." Sasha turns her attention completely to Lionel. "Clarissa hasn't told us a thing other than that you exist."

Lionel glances my way and I must be wrong, but I swear there's a glimmer of hurt in his eyes before he looks back to Sasha. "What do you want to know?"

"Let's start with the basics." Sasha leans forward to rest her chin in her hand as she gazes at Lionel. "What do you like to do for fun?"

"We play games on our computers," answers Lionel.

"She meant what do you do for fun that's not job-related," I clarify, taking a fortifying sip of wine.

"What game do you play?" asks Maddie, sitting up a little more.

"Are you interested in gaming?" Angela asks her, surprised.

Shrugging, Maddie says, "I like to play the racing games with my neighbor sometimes."

"The neighbor you have dinner with all the time?" asks Angela, infusing the words with clear meaning.

"Yes," mumbles Maddie into her drink. I understand why Angela hinting that Maddie isn't entirely available annoys her, but at the same time, I'm grateful for it. If they think she's semi-taken, maybe they won't take her flirting seriously, and I won't have to analyze the bubble of possessiveness that rose in my gut when Maddie touched Quintin just now.

"We play LoL," Quintin says in answer to Maddie's question, "but lately we've been getting into tabletop gaming when we have time off."

I flush with happiness at this statement. The tabletop gaming is a very recent development—as in, since this week —and he's including me in what he considers a fun time. And it wasn't even sex. Well, we did fuck during that one game, but we've played since then and it's been totally non-sexual. I sit up a little straighter, both excited and honored that this popular, talented gamer is even hinting at our friendship.

"Clarissa and I have been planning a little movie night since our last one got cut short." Sasha pauses and looks at Lionel as if she's just now realizing, and laughing, adds, "Well, you know all about that."

"That we do," says Lionel, outright smirking as he raises an eyebrow at me.

I focus on the glass in my hand and try very hard not to think about the reason I had to leave movie night. This conversation is dangerous enough without me getting all hot and bothered thinking about them playing with the egg they gave me.

"We should plan something soon." Sasha glances to me

quick before turning her attention back to Lionel. "Some night when you're not working."

"Uh, maybe." Lionel flicks his eyes toward me in question.

"So, what do you all write?" asks Quintin, looking around the table.

Thank you, Quintin, I think. *Saved by a subject change.*

Maddie tells him about her billionaires and Angela spills the details about her small towns. Then Sasha launches into her spiel about romantasy, and how they might enjoy her books because they include quests, magic and, of course, dragons.

I have a hard time focusing on what Sasha says, though, because Lionel shifts subtly under the table until his knee is brushing mine. Once we're touching, he walks his fingers from his knee to mine.

My eyes flick to his and then around the table, waiting to see if anyone notices and calls us out.

When no one does, Lionel slowly walks his fingers up my thigh. My own hand slips beneath the table and clasps his, moving it back to his own leg. But instead of letting go, Lionel links our fingers, and now we're sitting around the table talking to my friends and holding hands. Like a real, honest couple. Which we most certainly are not.

"Yeah, maybe we'll give that a go," says Lionel, when he can finally get a word in. "Although we'd really love for our first romance book to be one of Clarissa's. So maybe after that. We'll see."

"Oh, you'll be in for a treat when you read Clarissa's," says Angela, rejoining the conversation.

"Whew!" Maddie fans herself dramatically. "Be prepared for some spice with that one."

Lionel quirks an eyebrow at me. "That's good to know."

My face feels like it's been sunburned, I'm blushing so

hard. I absolutely don't want my boyfriends to read my books and realize that I've basically been transcribing all of our sexual interactions for my characters. They almost certainly wouldn't want anyone to know all of the details of their moves, especially when they've hired me for a job that no one else knows about.

I need to nip this in the bud right now.

"It's getting late, we should probably head out." I practically rip my hand out of Lionel's as I stand.

"Sure," says Quintin, also standing but being much more chill about it.

"See you all later." I grab my bag and beeline for the door. My boyfriends can come or not. It's up to them. Although I hope they do, because god only knows what secrets will be divulged if they stay behind.

"Why don't I come over on Saturday to see the new place, and we can finish our movie?" calls Sasha.

Instead of responding, I just toss a wave over my shoulder. This was exactly why I didn't want these two worlds to collide. I want all of my worlds to stay neatly separate. No touching.

"Give me your bag." Coming up behind me, Quintin grabs my bag off my shoulder and hooks it onto his, not even caring that he's wearing all black and my bag is pink with cute little birdies and flowers embroidered on it.

"You didn't have to come out to the bar," I say. Before they can defend themselves, I point out, "You could have met me at the station that's right by our house if you're still worried about me walking home at night."

"You'd told Ender you didn't have a lot of friends, but you had this group." Lionel shrugs. "We wanted to make sure they were nice."

"And I notice you both put on jeans to come out tonight." It had been one of the first things I'd noticed, actually, but I hadn't wanted to say anything because I can already feel their interest piquing now that I have brought it up.

"Do we get a reward for putting them on again?" asks Quintin. "We even did it without being told."

"And without being bribed," I point out.

"Oh no, we still want our bribe," says Quintin.

"In fact, we should get extra because we put them on proactively," Lionel bargains.

"I'm not sure you understand how bribes work." I don't know if I'm more annoyed or amused. Both in equal measure, probably.

"I'm not sure you understand how this works." Lionel takes my hand as we ascend the steps to the platform.

"You're going to have to tell people about us eventually," adds Quintin.

I turn the tables back on them. "Oh, so you've already told your friends and family about me?"

Both of them open and close their mouths as they look to each other.

"That's what I thought." I step onto the train and sit in one of the four seats facing each other. They can follow or not.

"We don't have a lot of friend-friends," says Quintin, following me onto the train. "More like work friends."

"And fans," adds Lionel, close behind.

"Exactly, that's what my critique group is. They're my friends, but on a super professional level. And you're not announcing to your fans and followers what's going on in our house." Never once on their streaming page or in their chat have they even intimated that any of them has a girlfriend, let alone one they all pay to live with them.

Both Quintin and Lionel give me a surprised look, and I realize I've said something I shouldn't. They're not supposed to know I've researched them. Or that I'm following them and listening to all of their streams so I can hear their voices because they calm me down when I'm stressed or lonely.

"What about your families? You haven't told them," I point out, directing the attention away from my slip-up.

"We all live so far away from our families that it's not likely they'll meet you," says Lionel, finally sitting beside me.

"Then why live here in an expensive city when you could live closer your families?"

"But we'd only be able to live near one person's family. This way it's more fair," argues Lionel.

"Besides, there's better takeout in the city," says Quintin, sliding into the spot across from me.

"You were just home visiting your families for a few days." I'm not letting them distract me from this fight. If they're holding me to a certain standard, they need to be held to the same one. "You're telling me not once in all that time did you have an opportunity to tell them that you hired a live-in girlfriend to share between you?"

"I wouldn't phrase it exactly like that," says Lionel.

It's exactly like that though. Of course, I don't say this out loud.

"And they didn't once ask during that time what is new in your life or if you're seeing anyone?" Now that I'm thinking about it, I'm a little hurt that they claim to enjoy spending time with me, but it seems like it's only in the bedroom, and they're not telling anyone about me. I'd thought we were getting closer, emotionally, these last couple of days with our dates and playing board games. I must have been wrong.

"Our families ... aren't the biggest part of our lives," hedges Lionel.

"I'm just saying, you're here talking about fairness, yet

you're upset I'm not telling people about you when you're not telling anyone about me."

"You're right." Quintin turns to watch the city go by out the window, and I can't tell if he's lost in thought or just done with this conversation.

We ride the rest of the way home in silence, and when we get off the train, I'm not sure what to expect. But both of my boyfriends take one of my hands as we walk down the sidewalk, three abreast, our fingers linked.

Maybe I shouldn't have said what I did. I could blame the extra drink, but I know that's not why I said it. I've probably ruined the vibe between us and the fragile friendship we were forming. And, of course, they'll probably tell the others. We still haven't had any of the real conversations we should have had at the beginning about what everyone's expectation are for this relationship, and now things are getting even more complicated than they were a few days ago. I'm sitting here, hurt that they haven't talked about me, when this is just supposed to be a job. Why I am having stupid feelings about this when feelings were never supposed to be a part of it?

Even worse, I do actually feel more comfortable walking home with Quintin and Lionel. Not that I'm going to tell them that.

Quintin unlocks the front door and waits for me to go inside.

"No, that shouldn't go there," I hear Miles say down the hall. "It's like you've never set a table in your life."

I glance at Quintin and Lionel, but they just wave me on into the kitchen.

"You're home!" says Miles. "We made you dinner."

"I'm supposed to say that to you." I kiss Miles, and he wraps me in a hug.

"Well, *someone* was supposed to text when you were

almost here so we could be ready," he says, frowning over my shoulder at Quintin and Lionel.

"My hands were full," says Quintin, setting down my computer bag.

"Just for that, you're on dishes duty." Ethan sets a casserole in the middle of the table.

"Fine," grumbles Lionel, rounding the table and dropping into a chair.

"Not cool," grumbles Quintin. "You two cook like animals."

"You're going to eat it and not complain," says Miles. "Stop ruining the nice thing we're doing for Clarissa."

"Everything looks absolutely delicious." I give each of my cooks a kiss in thanks. It doesn't look terrible, and after a couple of drinks and no food, I'm starving. "I'm sure you both did a wonderful job."

"At least someone knows how to appreciate us," says Miles.

"What's the special occasion?" I take a seat and admire the effort my boyfriends have gone through.

Ethan dishes out square pieces of casserole onto each plate, then spoons out green beans to everyone, while Miles tosses each of the guys a roll. Mine he sets on my plate nicely.

"I looked up the term you used, Artist Date, and it said you should do something you don't normally do," says Ethan. "For us that's cooking."

"What did you think? Is this something you'll continue going forward?" What I'm really asking is, *Will you keep cooking so we don't order so much takeout?*

"No," says Ethan immediately. "But it was nice to do this one time. Maybe for special occasions."

"Well, I appreciate it," I say, taking a bite. "Now tell me about your evening."

Chapter Twenty-Three

I'm warm and cocooned, and having the best dream. But when I try to roll over beneath my blankets, long fingers wrap around my thighs to hold me in place. Holding me open for probing kisses and a tongue.

"I've missed you," says Helix from under my covers.

I'm not sure if Helix is talking to me or to my pussy specifically, but either way, I shift a little to help him find the perfect spot that has me humming in bliss.

"Sounds like someone missed me too," he says, his breath hot on my clit. "Were my teammates not taking care of you properly while I was gone?"

Fuck, it's not even dirty, but Helix checking in on me about how his friends having been fucking me makes me feel both a little bit used in the sexiest of ways, and cared for, because they're sharing the responsibility to make me always feel wanted.

He flicks my clit with his tongue, pulling a moan from me. "That's not an answer," he says, drawing back.

Reaching down, I grip Helix's hair to tug him back to where I need him, but he resists, chuckling.

"They did," I finally say, my voice hoarse from sleep, "but they aren't you."

All of my boyfriends touch me slightly differently, all in good ways, but sometimes I just need a specific touch. Besides, it's felt like part of us, of me, was missing with Helix gone.

Helix laughs again. "You're so good for my ego."

Then he drags his tongue from my entrance to my clit, latching on to suck at the sensitive bud. He bites down lightly, restricting the blood flow until it's almost uncomfortable, before releasing the pressure. The blood rushing back in sends waves of pleasure through my limbs.

It's not enough though. Not when I know what he's capable of giving me.

"More." I tilt my hips up to Helix's eager mouth. My boyfriends have been making me so needy with this constant servicing.

My fingers grip his hair tighter as he feasts on me, angling closer as he slips two fingers inside me. It's not a cock, but it's better than empty as he builds me up to a perfect morning orgasm. I can't imagine a better way to be woken up.

My orgasm is just out of reach though, and he withdraws his fingers. It's as if he's intentionally holding back, extending my missing him by not being fully inside me yet. His being home won't feel real until he's fucked me.

Hooking my leg over Helix's shoulder, I encourage him to take more. To give me everything. He's flared up these needs that had lain dormant for so long, and now that he has, I need him to help me sate them.

Helix gets the message because he moves down, he's fucking me with his tongue exactly the way I wish he would with his cock. I'm so close. I just need a little more.

When he presses a single slick finger against my

puckered asshole, my hips jump of their own volition—first in surprise, and then pleasure, as he eases past my body's natural defenses until he's a knuckle deep. With both holes penetrated, my hips keep moving, fucking both Helix's tongue and finger at the same time until I'm coming.

Helix removes his finger, but he's still lapping up my juices as my pussy pulses. Then there's another, larger point of pressure at my ass, sliding home smoothly in the wake of his finger. Once it's in place though, it doesn't move. It just fills me as I ride out the last waves of my orgasm.

"What did you do?" I'm breathless as Helix kisses my clit once more before crawling up the bed to place another soft kiss in the corner of my lips.

"Butt plug." Helix captures my mouth in a breathtaking, needy, and distracting kiss that keeps me from asking any further questions.

Especially as he re-fans the embers of my orgasm, building the heat back up until my hips are moving against him, seeking what I really want. Still lost in the kiss, I lift my leg and hook it over his hip, silently begging for what I need. He doesn't give in though, instead teasing me by sliding his hard length against my still-swollen clit.

I moan, frustrated by Helix's refusal to fuck me while also reveling in the feel of him against my aching clit. The shifting of my leg changed the position of the toy in my ass, ramping up my need to be fully filled and stretched by him. It's been a while since one of my boyfriends has filled my ass with a toy, and I'd nearly forgotten the feel of it moving within me.

"I knew you'd appreciate a new toy after our being away this week," says Helix as he finally relents and sheaths himself in my wet pussy.

"I'm glad you're all home." The house felt weird with

only a few of us here. Now that Helix is home we can get back to a semblance of normalcy.

"Me too." Helix bottoms out with each steady stroke, ensuring his pelvic bone grinds into my clit with each thrust to provide that extra touch of stimulation.

Words are erased from my mind as Helix folds my knees up higher, nearly beneath my chin, and jackhammers me into the mattress. Each thrust and fold of my body shifts the butt plug, driving me wild. Folded in half in this way, the toy feels larger as my ass clenches around the plug.

When Helix rolls his hips, he hits my g-spot perfectly and my world explodes.

"Fuck," Helix groans through clenched teeth, "your pussy is like a vice around my cock. Milking me of all my cum."

All I can do is lie here and enjoy the spasms rushing through my body. My first orgasm is obviously good, but my second is always better, probably because my body is still sensitive and revved up from the first one.

"I have training." Helix pulls out of me and rolls over to the side of the bed.

"You're taking this toy out of me first, right?" I watch as he stands to tug on his sweatpants.

"Nope." Helix leans down to plant a last quick kiss on my lips. "Don't get the tail wet either. That means no shower."

"Wait," I sit up, feeling the toy shift inside me, "a tail?"

All Helix does is wink before disappearing down the hall, leaving me alone in my bed.

Rolling onto my hip, I look behind me and can see something orange, but it's difficult to get a good look. Scooting across the bed, the toy drags a little, shifting, but not getting pulled out. Then I look in the bathroom mirror.

Right there, protruding from my ass, is a short fluffy tail. It looks almost fox-like.

This is ridiculous. I can't spend the whole day wearing a butt plug, let alone one that doubles as a tail. I should take it out. My boyfriends have done it before so it shouldn't be difficult. I'd have to make sure I get the angle right though or it'd be even more uncomfortable than spending the day with it in.

Maybe it'll be fine for a little while. Worst case, it if gets too annoying, I'll convince one of my other boyfriends to pull it out.

Not being able to shower is a challenge, though. I clean myself up as best I can with a washcloth. There's still a lingering scent of sex, but hopefully nothing a dash of perfume and deodorant won't cover up.

I attempt to pull on some panties to properly get dressed, but the tail gets all bunched up. That crosses off pants then as a potential outfit too. I grab a skirt and a sweater. If I'm walking around bare underneath my skirt, I'm at least going to feel well-covered on top.

Miles and Helix are eating cereal in the kitchen. They all seem to live on the stuff, along with energy drinks. I'm not sure how they look so sexy naked without putting healthier foods into their bodies. Right now though, their focus is on *my* body. I'm almost certain Miles knows what Helix did. About his leaving this toy in my ass.

"Sit down and join us," he suggests with a wicked gleam in his eye.

He definitely knows.

"I'd rather stand." Pouring my own bowl of cereal, I lean a hip against the high countertop and keep an eye on them as I slowly eat.

Mid-bite, there's a sharp vibration in my ass, nearly surprising me into dropping my bowl. They both keep their faces completely neutral, so I'm not sure who did it. Who has the remote for the toy tail?

"Are you sure you don't want to sit down?" Miles pulls out a chair next to him.

They must have vibrated the tail to get me to come over, so I shuffle to the table and half-kneel on the seat of the chair so I don't have to put all of my weight directly onto the plug. Even if I smooth down the tail, I'd still be pressing it deeper into my ass.

"What a good little fox," praises Helix.

"What do you mean fox?" asks Miles, rinsing out his cereal bowl and putting it in the dishwasher.

"You should show him, Clarissa." Helix grins. "I'd tried to order a cat one since I've always wanted a cat, but I couldn't find one. So we have a little fox now."

"No, it's embarrassing," I grumble. I like these guys, and I really love the toys they use, but I still feel weird about initiating anything with them. And this would definitely initiate something.

My fox tail vibrates again, soft and teasing. I shift a little on my chair.

"There's nothing to be embarrassed about," Helix reassures me. "He's going to love it, and you'll make his day. I bet he'd ensure you love it too."

Helix has a good point. They've never been mean to me, and Miles probably would get a laugh out of it. But I'm also not sure I want him to laugh at a thing that's supposed to be sexy. Although I'm not fully certain that this *is* sexy. It probably is funny, and I don't want him to think of it and start laughing whenever he fucks me in the future.

The vibrations change to a new pattern, and all I can do is shift as Helix—I'm now certain he's the one controlling the plug—coaxes me to get wet. I decide I can try to find the pleasure in this moment. They want me to be comfortable and excited about the things they're excited about.

On a heavy sigh, I stand up and lift my skirt slightly to show off the tip of the tail that's hanging between my legs. I also stick out my tongue at Helix, who just winks at me.

Chuckling, Miles takes the hem of my skirt from my hands and lifts it even higher to flash more of my bare ass.

"How did you know foxes are my favorite?" Miles runs the tail over his palm, letting me feel the slight pressure from his touch as he leans forward to whisper in my ear, "You're my favorite too."

The way Miles wriggles the toy in my ass, continually shifting around the vibration so it's never the same for too long, keeps me on edge. There's not enough of anything to fully get me going, but having his eyes on me, knowing that he's loving the view of playing with my new tail, is exciting enough to add to the moisture collecting between my thighs.

Setting my palms flat on the table, I lean forward to give Miles a better view. Not only is the toy on display, but he can probably see the way my pussy is glistening for him. He could so easily fuck me, and the longer he holds off, only looking, the more on edge I become.

"Do you like having a little tail?" Miles tugs it a little harder so the toy pulls out of my ass just a little before he lets go and it's sucked back in. He repeats the movement, pulling it out a little farther and then easing it back in, watching the way each stroke quickens my breathing.

"Don't be shy, Clarissa," says Helix. "Let us in."

"Yes," I whimper as Miles continues playing with the

toy, as if he's trying to figure out the code or pattern he can use to conquer the game of getting me off.

Miles circles his finger around the entrance of my bare pussy, causing me to spread my legs to give him more access. It's not a conscious choice, it's a bodily need. He pulls out the toy, then eases it back in before swiping his finger across my weeping hole again.

"I can tell," says Miles. "You're getting wetter the more I play with it."

He keeps playing, trying new patterns, speeds and depths, never settling on one rhythm, and it's driving me nuts. It's too much teasing and not enough satisfaction.

Turning my head, I'm about to tell Miles off for his lack of follow-through, but freeze when I notice the way he's licking his fingers. The very ones that were just circling my pussy. Depravedly, I consider asking him to feed those same fingers to me.

"Did we get a little fox?" asks Quintin, coming into the kitchen.

"We did," says Miles. "Isn't she adorable?"

"I'd says she's looking hungry," says Quintin with a smirk.

"I agree. This pussy definitely looks hungry," agrees Miles as he eases a single finger into me.

It's not enough. Two would be better. Perhaps three. With my ass stretched and played with, my pussy feels left out and empty. Especially when Miles pulls out his finger and holds it up for his teammates to see how coated with my juices it is.

Miles makes a show of sucking the juices from his finger. Sticking it all the way into his mouth the way it'd been stuck into my pussy, then pulling it slowly out, licking it clean.

"Looks like our girlfriend's pussy is super hungry and

needs something more than your skinny finger," suggests Quintin.

"You're probably right." Miles tucks the hem of my skirt into the waistband so I'm even more on display.

The way they're teasing me and drawing out my anticipation is frustrating, yet exciting. At any moment they could fuck me. I never thought I'd be in this position. Not only leaning against my breakfast table waiting to be fucked by a boyfriend while two others watch, but *eager* for it.

There's a nudging at the entrance to my pussy and I'm fully prepared for Miles to continue teasing me, but he doesn't. He shoves his full length inside me in one strong stroke, nearly sending me face-first into the table. I brace myself again, keening at how good he feels.

This was exactly what I needed. My pussy practically sucks his cock in, not wanting to let it go when he pulls back.

"I don't know, I still think our girlfriend looks hungry," says Quintin, sitting on the chair right next to us with his sweatpants tugged down around his thighs so his hard cock is on full display.

I watch Quintin's cock as he strokes it, enjoying the way I'm taking his teammate's pounding. He's probably starting the line to fuck me next.

Miles grips my hips and turns me away from the table so I'm forced to rest my palms on Quintin's thighs. I'm inches from Quintin's cock and know exactly what he's suggesting. I glance up into Quintin's eyes to see if he's thinking the same thing as his teammate.

He's waiting, not moving as he lets me make the decision. As he put it, he's letting me decide how hungry I am and if I want to swallow his cock. Licking my lips, I note the tiny bead of pre-cum on the tip of his cock. It felt amazing the last time I'd had one of my boyfriend's cocks in my mouth and one in my pussy, so I lean in and take it all.

Quintin groans as my lips wrap around the tip of his cock and my hands around the base. With Miles holding me up, I grip Quintin firmly but gently, sliding my tongue from the root to the tip and back down again, swallowing down that salty drop of pre-cum before slipping just the tip into my mouth.

Miles has other ideas though. He reaches down mid-thrust and snags my hands off Quintin's cock, holding them behind my back. Then on his next thrust, he sends me face-first into Quintin's cock, ensuring I gag.

I'm so full of cock and the toy, with the eyes of three of my boyfriends on me. They're using me exactly how they want, and it's exactly as I want as well. To be the center of their attention so I can only be in this moment and nowhere else. They've taken all of the control, but in a way that ensures I fully enjoy their playing with me.

I'm sure there's no way this moment could get better, when Miles uses his free hand to play with the toy. Now, not only is it vibrating, but the toy is fucking me in sync with Miles's cock as I'm thrust over and over onto Quintin's cock.

It's overwhelming, and I love every bit of it. Before, it was all teasing and not enough satisfaction, but this is all satisfaction as they fulfill desires I didn't even know I had before moving in with them.

"Fuck, I'm going to blow my load, and I forgot a condom," groans Miles. "Anyone know if she actually got on the pill?"

"I've got her mouth, so it's not a problem for me." Quintin wraps his hand in my hair so he can fuck my face as Miles slows his thrusting, waiting for an answer.

"Stop fucking her for a minute so she can answer," growls Miles. "Waiting is torture."

"No, I'm so close," says Quintin, his grip on my hair tightening. "Let me see you wiggle her little tail again."

Miles stops thrusting, letting his cock stopper my sopping pussy, and I miss the steady pace. At least he's still filling me, stretching me as he plays with the vibrating tail for Quintin to admire as he fucks my face faster. Until I'm pulled down hard and Quintin's cock hits the back of my throat, so deep I don't even have to work to swallow his cum as he spills his release in hot, thick spurts.

"I hope that was worth it, because I'm getting blue balls over here," complains Miles, continuing to play with my ass as I choke and struggle to breathe.

"Oh, it really was perfect," says Quintin, slowly lifting me off of his softening cock, finally letting me catch a breath.

I gasp for air, licking up the last few drops of cum that coat his head.

"Are you on the pill?" asks Miles, slapping my ass.

"Yes, please, I'm so close," I groan. If I had a free hand, I'd already be getting myself off.

"Don't worry, we're going to take care of you." Miles fucks me steadily, his hips slamming into my ass with each thrust. He twists the toy nearly out of my asshole, then slams it back in, keeping time with his cock.

The simultaneous fucking sends me over the edge, and thank god Miles is still holding my wrists in his free hand or I'd fall face-first into Quintin's lap. It's magical. All I can do is close my eyes and bask in the glow of so much pleasure as Miles's cock throbs in my pussy with his own orgasm.

"That was a great come face." Turning to Helix, Quintin says, "Did you see that?"

"I wouldn't mind seeing it again." Helix's watch beeps, and he adds, "But it's going to have to wait."

"Game time." Quintin claps his hands and pulls up his sweatpants as he hurries out of the kitchen.

"Your pussy gripped the life out of my dick," says Miles as he helps me stand up straight and regain the feeling in my arms. He hugs me from behind and kisses my neck. "Thank you."

Helix goes to follow Miles out of the kitchen, but stops to untuck my skirt and cover me back up.

My body is still vibrating from the powerful orgasm, but the way Helix is looking at me, I'm already preparing for another round.

"Don't forget that you can't get that tail wet," he says, wrapping his arms around my waist to hug me tight. One of his hands drops down to pat my ass as he adds, "I can't wait to see that cum dried on your thighs later."

With a last kiss, Helix walks out of the kitchen, leaving me standing there with his teammate's cum drying on my thighs and a toy still in my ass. At least it's stopped vibrating so I can focus again on my surroundings. Which includes cleaning up my dishes from breakfast.

And figuring out which scene I'm working on today while my boyfriends are gaming. Thank god I have a standing desk now since I'm not able to sit down.

Chapter Twenty-Four

Thankfully the toy in my ass stays silent while I'm drafting out the wounds and character descriptions for a new book. My first manuscript is with the editor, and I need to keep my mind occupied while I wait. Hence the new book, since my gamer boyfriends provide so much inspiration.

Still on for movie night? Sasha texts, distracting me from my flow. *I'll be over in an hour.*

Wait, what?

I'd completely forgotten that Sasha had suggested tonight as I'd ran out on our critique group. Yikes, I'm nervous about having a friend over to the house for the first time.

I open my minimized window to check how long my boyfriends have left in their game. I wouldn't care, except that they still have this toy in my ass. And I should probably give them a heads up that I'm having a friend over. They shouldn't care since they've repeatedly said this is my home too, but I don't want them to come out naked and looking for a fuck while Sasha's here. Talk about awkward.

I hurry downstairs and knock on their door. I've never

bothered them when they're gaming before, but this is important. And they should be finishing up this match soon.

Helix opens the door a crack. "What's the emergency?"

"My friend is coming over tonight for a movie."

"Did you need us to be there?" asks Helix, annoyed as he looks back over his shoulder into the computer den.

"No, but I need your help with something before she comes over." I point to my ass since I don't know how much of our conversation can be picked up by their microphones. I don't want the fact that I have a toy in my ass to be live streamed to over thirty thousand viewers.

"Oh!" Helix lets out a laugh when he realizes what I'm referring to. "Give us a few minutes to finish our stream and then one of us will be up to help you."

"Thank you," I whisper.

He'd said they would be a few minutes and every minute counts right now since Sasha will be here in less than an hour. I rush through the kitchen and pick up, tidying our normalized chaos. Then I move to the front door to organize the shoes scattered haphazardly in the middle of the hall.

"Ready?" Ethan steps out of the computer den with an excited smile.

"Yes, I was just straightening up." I drop the last pair of shoes. "Can you just take out the toy so I can shower and get ready?"

There's an answering vibration in my ass and I close my eyes, not in the mood for this right now.

"Actually, there's something you could help me with first." Ethan grins.

"But she's going to be here any minute." I glance at the door as if Sasha will walk through it at any moment, even though I know rationally that we still have time.

Unless she's early. Which would be just like her.

"Then we better be quick." Ethan heads up the stairs and all I can do is follow.

When I walk into my bedroom, he's already pulling his shirt over his head. He seems to have a plan for how this will go.

"My teammates told me about your cute little tail and I've wanted to see it all day." Ethan pulls my own sweater over my head. "But I always want to see you."

Although Ethan talks of my new tail, his focus is all on my tits. And even though we're in a rush, he takes his time kissing me and teasing his fingers over the outside of my bra. Distracting me from the fact that we're on a time crunch.

His touch is addictive. With the vibration in my ass kicked up to a higher level though, I need more. I drop my own skirt to the floor before reaching out to do the same with Ethan's sweatpants.

"Someone's an eager beaver." Ethan and reaches around to tug gently on my tail.

"For you, yes." I step even closer. I don't want any space between us.

"Good." Ethan drops his palms to the back of my thighs and lifts me until I'm straddling him on the bed. "Then fuck me. Show me exactly how much you want me."

Ethan lines up his cock, then I drop quickly onto him, groaning in satisfaction as his cock stretches out my pussy while the toy's vibration in my ass kicks up a few notches. I ride him fast and hard, the toy's buzzing urging me on, racing me to my own finish.

Once I'm coming, Ethan flips us over and pounds me into the mattress. The continued vibration in my ass extends my orgasm, and after a moment he's coming too.

"That vibrating in your ass comes through onto my cock in your pussy and it felt amazing." He collapses onto me before rolling to the side. Our arms still touching.

"Okay, that was worth it." I roll into his shoulder, laughing a little. I'd been so stressed about Sasha coming over, but a good, fast fuck calmed me down.

"Good." Ethan plants a hard kiss on my lips. "Now lift your knee so it's easier for me to pull out your toy."

My ass feels empty after hours with the buzzing fox tail plugging it up. I almost miss the toy, unsure when I'll get to be a fox again. I know it will only be a few days before my boyfriends will have found a new toy they want to try on me.

"Thank you." I kiss Ethan slow, allowing myself to really enjoy the slide of his tongue against mine.

"Now go shower," says Ethan, pulling away. "You have a friend coming over tonight."

"I do." I grin and rush into the bathroom.

Letting the water heat up, I tie back my hair so it won't get wet. I don't have time to dry it, and it doesn't matter if it's not freshly shampooed for a movie night. Tonight is going to be low-key, casual, and just what I need to stay calm while my manuscript is with my editor.

"Put your knee up on the counter," says Lionel from the doorway.

I'm not sure how much time I have before Sasha comes over, but saying no never crosses my mind.

He's already behind me, lifting my knee as he's sliding into my ass. His cock was already primed with lube and I've had the toy in all day, so it doesn't hurt. It feels incredible.

"You're going to have all of our cum on you before you shower it off." Lionel sets a small toy against my pussy, running it between my lips before settling it on my clit.

"Fuck, yes." I plant my hands on the counter and squeeze my eyes closed. The vibration is so intense it's almost painful, and he didn't ease me into it.

"It's driven us crazy knowing you were wearing a tail all

day. I bet that toy didn't feel nearly as good in your ass as my cock does." Lionel clicks the power up on the toy so it's even more powerful.

"Yes." It's all I can manage to say. My entire focus is on what Lionel is doing to me.

He pounds my ass and ups the vibration strength one more time until it's almost unbearable. Then I'm not only bucking against the toy and his cock, I'm coming so hard I squirt. All over his hand, the toy, and the floor. If I had any mental capabilities left, I'd be embarrassed.

Lionel slams into me twice more before coming too, biting my shoulder as he groans out his own release.

The toy slowly lowers in intensity as he lavishes kisses on my shoulder and along my neck, soothing the sting of his teeth.

"Your movie night is going to go awesome. Don't even sweat it," says Lionel with a last kiss before helping me into the shower.

The water is so hot I can barely step beneath it. Just the way I like it. The heat releases all of the remaining tension in my muscles from being fucked in so many different positions today. But my boyfriends were right. I'd needed the distraction, and now my limbs are loose and there's no space left in my mind to be worried about what Sasha will think of our house. Or if she'll discover my secret. If we're going to be friends, she's going to see the good and the bad about me at some point anyway.

I scrub extra well on my inner thighs to ensure I clean off all of the dried cum. Sasha will never be able to guess that I took two cocks right before she arrived.

Dressing in comfy sleep pants and a cozy hoodie, I can't help but smile when I notice that the little puddle I'd made earlier with Lionel has been cleaned up. My boyfriends really are taking good care of me.

My relaxed attitude seeps away as soon as I step downstairs, finding my roommates running around picking up the house.

"What's going on?" I stand in the middle of the kitchen as action swirls around me. "Sasha is only coming over for a movie. It's not a big deal, the house doesn't have to be pristine."

If they pretend it's more than just a casual movie night, I'm going to stress out again.

"We're just making sure we've picked up all of the, uh, toys." Helix's arms are filled with not only action figures, but different colored sex toys. Some of which I recognize, and others I don't.

"Oh, thanks." I blush. I hadn't realized that my roommates stored them in random places all over the house. I'd assumed they kept them all organized in their rooms.

"It's going to be hard, but we'll try to control ourselves while your friend is here." Miles wraps me in a hug, squeezing me tight.

"You act like it's a challenge." I laugh into his shoulder, wrapping my own arms around his waist and enjoying a moment of quiet cuddle in the midst of the current chaos. "Especially when I'm dressed like a troll."

"Oh, it definitely is." Miles chuckles, and even as we hear a knock at the door, he holds me a moment longer. "You're my favorite troll."

"I'm going to go let her in." I rise onto my tiptoes to kiss Miles's cheek before breaking his embrace.

I take one last deep breath, then open the door to Sasha. I blink as I take in her outfit. I thought we were doing a movie night, yet she's dressed for a girls' night out in skinny jeans and a sparkly, low cut tank.

"Welcome!" I raise my arm to gesture into the hallway. It's over the top and ridiculous, but I'm not sure how to act. I never had people over to my last apartment, and I'm worried I misread her text earlier.

"Thanks." Sasha steps inside, immediately examining the space.

By the time I lock the front door, Sasha is already down the hall in the kitchen, setting her bag on the kitchen table. The same one my roommates have fucked me on multiple times because they were too impatient for us to go up to a bedroom.

"Where are your roommates? I thought they were going to be here." Sasha pulls out her workbook so we can analyze tonight's movie.

"I'm not sure where they went." They'd been rushing around only a moment ago and I thought they'd still be right behind me. Maybe they wanted to give us privacy.

"Oh." Sasha frowns, but then regains her composure. "Well, shall we get started? Where are we watching the movie?"

"We have a theater downstairs." I lead the way into the basement, realizing we have a projector instead of a normal tv, and I've never set it up. I'll have to get one of the guys to come help with it.

"I guess that's one of the benefits of living in such a big house. A room just for movie watching," says Sasha behind me.

"But then you'd have roommates, and I thought you liked living alone." There are definitely things I miss about it, but at this point I don't think I'd like it anymore. It'd be weird to go back to the silence, not having others around to help cook or clean or laugh with in the evenings.

"I do, but there are certainly benefits to your situation."

Oh, Sasha, you have no idea.

I stop short on the bottom of the stairs and Sasha runs

into my back, nearly sending me tumbling onto the basement floor.

Helix and Miles are both down here.

"We thought you might need help setting up," says Helix, currently loading our streaming service onto the screen.

"And you can't watch a movie without snacks." Miles tops off a bowl of chips, then comes around to shake Sasha's hand.

"I'm Miles, and that's Helix," he says. "I think you met a couple of our teammates already."

"At the bar," clarifies Helix, also shaking Sasha's hand. Like it needed clarifying.

"So then there's just one more of you I haven't met yet," Sasha points out, still clutching Helix's hand.

"I doubt you'll meet Ethan," says Miles, coughing to cover his snicker as Helix yanks his hand back.

"Do you want to join us for the movie?" offers Sasha.

"Well, Clarissa had mentioned this was kind of a work session for the two of you," says Helix, "so we're going to get out of your way. But text us if you need anything."

Miles leans in as they pass as if he's going to kiss me. It's normal, but at the last minute we both realize that we have a guest who doesn't know our situation, and I turn slightly away from him as he awkwardly pats my shoulder instead.

"Alright, what movie do we want to analyze tonight?" I flip through potential options, breathing a sigh of relief at the averted crisis as the guys make their way upstairs.

"Let's do the one about the fashion designer from the south who is accidentally still married to her husband," suggests Sasha, settling into the sofa.

"Sounds good. There are a lot of tropes in there to discuss. Especially because it's kind of enemies to lovers, but also a second chance romance." I cue up the movie and take a look at the array of snacks my boyfriends provided. They actually did a decent job—chips and salsa, popcorn, some sodas, a bowl of chocolate candies. I shouldn't really be surprised, though. Before I moved in, they pretty much survived on snacks.

We watch the movie in silence, and my focus wanders to what my roommates could be doing right now. Slipping my phone out of my pocket, I check the their subscribers' chat, since I can't see if they're live streaming from my phone.

There seems to be a conversation about an upcoming ARAM, and one of their followers is claiming a female gamer could never be an AP Carry. Some of the others are bringing up strategies of the other team, such as their tendency to camp. And still others keep commenting, "BM".

My fingers hover over the keyboard. I've always lurked as other subscribers chatted because I don't want my boyfriends to find out I'm basically spying on them, and because I'm still getting a grasp on the lingo and how to play the game. But no one should bash a player simply because they're a woman.

"BM. Toxicity is not allowed," posts Hel.

The chatbot states that the asshole has been removed and banned.

"We're not afraid to enforce the rules," posts Faker.

I delete everything I'd been typing because my boyfriends dealt with the misogynist quickly and didn't let it get out of hand. They stood up for her before I could, and now I want to thank them for being so awesome.

"Who are you texting?" asks Sasha, her attention on me and not on the movie.

"Oh, no one." I set my phone facedown on the coffee table and grab a handful of popcorn.

"Last time we watched a movie, you were texting your roommates, and then suddenly had to leave," she points out.

"I think they're gaming, actually." Or at least chatting with their fans. "I'm not sure though."

"Is something happening between you and one of your roommates?" Sasha fully turns to face me on the sofa, the movie forgotten.

"What? Why do you ask?" I focus on my popcorn, chewing one kernel at a time. My stomach is somersaulting. I was afraid she was going to do this.

"You've never gone out much, and as soon as you moved in here, it seems like whenever we're hanging out, you're texting someone." Sasha leans forward to snag a couple of chips.

The way she phrases it makes me feel shitty, like I'm a bad friend for ignoring her when we're supposed to be spending time together. I wouldn't like that if she did it to me.

"Besides, your writing has improved so much, you must be getting inspiration from somewhere. And if you're not watching porn, you must be sleeping with someone," she says, watching my reaction carefully.

"Is that what you'd do?" I'm not sure if I'm ready to have this conversation with anyone. It has to happen at some point, and it makes sense that Sasha would be the first person I tell about my unconventional relationship, since she's my closest friend here, but it still makes me nervous that she might judge me.

"Sleep with someone for inspiration?" asks Sasha, as if she's considering the idea. "I suppose I would, although I work a lot, so it'd be challenging. I'd have to make sure they don't get attached because I'm focused on my career right now and if I keep rapid-releasing and following the data, I should be able to set up my entire career to succeed. I don't have time for a relationship, so if I were going to sleep with someone for inspiration, it would have to be casual."

"That's very practical." Maybe Sasha wouldn't judge me, then. Maybe I should come right out and say it. Tell her I'm sleeping with, and sort of dating, all five of my roommates. But there's a difference between her willing to sleep with one guy for inspiration and my sleeping with five.

She shrugs. "You're just as practical, right? Focusing on your career. Why else would you move from your own apartment into a house with five random gamers?"

Nodding, I weigh my options carefully. Finally, I say, "Living here does help so I can put all of my profits toward my next book since I don't have any bills now."

"You don't have any bills? What about rent?"

"Oh, uh, actually, I don't pay rent since my roommates earn enough to cover all the bills. They buy the groceries too." I pick an invisible piece of lint from my hoodie, nervous. That was a huge piece of honesty, and I need to gauge how she reacts before I tell her anything else.

"They're paying for you to live here?" Sasha's eyebrows nearly disappear into her hairline.

"Uh, yeah, we ... sort of worked out a deal." *I should have kept my mouth shut.* I wish I were anywhere but here right now. But I've come to realize lately that the more time I spend with my boyfriends, the more time I *want* to spend with them, and at some point I need to not keep them a secret anymore. I'm certainly not starting off by telling my parents, they're too judgmental, so it makes more sense to confide in a friend, another spicy romance author who might be more likely to understand.

"What sort of deal?"

"We're ... dating," I mumble, reaching for more popcorn even though I don't want it. My nerves over this whole conversation are making me feel sick, but at least snacks will occupy my hands.

"So you met, and at some point they liked you enough to ask you to move in and let them take care of you financially," states Sasha, her shock almost tangible.

"... basically." Sasha doesn't have the exact timeline, or the specifics of how and why we met, but she has the gist.

"Which one are you sleeping with then?" She leans forward, clearly hoping for some details.

I cringe a little. It's one thing for me to think about it that way, as just sleeping with my roommates for room and board, but hearing Sasha say it out loud doesn't sit well. Besides, I'd said "dating", not "sleeping with". She made that leap all on her own.

"All of them." I shove the rest of the handful of popcorn in my mouth to avoid saying anything else, and immediately regret the decision as the popcorn turns to sawdust in my mouth. I sip at my soda, trying to swallow the mouthful of popcorn down. I very intentionally do not look at my friend on the other end of the sofa, instead training my eye back on the movie.

"All of them?" I've clearly shocked Sasha. I'm a little thrilled at having managed to shock her, even as I'm mostly mortified to even be having this conversation.

Nodding, I watch the main characters argue at a bar.

"And they're okay with that?"

"It was their idea." And while I was against it in the beginning, now I love how we all fit together. I wouldn't want to give any of them up, to have to choose one boyfriend over the others. Individually they're all fantastic, but as a team they're perfection.

"Wow."

We sit in silence for a minute. I'm still pretending to

watch the movie, afraid to look over at Sasha, but eventually I have to say what I'm thinking.

"Do you think I'm the worst?" Sasha is my only close friend in Chicago, since although I see Maddie and Angela every week, we don't actually spend any other time together. And if I don't count my boyfriends. I don't want to lose her in my life. How many other people out there understand what it's like to have the drive to succeed that we have? And I can't deny that having Sasha in my corner could open a lot of doors for me professionally. As it is, she's the only reason I ever have an opportunity to connect with other writers. Without her, I'm back at square one both socially and when it comes to networking.

"No! In fact, it's a great idea, and the fastest way to research for your books. This shows real dedication to your craft. I'm impressed." Sasha nods, and glances back to the stairs.

I whip around to check the stairs myself. Only to sag in relief. My boyfriends aren't standing there overhearing every word I say.

"Thanks." A sense of pride washes through me at Sasha's words. She's such an impressive author, and my doing something she approves of feels like confirmation that I'm on the right path for my own career.

We both turn our attention back to the screen, and the relief I feel at having gotten that elephant out of the room allows me to actually pay attention to what's happening in the movie. Now that my secret is out, the tension created by me trying to keep it in and Sasha trying to pry is out has dissolved, and I'm able to enjoy just watching a movie with my friend.

Halfway through the movie, my roommates come down carrying boxes of pizza.

"We brought sustenance," announces Lionel cheerfully.

"Pizza *and* snacks? You guys are amazing," I say. "Thank you."

"We couldn't let you two starve." Quintin places a stack of paper plates on the coffee table.

"Or yourselves," I tease. My boyfriends have clearly calculated out the amount of food they would want for a movie night instead of how much two lone women can consume.

"You know us so well." Miles drops onto the sofa next to me and snags a slice of pizza, offering it to me and then getting one for Sasha before taking one for himself.

"How did training go?" The slice is still hot, and I lean forward to grab a second plate the same way Ethan does for more stability and to protect the grease from seeping through.

On my first bite the cheese strings from my mouth to the slice. Not too long ago, I'd have been embarrassed by the indelicate way I'm eating, but I no longer feel like I have to hide my imperfections from any of them.

"Fine, no issues." Quintin plops down on the other side of Miles. "How's the movie?"

I know for a fact that it wasn't fine based on the chat, but maybe the team deals with that sort of thing regularly so it doesn't register as a big deal to them. It is a big deal to me though, that they shut down the sexism the minute it happened. I wish I could say something about it, but of course I can't without outing myself as a subscriber.

"Good, I'd say we're learning a lot." I look to Sasha for confirmation, and she nods but says nothing.

Lionel and Helix grab slices of pizza and sit on the other side of Sasha.

"Ethan didn't want any pizza?" I'm used to us all being together and don't want him to feel excluded.

"We left a pie upstairs for him," says Quintin. To Sasha he adds, "He's not big on company."

"I'll check on him later, then." I'll probably spend the night in his bed since it's comfier than mine and if I'm spending all this extra time with these boyfriends, Ethan deserves some quality time too.

"He'll like that," says Miles, subtly shifting closer. "Now catch us up on this chick flick."

My boyfriends aren't completely sold on the plot as we explain it, but they also don't complain, which I appreciate. It's not really their thing, which is why I hadn't invited them to watch with us. That, and I assumed they'd be gaming the entire time, but it's nice that they're putting in the effort to be nice to my friend.

"Drinks," says Lionel, seeing that the two sodas they'd left for us earlier are the only beverages down here. "We forgot drinks. I'll go get them."

"Do you want help?" offers Sasha.

"No," says Lionel quickly. "You're our guest. We can't make you work."

He dashes up to the kitchen, returning with an armload of sodas and waters, which he passes out to the group. Then he moves the coffee table forward until it hits the wall below the projector so he can sprawl out on the floor.

Helix moves a little closer to Sasha on the sofa so he has a better view of the movie and can stretch a bit too.

We continue watching in silence until Helix pops up off the sofa and says, "I need an energy drink. I'll grab a couple in case anyone else wants one."

"I'll help you," says Lionel, hurrying up the stairs with Helix.

"We might as well stretch out then," I say. If they're going to keep running up and down the stairs, we don't have to be squished. Especially since the guys are sitting awkwardly close, but not touching me. Usually we end up squashing together cozily down here, mostly because my boyfriends insist on touching me whenever possible. It's weird sitting next to them but not making physical contact.

"Good idea." Sasha moves down into the spot recently vacated by Helix until she's stretched along one side of the sofa.

"I thought you were getting more drinks?" I ask when Helix and Lionel finally come back down, their hands empty.

"Oh. Yeah. Actually, I want to be able to sleep tonight so I don't need more caffeine," says Helix, looking for a place to sit as Lionel returns to his spot on the floor.

I frown at him. Helix's motto is usually the more caffeine the better, any time, anywhere. I hope he's feeling okay.

"You can sit down here," says Sasha, moving her legs a little to make space on the sofa.

"Oh, uh, that's okay. You look too comfy to make you move. I'm just going to sit over here." Helix pulls me to my feet, takes my seat and then pulls me back down onto his lap, wrapping his arms around my waist to keep me in place.

I'm now doubly glad I told Sasha that I'm sleeping with these guys. If I hadn't, she would definitely be figuring it out now.

"Is it just me, or is it suddenly a bit chilly in here?" Sasha wraps her arms around her middle.

"I'll grab you a blanket." Quintin takes a blanket from a basket in the corner and drapes it over Sasha, then moves back to his own space on the other side of the sofa.

"Thanks." Sasha wiggles her feet, adjusting the blanket until she's covered. "Do you want to come back up here, Lionel?"

"I'm good," says Lionel.

We all watch in silence as the movie wedding begins, Helix holding me close. Even Miles leans closer, his hand resting on my knee.

As soon as the movie couple finally kisses, Helix moves me off his lap and says, "We'll let you ladies discuss whatever you need to, and we'll take care of these boxes."

"Oh, thank you." In all the time I've lived here, these men have never once jumped so fast to clean up after a meal. They usually say they'll get to it later, which historically meant tomorrow at best.

"No worries," says Miles, as they all collect boxes and plates and disappear up the stairs, leaving me and Sasha stretched out on the sofa.

"So, yeah, you're definitely sleeping with them," says Sasha with a little laugh.

"And then the inspiration flows," I joke. Partly because it's true and partly because if I can pretend it's not a big deal, I won't have to admit that I'm falling for them.

Because I can't deny it anymore. I am one hundred percent falling for all five of my boyfriends.

"Before we start analyzing, where is your bathroom?" asks Sasha.

"Up the stairs and on your right when you step out of the kitchen."

Without my boyfriends down here holding me, Sasha is right, it's a little chilly down here. I pad over to the basket to snag my own blanket so I can be cozy while we chat.

"Get the fuck off me!" The shout from upstairs raises alarm bells in me.

It's not like my boyfriends to fight. I drop the blanket and hurry up the stairs.

As soon as I step into the kitchen though, I'm even more confused. My boyfriends are scrambling around to one side of the kitchen table, keeping Sasha on the other in a weird game of tag.

"Someone yelled," I say, surveying the group. "Is everything okay?"

"No," thunders Miles. "I don't know what you've told your friend here, but we're not servicing her."

"She needs to leave," says Lionel, pointing at Sasha.

"Back up. Start over." We were all just hanging out together downstairs and everyone was fine. How did Sasha's coming upstairs to use the bathroom start ... whatever this is?

"Tell your roommates to sleep with me." Sasha folds her arms and glares from me to my boyfriends.

"You tried to sleep with my boyfriends?" I take a step back, her words hitting me like a physical blow.

"It's not fair that you get five guys taking care of you while some of us are out here working hard for our success," says Sasha, anger radiating from her. "I deserve their help too."

"You don't think I'm working hard?" I'd thought Sasha could see all of the hours I've spent honing my writing craft. I've given up my apartment and changed everything about my life in order to pursue my dreams. Nothing about that was easy.

"All I'm saying is if you can use these gamers to improve your writing this much, imagine what they could do for someone who actually has talent."

I don't even know how to process that. I'd thought we were friends, that Sasha respected me, but she is quickly proving that none of that is true. "You think you're better than me so you're going to fuck my boyfriends to prove it?"

"Look, you know as well as I do that we need to do whatever we can to get ahead in life and follow our dreams, especially when it's something as high-stakes as publishing.

You're doing it yourself, so you can't judge me for doing the same."

"I wouldn't sleep with someone else's boyfriend, and I specifically told you we're dating. So you've tried to hurt me deliberately," I say, my own rage building. "That's something I would never do."

"I've shared all of my methods to get ahead in this career with you, and now it's you that's hurting me by gatekeeping," argues Sasha.

"I'm not sharing them," I snap. "They're my boyfriends."

There. I've said it aloud, and I'm going to fully stand behind that statement. I don't want to share my boyfriends with anyone, even though they share me with each other. I like being with them, joking, working, fucking. Even the tough, annoying things in life are better when we're all together, and I don't want to break up this not-so-little family that we're forming.

"We think you should leave," repeats Miles, crossing his arms.

"You can forget me helping you in the future, then." Sasha grabs her bag off the table and huffs down the front hall and out the front door.

The guys and I all stare after her, the energy in the room slowly returning to something resembling normal. "What did she mean by gatekeeping?" asks Helix.

"I'm going to bed." I suddenly feel bone-tired. "Can you finish picking up the snacks downstairs? Thanks."

I slowly climb the stairs and instead of turning into my own room, I walk right into Ethan's without even knocking.

Chapter Twenty-Five

"What did you and Sasha fight about?" asks Ethan, stroking my hair as I snuggle onto his shoulder.

"I don't want to keep talking about it." I roll away. He'd been asleep last night when I snuck into his room, but this morning I told him I had a fight with Sasha and now all he wants to do is talk, which is not properly distracting me from all of the emotions swirling around inside my head.

"You wouldn't have come in here if you didn't want to talk." Ethan rolls me back toward him and tugs me until I'm sprawled out on his chest. "You would have gone to Lionel or Helix, who would have fucked you into forgetting what happened."

"I'd thought Sasha was my friend, and I'd confided in her that I'm, you know, seeing all of you," I tell Ethan's chest. "I didn't know if she was going to be supportive or judgmental. And at first I thought she was cool with it. But then she called me a bad writer."

I've never thought of myself as the perfect writer. There's always room for improvement, which is why I'm part of a critique group. But I've been working hard and following all of their advice. Doing as much research as my body can possibly take. Surely a truly bad writer wouldn't work so hard to improve.

"And she hit on the guys in the kitchen while I was still downstairs." I can't believe she thought I would let her fuck them for inspiration. Refusing to play along with that scheme is hardly gatekeeping. They're *mine*.

"Are those two things equal in your eyes?" Ethan lifts my chin up off his chest to look into my eyes.

How do I answer? Both things hit my feelings like a personal attack. Insulting my writing is basically her slicing up the core of my being, my deepest identity. But I also feel more and more that these men belong to me, and being their girlfriend is also becoming a large part of my identity.

"No," I whisper. "I don't think so?" I glance up. "This is all so confusing."

"It's not supposed to be." He leans forward to brush a soft kiss against my lips. "But I'm glad you at least told someone about us."

"Yeah, I'm not sure I'm doing that again." I roll off of him to stare up at his ceiling. "Look how well it went."

Ethan's phone pings, and he checks it, swiping and tapping at the screen. Probably work then. They all work so hard, and don't get much downtime. I should do something nice for them soon so we can have quality time together. Maybe a weekly date night with no phones and no work.

"I hope you change your mind on that." He plants another kiss on my forehead before rolling out of bed. "And quick too."

"Why do you say that?" I sit up, letting the blanket pool at my waist to bare my breasts, which makes him pause at the door.

"Because we just announced that we have a girlfriend to all of our followers." He disappears into the hallway, leaving me alone in his bed.

"What?" I call after him. "You didn't want to talk to me about that first?"

When Ethan doesn't answer, I crawl out of bed and move over to my own room and my computer. I don't know where I left my phone. Probably in the basement, but I don't want to go looking for it. I'm not ready to run into all of my boyfriends yet after the embarrassing situation that was last night.

I'm not sure where they posted the information that they have a girlfriend. Or how much information they've given. I do a basic search with their names and girlfriend. A few older articles come up, saying they aren't dating anyone, but a few chat forums show up as links with other gamers either freaking out that these guys have a girlfriend or posting they don't care and it shouldn't matter.

These comments include the link to their streaming site, and when I click over there, I see it. In their "About" section, it simply says, "In a relationship". No other information is provided.

I'm not sure how I should feel about this. They've clearly stated that they're in a relationship and they're not interested in either hitting on or being hit on by any of their subscribers. However, they also haven't named me, which is nice for my privacy but also makes me wonder. If they were involved with someone famous or successful, would they tell everyone my name and be proud to claim me as theirs?

I pull up the web version of the subscribers' chat. My subscription was about up the other day, so I renewed for another month. It's not that much money and I like knowing what they're up to.

Their subscribers are freaking out there too. Apparently, because my boyfriends never share anything from their personal lives, the fact that they've shared this is sending everyone into a tizzy.

Miles's pinned post floats at the top of the chat, no matter if I scroll backward or forward. "Yes, we have a girlfriend. No, we will not be divulging additional information about her at this time."

I really wish they'd talked to me about this first. I mean, we'd talked about it briefly the other night when Quintin and Lionel walked me home from critique group. But when I'd called them out on not telling people about me and our relationship, I'd thought they would tell their friends and family first. Not their millions of fans and followers.

I climb into a scalding shower to wash off the bad vibes from last night and organize my mind about what I'll say to my boyfriends when I confront them. And hope they don't bring up Sasha's comment about gatekeeping again.

I could tell them to ignore her because she's just jealous that I have five boyfriends and she has none. But if I wait too long, my boyfriends will be shut up in their computer den and I won't be able to talk to them for hours.

"We need to talk," I say as soon as I step into the kitchen, but immediately freeze at the sight before me.

The table is set with real plates, stacks of pancakes, and bowls of both fruit and eggs. I've never once seen any of my boyfriends eat anything more substantial than a bowl of cereal for breakfast. Usually they grab a protein bar if they're feeling healthy, but pair it with an energy drink. This is the most startling thing I've seen since moving in, and they've bought me multiple sex toys.

"What do we need to talk about?" Miles hands me a cup of piping hot coffee.

Of course it's in my favorite mug, the one with the little birds singing all around it. Don't they know this thoughtful little display of theirs is throwing me off my game when I'm ready to be mad? How do I tell them I'm upset when they're doing something so sweet?

"What's with all this?" I point accusingly at the loaded table, then sip my coffee. It's delicious.

"Breakfast," answers Miles.

"Sit down," says Helix. "Eggs go cold surprisingly fast."

"I can tell it's breakfast," I say as Quintin practically ushers me into a seat. "Why did you all make breakfast?"

"So, we did a thing," says Miles sitting down as well.

"I already told her," says Ethan, casually helping himself to a couple pancakes.

"You told her?" asks Lionel. "Ender, you've left us overextended!"

Ethan shrugs. "She was with me when we decided and posted."

"And you didn't ping us?" asks Helix. "Or tell us while we were cooking all of this?"

"I thought we were making breakfast to make Clarissa feel better about her friend hitting on you last night," says Ethan, his brows drawing together in confusion.

"No, we did it because we wanted to break the news to her about our subscribers," says Miles.

"Wait, I thought we were doing it because we crashed her critique group thing," says Quintin.

"I thought it was because we hadn't told her we were going on vacation." Lionel casually pours syrup over his scrambled eggs.

Miles pinches the bridge of his nose in exasperation. "Fine, it can be for all of those reasons."

"Oh no, this can only be for one of those things," I say, accepting the syrup from Lionel and dousing my pancakes. "This is a nice breakfast, but it's not nice enough to cover *everything*."

"Then it's for my reason, since I was the one who suggested the breakfast thing," says Miles. "And we'll have a strategy session later to deal with the other things."

"Fuck, that's going to be a long session," grumbles Quintin.

"Can we order takeout for it at least?" asks Helix.

"Sure," says Ethan, scooping a line of egg down the middle of a pancake and rolling it to eat like a taco.

"Are you going to get to the apology part of this meal?" I'm annoyed about them not involving me in this announcement, but I also feel guilty about needing to apologize myself for using them without their knowledge as research for my book. The better I get to know these guys, the worse I feel about keeping this a secret. Maybe I'll plan an elaborate apology blow job for each of them.

"This is the apology," says Miles, surprised.

"You need to say the words too." I don't have a lot of dating experience, but I'm pretty sure all apologies have to include the words *I'm sorry* at some point. Although that'll be hard with my mouth full of cock, so maybe a blow job and something else.

"I'm not sure that's true." Miles looks around the table to his teammates for guidance.

"I'll wait for as long as you need." I sip my coffee. "But you should take down the notice that you have a girlfriend until you apologize."

"Yeah, that's not going to happen," says Miles, setting down his fork and crossing his arms.

"So you're afraid of looking bad in front of your followers, but not afraid of what I'll do, or not do, until you apologize?" I set down my own silverware and mirror Miles's posture.

"Woah, woah." Helix throws up his hands. "Let's not poke at each other."

"Yeah, let's not jump to anything drastic," says Lionel. "We can sort this out."

"Sure, and while this is a nice gesture," I wave to the breakfast spread, "I need the words too."

"Okay, yeah, we can do that," says Lionel, nodding. "Go ahead, Arrow."

"What?" Quintin seems shocked. "Why am I doing it? I wasn't the one who made the post."

"We made this agreement together," says Miles.

"Look," says Helix, leaning forward and pointing his fork at Miles, "we need a glass cannon, and you're the one who physically typed out the post."

"Fine, fine," grumbles Miles. "I can do this."

"Ready when you are." I'm not even sure why I'm fighting, since this gesture is absolutely amazing. While my using them for inspiration is harmless and they'll never find out, I'm not sure they understand the impact of what they just did to me on their channel.

When I'd talked to Quintin and Lionel about being fair, that if they wanted me to tell my critique group and friends about our dating situation, then they had to tell theirs, I never thought they would take that as meaning they should announce it publicly to the whole world. I'd thought we could start small and make those big-step decisions together, but they made that choice for me. For us.

Since I've moved in, we've all been making our own choices separately, but if we're doing this for real, we need to decide things together. Like a real couple. Or whatever a relationship between six people is called.

Miles takes a deep breath and grips the edge of the table. "We're sorry."

The rest of the team nods in agreement, waiting for me to tell them it's okay.

"Sorry for what?"

Miles drops his head into his hands with an exasperated sigh. "For all the things we listed before."

"But I'm not sorry that you told your friend about us," adds Quintin.

"No, definitely not for that," agrees Lionel.

"Although it wasn't fun when she tried to kiss me," says Miles.

There isn't anything Miles could have said to get me to completely forgive them faster. Or make me feel worse. I'm the one who put them in that position by believing that Sasha was my friend.

Getting up, I slide onto Miles's lap and wrap him in the tightest hug possible.

"I'm sorry that my poor judgement in friends caused you to be put in such an uncomfortable position." I kiss him on the cheek.

Miles wraps his arms tight around my middle and rests his chin on my head. "Thank you."

"And that's how you give an apology," I tell everyone, looking around the table so they can all make a note of my skills. Even as my secret of using them weighs heavy on my chest, I just hold Miles, silently willing him to accept my own unspoken apology.

My boyfriends all chuckle, and we tuck into the amazing breakfast they prepared. It's a challenge with Miles still holding me, but I don't mind. Sometimes I just want to be held too.

My feet slow as I round the corner to our usual table in the dive bar. I haven't heard from Sasha since she came over for movie night five days ago. My anxiety has been going haywire with my uncertainty about seeing her again.

Maddie and Angela are at the table chatting and my shoulders immediately relax. Although just because Sasha isn't here right now doesn't mean she won't show up.

"Loved the pages on the new book," says Maddie, leaning back in her chair.

"Writing a new one is probably a good distraction for while you're waiting for your editor to return your manuscript," says Angela.

"To say I'm on edge these days is an understatement." I huff a laugh, but I'm nervous and distracted, still glancing around the room in case Sasha is approaching.

"And it never gets easier," says Maddie. "We just learn how to mitigate the anxiety."

"Thanks for ordering for me." Nodding at my usual glass of wine, then looking over to Sasha's empty chair. "No Sasha tonight?" I try to keep the sound of hope out of my voice.

"Your welcome. I figured we should since The Moat is so busy tonight, and no. She said something about going home to visit family." Angela shakes her head, and I feel the tension leave my body now that I know I won't have to see Sasha tonight. "I'm surprised she didn't tell you. I'd thought you two did a lot of things together."

"We mostly get together to write." I shrug. *Or try to fuck each other's boyfriends, apparently.*

"Well, your writing has certainly changed so if it's from working with Sasha keep it up," says Maddie.

"Thanks." I bite my lip. I'm not sure if I should ask, but it'd help my peace of mind, so I say, "Do you know when Sasha plans to be back?"

"She didn't say." Maddie glances over at Angela. "Did something happen between you two?"

"Kind of," I mumble. Then, without even consciously deciding to, I end up spilling the whole story about how Sasha had called me a bad writer and kissed my boyfriend.

"Oh no." Maddie reaches across the table to hold my hand. "I'm so sorry. You're not a bad writer, and I'm glad your boyfriend made it clear that he's in a relationship. He sounds like a good man."

I nod, appreciating their words, but it's still hard to believe. My boyfriends are so famous in their own little circle, it almost feels like it's a matter of time before someone tries to take them from me again. And although they originally only hired me to be their girlfriend so they can use me whenever and wherever, I feel like we've moved past that emotionally and are in a real relationship.

"Soooo." Angela casts a glance at Maddie. "Which one of those two guys who came by last week to pick you up is your boyfriend?"

I cover my face for a moment in embarrassment. This is so awkward to talk about, but my boyfriends and I had talked about it over breakfast and we're going forward with telling people about our relationship. They don't need to know that I'm getting paid for it though.

I take a deep breath and spit it out. "Both of them are my boyfriends. Well ... two of my boyfriends."

"Wait, you mean there's more?" asks Angela, her eyebrows raised. "How many boyfriends do you have?"

"Five," I mumble into my glass of wine.

"Are these all of your roommates? You'd said you have five roommates," says Maddie.

"Yeah, it kind of just happened after I moved in." This is technically true. First they hired me, then I moved in, and then we started sleeping together. I can't pinpoint exactly when I fell for them and this all became real, though.

"Whew!" Maddie fans herself. "No wonder you're writing such hot scenes now, with boyfriends like that!"

"Some people struggle seeing other people have success and happiness," says Angela, reaching out to pat my shoulder. "I hope you and Sasha can get past what happened to continue critiquing together. But if you can't, we understand and we can have that difficult conversation with her."

"I'm not sure what's going to happen with her, to be honest. I'd thought we were friends, but then she did this so I'm not sure if that was ever true." I pause to sip more wine. Tough nights like this require more alcohol. It might be a three-glass evening. "But thank you. It means a lot to have you both in my corner. I'm just glad she's not here so we can both have some space away from each other."

"Well we're here for you," says Angela. "Just let us know what you need and we're ready to help."

"Thank you. I really appreciate that. I think for now I'm just going to throw myself into my work." *And prove to both myself and Sasha that I'm a good writer.* I pull out Angela and Maddie's chapters that I'd marked over the last couple of days, shuffle through them and put Sasha's back in my bag.

"Yes, let's get some work done. After all, that's why we're here." Maddie pulls out her marked pages too. "Then after, we can have another drink and you can tell us all the details about these five sexy gamer boyfriends of yours."

"Sure." I laugh, and we settle into our discussion. They have no idea they've already read the dirtiest details.

Without Sasha, we get through our comments surprisingly quickly, and while there is still a lot of constructive criticism, there's no pushback, and there are a lot of compliments too.

"Oh goody, the eye candy has arrived." Maddie blindly stuffs the copies of her chapter into her bag, her gaze focused on something behind me.

Turning in my seat, I spot all five of my boyfriends filtering through the tables as they approach. Even Ethan.

My boyfriends had promised—or threatened?—to come pick me up, and I'd told them repeatedly I could handle it.

Apparently, they didn't believe me.

Shuffling my own papers into my bag, I tamp down the worry that zings through me. I don't think Maddie would also hit on my boyfriends in front of me, especially after hearing about the Sasha incident, but I'm still on edge.

"Here to collect your girlfriend?" asks Angela, loudly.

All five of my boyfriends break out into the biggest grins.

"So you're telling everyone about us now?" asks Miles, sliding into Sasha's empty seat.

"Says the guy who announced it to millions," I shoot back as the others snag empty chairs from nearby tables and pull them up.

"Wait, what?" asks Maddie, confused.

I don't blame her. She's not in the gamer scene, so she doesn't realize that some of these players have so many followers. I didn't know anything about it either, until I moved in with these guys.

"We made a small post on our socials so girls wouldn't hit on us." Quintin side-eyes me to judge how I handle this information.

Sasha isn't here, but I'm still keeping a close eye on Maddie and Angela even though I'm pretty sure I don't have anything to worry about. We talk a lot about sex and they've made some wild comments, but I shouldn't immediately assume they'll hit on my boyfriends right in front of me. Although Sasha had been just fine with doing it behind my back, so I'm still cautious.

"But we learned from that, didn't we?" I say, grinning. I can't help but provoke them. I'll pay for it later, but I know that will be more of a reward than a punishment.

"Yes, we did," agrees Miles.

"It's still cool though, when you tell your friends," whispers Ethan, leaning close.

I roll my eyes, but my heart still flutters a little harder because the more people who know, the more real this entire situation becomes. And the harder it will be to walk away. I'm not sure if that's what I want anymore. Not if it means no longer being part of their lives.

Chapter Twenty-Six

"I don't give a shit about Mom and Dad, but I wanted to tell you something."

I nearly walk into Ethan pacing the upstairs hallway, his phone pressed to his ear. When I try to go around him though, he snakes out an arm to tuck me against his chest as he continues talking to whoever is on the other side of the line.

"No, it's nothing like that," says Ethan, shaking his head so his chin rubs against my hair. "I didn't want either of you to hear it from someone else, but I'm dating someone."

Now that they've told the entire world, my boyfriends are slowly calling their families and telling them. I'm not sure if they're explaining that they're dating a woman who is also dating four other guys, but at least they aren't keeping our relationship a secret anymore.

I wrap my arms around Ethan's waist and squeeze him tight in case he needs a little more confidence to keep this conversation going. I haven't even told my parents yet. I'm not sure what will freak my parents out more, that there are five boyfriends or that they're professional gamers.

"She's actually my roommate." Ethan plants a kiss on the top of my head as his sisters squeal in excitement, their voices carrying even though they're not on speakerphone. "Yeah, the one who wrote that romance book you're ARC reading."

My stomach squirms. I want to ask what they think of my book so far, but don't want Ethan to learn too many details.

"No, I haven't read it yet. I'll have to buy a copy since I wasn't lucky enough to receive an ARC."

Ever since we started our stripping game, my boyfriends have started learning more writers' jargon and are always throwing in a few author terms to show me they're listening. It's super cute.

"Oh, wow, spicy, huh?" Ethan winks down at me.

And that's my cue to leave. I can't not blush every time I talk to anyone about the spice levels of my new books. It makes me miss writing sweet romance a little bit because the topic never came up. But I'm not about to give up on all of my very hands-on research.

As his sisters talk, Ethan's eyebrows keep raising ever higher. *Yep. Definitely time to walk away.*

Planting a kiss on his shoulder, I slip out of Ethan's grip and head into my room. My second book isn't going to write itself. And book one is already seeing enough reads that I should get book two out soon.

"Hey, Clarissa," says Helix, sticking his head into my room. "Would you mind coming downstairs a minute?"

My mind is so deep into my book that it takes me a full minute to register not only that Helix is talking to me, but what he's saying. I'd ask what he needs, but he's already disappeared.

I find my boyfriends in the kitchen, either leaning against the counters or sitting at the table. None of them smile when I come in, and my stomach flips. I can't remember a time when at least one of them didn't smile or reach for me when I walked into a room.

"What's wrong?" My mind is flying through the possibilities. Maybe one of their conversations with their families went wrong and they're making them move home.

"We read your new book," says Quintin, his gaze hard.

"It was very enlightening," says Miles.

"Oh?" I start to sweat and my feet itch to step slowly out of the room. This cannot be good.

"We weren't aware that we were providing so much inspiration for you," says Ethan. "And your readers."

"I'm a writer." I look anywhere but in their eyes. "We get inspiration from everything around us."

Granted, I did go into this situation knowing that I would use it for inspiration and write about everything that happened between us. But they shouldn't be so upset. It's not like I named them personally.

"But it wasn't just inspiration, was it?" says Helix, standing up straighter and crossing his arms. "You wrote thrust-by-thrust descriptions of the ways we've fucked you."

"No one knows it's you though." It's a weak defense, but it's true. Most people will think I've just dreamed up these scenarios. They'd never imagine that each of these fucks happened with one of my boyfriends. My readers don't even know I have any boyfriends.

"Your critique partners met us, and they've read your

book," Quintin points out. "I'm surprised they haven't asked you about it yet. Either way, they probably will soon."

He's right. Sasha had guessed it.

"They'll mark that your writing went from no sex at all to your characters getting dicked down regularly, and they'll notice that the change happened when you moved in with us," adds Lionel.

"I don't know that that's true," I protest. Besides, it shouldn't matter what other people think. Not if my boyfriends really like me. "It's already done, so it's not like I can undo it. Do you want me to apologize? Because I will."

"What we want is for you to have been upfront about using us from the moment you moved in," says Miles.

"You could have been honest about using us for your research so we could have a choice if we end up in your smut or not," says Ethan.

They're acting as if I'd gone into this intending to hurt them. The whole reason I met them and moved in here in the first place was because Helix posted that stupid flyer about hiring a live-in girlfriend.

"You all used me too," I point out, growing angry that they're not acknowledging their own part in how we got here in the first place. "You fucking hired me to be your live-in girlfriend. You've paid to fuck me for this entire time. Do you really think I would have moved in with you if you weren't paying for my rent and food?"

If I hadn't found this situation, I wouldn't be able to afford to live in the city and I'd already have had to move back home.

"We told you upfront what we wanted, and you agreed to it," says Helix. "But you didn't give us the same respect."

"We thought you might be starting to really like us-like us," whispers Ethan. "I mean, you told your friends about us."

My heart breaks at Ethan's words, because it's true. No matter how much I tried to keep things between us professional and told myself I was only doing this because I didn't have any other options, at some point I fell for them. Not just individually, but as an entire team too. Even with just one of them gone from the house, the entire vibe of our group felt off and I hadn't been truly settled until we were all back in the house together.

We're at a standstill.

"What happens now?" I'm more than a little scared of the answer. I wish I could step into their arms and be held and told that it's all going to be okay. But I'm afraid that it won't be.

Miles clears his throat. "We think it'd be best if you moved out."

"You're fired, effective immediately," says Helix, glancing away like he can't stand the sight of me. "You should be out by tomorrow." They all stand and file past me out of the kitchen.

"What the hell?" I can't believe they're acting like this after all the shit they've pulled, no clear expectations. I should have asked more questions at some point, but they put out the add and they knew what they expected going into this If they didn't, then they had no business advertising for the position. Besides, they were clearly ashamed of me and their hiring me because they hadn't even told their families that I exist up until recently. "Where do you expect me to go?"

"That's not our problem," says Quintin, leading his teammates out of the kitchen and barricading themselves in their computer den.

I can't believe it. My boyfriends—ex-boyfriends now, I guess—are kicking me out of the house. The place they've said I should think of as my home. Shoving me out on the streets like they don't care what happens to me.

Holding on tight to my anger, I barge out the front door and to the nearest store to pick up boxes. As soon as I let go of the anger, I know I'll fall apart, and I will not give them the satisfaction of seeing that. Of knowing how much they're hurting me.

Chapter Twenty-Seven

"Clarissa, honey!" my dad calls to get my attention at the train station.

"Thanks for picking me up," I mumble into his chest as he envelops me in a bear hug.

"Of course. It's not every day that our little girl comes home for a visit," he says, leading me to the truck. "We love having you around for as long as the big city can spare you."

I don't have the heart to tell my parents that I got kicked out of my house. Or that five of the most amazing men I've ever met broke up with me.

Hopefully I can milk this "visit" pretense long enough for some of my royalties to roll in from my new book, which is doing really well. Then I'll have a deposit for a new apartment so I can start over again. Maybe not in Chicago. I won't be able to look at the city the same way, and I'll always be afraid of running into my gamers somewhere. It'd be just my luck, even though they don't get out much.

First, though, I need time to lick my wounds and save some money.

"I love being around you too, Dad." I smile across the truck bench at him as we wind through familiar streets to the house I grew up in. It doesn't look like anything has really changed here since I moved away.

"Your mom has a whole list of people who want to visit you while you're here. Everyone is so proud of you, moving off to the big city and pursuing your dream."

Great, way to make me feel even worse. Sure, my dreams are starting to come true career-wise, but life-wise, I'm falling apart. And now I'm going to have to pretend that everything is normal and nothing is wrong. Not only to my parents, but to the whole town.

"Can't wait." I try not to sound sarcastic, but fail. As Dad shifts into park, I add, "Sorry, I'm just tired from the train ride. I'm going to lie down for a bit."

"Of course, honey," says Dad, his easy smile returning. "We'll call you when dinner is ready. You've been working so hard on your last book, and now this one. I'm glad you came home for a little break and some rest."

I trudge down the hall to my childhood bedroom. My room is exactly the way I left it before moving to Chicago, and while I'm physically right back where I began years ago, mentally, I'm nowhere near here. This bed isn't nearly as comfortable as the one I left in Chicago. Which makes it doubly worse than the beds that my boyfriends—my ex-boyfriends—own. Maybe they'll ship me one of theirs on accident when they send all of my stuff. Since there was obviously no way I could move all my belongings on the train, I'd left the guys a note to send the boxes to me at my parents' address.

Pulling my laptop out of my bag, I set it up on the pillow next to me. The gamers' streaming page is already up. They're not live right now, but I can still see where it says they have a girlfriend. They posted it so recently, I'm not surprised they didn't immediately take it down. That would cause more drama in their fandom. It's only a matter of time though, and I feel the compulsion to continually check until it happens.

I don't have the heart or energy to pull up their chat though. Every inch of my body aches and all I can manage is to lay here and barely hold back tears.

"Welcome home, hun," says my mom, knocking on the door of my childhood bedroom as she walks inside without waiting for a response.

I slam my computer closed and roll to face her. There's no energy to get up or put on a happy face right now. My world has dropped out from under me, and I don't know what I'm going to do. I don't have the energy to make any big decisions right now.

"Oh no, hun, are you sick?" Mom sits on the edge of the bed and lays the back of her hand against my forehead. "You do feel a little warm."

Probably from the fact that I've been hiding under my blankets since I got home. But I'll go along with her and pretend to be sick if it gets me out of being dragged around to visit all of the neighbors and her friends. I can't smile as she lists all of the accomplishments of people I sort of know, or look people in the eye as she tells them I'm living my dream in the big city. It's all lies. Sure, my book is taking off, but I can't even be happy about that because it's just a reminder of how I messed things up with my boyfriends for my career.

Now all of my readers are falling for the fictional version of the guys and their bedroom moves the same way I did. But they can all just close the book and revel in the happily-ever-after.

There's no happily-ever-after for me.

"Probably from the travel," I mumble. Maybe she's right and I did catch something on the train. Real-sick or fake-sick, I just want to be left here in this less-comfortable and too-small bed and be miserable until I have absolutely no choice but to look for an apartment.

"I'll call Mrs. Nesbitt and tell her we can't make it tonight." Mom straightens my covers, tucking them up under my chin. "I'll heat you up some soup."

"Thanks," I say as she leaves, closing the door behind her.

I don't love lying to my parents, but it's not like I can tell them I was in a secret relationship with my five gamer roommates who they disapproved of, and we broke up and now I'm heartbroken. Which shouldn't even be true because the relationship was just supposed to be a business arrangement. They would cover my room and board so they could fuck me whenever and however they wanted, and I would use all of their sex moves in my new spicy romance novels. There were never supposed to be feelings involved, and they weren't ever supposed to know that I was using them as inspiration.

I've played sick for a full week without my parents getting suspicious. They're so distracted by my being home that they don't ask any other questions. Which is perfect, because now I can extend my visit without it being weird by saying that I didn't really get to spend time with them for the first bit.

Not that I'm excited about socializing with their friends. But I'll have to do something soon. Pretend to get my life back together. Fake it until I make it, and maybe someday it will be true. I can officially say that I have what I wanted: a successful author career. Readers have been devouring my newest book and are already asking for another. Which I sort of have, even though I haven't worked on it since I moved home. I have tons of ideas, and notes to work off of for inspiration, but then I'll have to put myself in the mind-space of being loved and cared for, when in reality I'm still in the wallowing stage of my breakup, moving about like a zombie while mentally burying myself deep beneath my childhood covers.

"I'm glad you're feeling better." Dad plants a kiss on the top of my head. "I'm off to work, but it's good to see you up and about."

"Thanks." *It doesn't feel good.* "See you tonight."

Left alone, I have the strongest urge to crawl back into bed, but I can't live under those blankets forever. At some point, my parents are going to start asking questions. Probably right as all of my belongings arrive from Chicago. I'd boxed everything up, but I'm still waiting for my exes to send it all to me. It's the least they can do after kicking me out of the house.

In an effort to resist the temptation to hibernate again, I set up my computer at the breakfast table. I stare at my manuscript icon, but can't bring myself to open it up. I can't make any of my characters happy when I'm so miserable.

I could solve my living situation problem though. I need a new place to hide from my parents, and a base to keep my newfound career going from.

Searching through all of the rental listings in Chicago,

even moving to the very edges, practically an hour away from the city proper, I come to the conclusion that living alone will be impossible. Even as my royalties increase, I won't receive any of those profits for at least two months. And I'm not even sure if this level of sales is sustainable. This is all probably a fluke, and in a month my sales will be back to their normal pittance.

Moving to a different city crosses my mind again. There's nothing holding me to Chicago. I don't have any boyfriends, and the only person I thought was my close friend actually doesn't care about me. My critique partners are good, but I could find new ones who are just as awesome in any other decently-sized city.

A new city also wouldn't remind me of places I've gone with my ex-boyfriends. I wouldn't be constantly holding my breath, expecting them to come around a corner at any moment even though they rarely leave the house.

I'd miss that house though. The old rambling style that's quintessential Chicago. Living close to public transport and knowing where everything is.

Somehow as my thoughts travel down this path, my fingers type in our address, and I'm already on street view. When I'd first stared at this door with that flyer in my hands, I'd seen a house in need of freshening up. But now all I can see is a house that's well-lived in. A true home.

And I'm glad my parents aren't here to see the few tears that escape because I really want to walk back through those doors again. Yet that's not going to happen. I'm moving on, and this will or won't become my villain origin story.

I should research other cities I could live in, but all I do is stare at that door on the screen. I'll never walk through it again. Never see inside.

As if of it's own volition, my mouse opens another

browser tab and pulls up my ex-roommates' streaming site. It's the only way I'll see inside our house again.

Or see them.

They look tired, and when I glance below their live feed and see their streaming schedule, it's no surprise that they're exhausted.

While the other day they weren't on and there was only their normal schedule, now their calendar is packed. They're playing for hours each day on live streams, and this doesn't even account for their training sessions or the ones they record and upload without a live audience. They've always gamed a lot, but they're pushing themselves harder than ever. They must be up for a big endorsement or have a huge competition coming up if they're practicing this much.

None of the quick comments whizzing by on the side of the live stream are talking about how tired they are though. Only about how hard they've been playing lately, never giving their challengers a chance to even get near their minions. How other teams are growing afraid of playing them because they're that good.

I'm not afraid of them though. All I want to do is gather each of my gamers to me and hold them until I'm not sure where my body ends and theirs begins. I would soothe away the purple circles under their eyes and remind them they should be eating and taking care of themselves.

That's not my job anymore though. They've probably already hung up flyers saying they're hiring again, looking for a new live-in girlfriend who can fulfill all of their sexual needs and won't betray them by telling the entire world of romance readers what they're like in bed, move by move.

Lucky bitch.

One of the comments catches my eye, mostly because a few of the other viewers comment on it, almost making a little conversation thread on the side.

"Is your girlfriend ever going to come on a live stream?" asks one of the viewers.

"It'd be cool to meet her," says another.

"I bet she's super hot. She has to be, because look at these guys," says another.

"She's taking all of the good gamers for herself. Not cool," says another.

The moment Helix sees the conversation thread in the sidebar he does a double take. His eyes darken and I can tell he's pissed. Probably other viewers can tell too, because he's not trying to hide it.

Immediately the chat says that the viewers who commented have all left the live stream. But Helix still looks pissed, and he flips up the mic on his headset before saying something to his teammates.

They all do the same, and now they're arguing amongst themselves. None of them looks happy and I wish we could hear what they're saying. In all my hours of watching their channel, I've never once seen them talk to each other privately. They're usually pretty casual and willing to give each other grief right on the air for all of their subscribers to see and know they're real people.

"What are you watching?" asks Mom, sneaking up behind me and knocking one side of my headphones loose.

"Just some videos," I say, hastily trying to close my laptop.

"Wait, are those your roommates?" Mom holds up the screen so she can get a better look at what's happening in the game.

I doubt she's ever seen a video game, let alone a computer game. It's embarrassing enough that she's caught me stalking my ex-roommates, but at least the sidebar chat is moving so fast there's no way she could see the comment about their girlfriend, or make sense of what they're saying now that they're back on their microphones. So much of the conversation in their world is coded with just acronyms, I don't even understand all of it, and I've spent months with and watching them.

"Honey," Mom settles onto the chair next to me, "do you want to talk about why you're really home?"

"I'm here visiting." I close my laptop and look at the table, the sink, anything in the kitchen other than my mom.

We've never talked about boys or relationships or anything. This is not the best time to start having personal mother-daughter talks. If she pushes too hard, I'm going to break down, and that will make both of us even more uncomfortable than we already clearly are.

"Your dad and I would be okay if you weren't just here visiting, you know." She hesitates, then rushes to say, "We could help you find a job and buy a car and get you back on your feet."

Of course Mom wants to rush in and fix everything, changing my entire life to look more like hers without even hearing about what I want. Or what I need. She might let Dad brag about me being an author to their friends, but she would be more satisfied if I worked a steady job that she understood and settled down to marriage and kids. I'm not saying marriage and kids aren't on the table, at some point in the far future, but the steady nine-to-five job will never be. She needs to understand that and respect me, and my life choices.

"I don't need a job, Mom. I already have one. I'm an author." I'm tired of fighting and I need this to be our last battle about this issue.

"And you can always be an author, but are you really selling enough books that you can get by? It can be a hobby. Something you do on the weekends or evenings after work."

"Mom," I say, sharper than I'd intended as I turn to face

her head on, "I don't want a different job. My new book is selling so well that readers are begging for another one. When my royalties come, I'll be able to afford my own apartment. In no world am I going to give up my dream of being an author to make you more comfortable."

Mom sits there with her mouth open, not saying anything, because I've never talked back to her like this. In the past I've ignored her, or gotten Dad to talk to her for me, but I wouldn't have nearly yelled at her to get off my back. But this breakup and the resulting need to assess my future have pushed me to my limit, and I can't be passive or go with the flow anymore.

"I'm not uncomfortable," she lies.

"Yes you are," I insist. "And that's okay, you don't have to be comfortable with what I do, but you also can't keep trying to talk me out of it."

"I just want you to have a secure future, and I've read how much the average author usually makes in a year. It's not much," she says. "I also want you to be happy, and clearly you haven't been happy this last week since you came home. Since you won't talk to either me or your dad, I can only assume it has something to do with your books."

"It's not my books," I whisper, deflating in my chair. "Not entirely anyway."

I turn away a little as I wipe a stupid tear from my lower lashes. I've shed so many tears over my ex-boyfriends since I've moved home, it's ridiculous. Not even when I was about to be evicted from my own apartment and had to scramble for a place to live did I resort to crying. Of course, then I didn't have to face the reality of moving home, and I wasn't also dealing with the worst breakup of my life.

"Then what is it?" asks Mom, throwing up her hands. "Because we're all out of guesses over here, and frankly, you're bringing down the mood in the house."

"I'm so sorry that my breakup is affecting you," I say sarcastically. It's easier than being honest and saying that I'm dying inside. "Let me just get over it and move on so you can get back to your happy little atmosphere."

"Oh." Mom pauses. "I didn't know you were dating someone." She glances to my closed laptop. "Was it one of your roommates? Is that why you're here instead of back in Chicago?"

"It wasn't one of my roommates," I say.

"Then why—" she starts, but I cut her off.

"It was all of them."

She stares at me for a moment. "... all of them?"

Mom has always been confident and straightforward. I'm not used to seeing her uncertain. I can practically see every preconceived notion in her head popping in succession.

"Yes, Mom, all of them." If she's going to dig in and make me feel bad, I'm going to do the exact same to her.

"Okay." Mom tries to physically gather herself back together in front of me, shifting in her seat and clasping her hands together between her knees. "Well, um, I'm so sorry that you're going through this breakup. Do you want to talk about it? Or should we ... should we eat ice cream and watch a sad movie?"

A small, sad laugh escapes me. Of course my mother is suggesting the most cliché breakup moping techniques. As if I haven't already been doing that all week when they've been at work.

"Or, umm," Mom casts her eyes around the room, probably waiting for Dad to show up so she can get him to give us a few ideas, "keep stalking them online? Leave some bad reviews on their website?"

Now I laugh for real. Because I've totally been stalking them. I'm not about to leave bad reviews on their website, though, even if that was a thing the site would let me do. I could do it on their social media, but they're usually pretty quick to block people. And there's no way I'm making myself look bad in public. I do not need an Authors Behaving Badly post about me simply because these five gamers who hired me to do a job broke my heart.

I also don't want to do something that would hurt them, no matter how upset I may be.

"Thanks for the offer, but that's not a good idea." Never in my life did I imagine I would be the rational one in a conversation with my mother.

"Okay, if you're sure," says Mom, standing. "But if you change your mind, let me know. We can borrow a few tricks from Karen down the street."

Mom heads over to the fridge, pulling out random containers for leftover night.

"While you throw yourself into work so you don't have to think about them, I'll heat you up some food. You can't make them regret their decision without becoming a famous author so they kick themselves every time they see your book on the shelves."

As soon as the words are out of Mom's mouth, I realize she's right. Throwing myself into work is a pretty good idea. So good, in fact, that I wonder if that's why my ex-boyfriends' schedule is suddenly so full. Maybe it's not a big upcoming competition. Maybe they, too, are reeling from the breakup.

I search through the public appearance page on their website and I'm not seeing any public appearances for a few more months. Even perfectionists like them wouldn't prepare for something six months in advance.

My phone beeps and I reach for it automatically.

It's a text from Sasha, of all people. *You weren't at critique group this week. Maddie and Angela read me the riot act. I'm sorry that the stress of publishing made me try to sleep with your boyfriends.*

Rolling my eyes, I text back, *That's a shit apology. Not accepted.*

Then I take a page out of my exes' streaming book and block her number. I don't need that kind of negative energy in my life, and I wouldn't put it past her to find out that we broke up and for her to apply for the job of their live-in girlfriend. Shaking my head, I try to dislodge that image from my mind. I'm not going to go there.

But Sasha's shit apology makes me think of my own. I didn't really give any validation to the gamers' feelings that I used and betrayed them. For all my pretending that I'm so good with people and know what I'm doing, I'm ruining a lot of things lately.

The live stream is over, probably in part because of the comment thread in the sidebar chat. So I pull up the private subscriber chat.

I don't want to out them on lying on their site that they're no longer in a relationship so I need to craft my message carefully.

"Your girlfriend is lucky to have five amazing boyfriends like you all."

Simple enough that most of the other subscribers won't pay much attention, but direct enough that they'll know I'm the one who left the comment, if my user name matching my pen name didn't already clue them in. I'm giving away that I'm one of their subscribers and they'll probably block me, but I'll need to stop subscribing anyway if I'm going to have a chance of getting over them.

All I can do is stare at the comment, waiting to be blocked.

Some of the other subscribers are already responding, confused because they didn't realize all of the gamers shared the same girlfriend. Others are berating me for bringing her up because the guys don't like to talk about their personal life, telling me that I'm going to be kicked out for talking about it and I should respect the rules and their desire for privacy.

It's such a mixed bag of emotions and replies, and I can't just sit here and wait for them to block me. So I do it myself. I pull up all of their numbers on my phone and block each and every one. If I'm going to have a chance of moving on, I need to start now.

I close my laptop again and join my mom in the kitchen, where she's heating up some leftovers. She even pours us some wine and lets us sit in the living room to watch a movie. We choose a comedy so neither of us cries.

Chapter Twenty-Eight

"Clarissa," says Dad, knocking on my closed bedroom door.

Rolling out of bed to answer it, I know look like a troll. Now that my parents know my sad situation, I've fluctuated between not caring about how I look and feeling super motivated to be so awesome that my exes will regret their decision.

Today is a troll day.

"Hey, hun," says Dad in his sad-but-trying-to-be-upbeat voice, "your mom and I thought we could all use a little family fun time. Why don't you get dressed and we can leave the house today?"

"Today's not a good day." I start to close the door so I can crawl back beneath my blankets, but he sticks his foot in the door.

"Coffee is brewed and we're leaving in twenty. See you downstairs." Dad heads back down the hall, calling, "I love you!" over his shoulder.

Grumbling to myself, I go into the bathroom to take the hottest shower of my life. After that, I'm pouring my coffee into the biggest mug I can find in order to endure this. If I'm not downstairs in time, Dad will come back up here and guilt trip me until I comply, so it's better to just go along with it. Especially because they really have been understanding with my staying here lately.

I'm not sure they'll be quite as understanding when my boxes arrive from Chicago, but I'll cross that bridge when it happens.

Mom hands me a travel mug as soon as I'm downstairs.

"I can't even sit and enjoy my coffee?" I grumble.

"Of course you can," says Mom. "In the car while we're on our way."

"Where are we going, exactly?" I settle into the backseat of the car, sipping the life-giving brew that is coffee. If they expect me to be upbeat or even alive, they'll have to wait until this entire thermos kicks in.

"It's a surprise," says Dad cheerily as he turns around to back us out of the driveway.

Great. I'm not sure I can take any more surprises. I just watch out the window as the small town I grew up in passes by, then disappears.

It takes over an hour, and I'm starting to have to pee because I drank that entire thermos of coffee.

By the time Dad finally pulls into a parking lot, I'm ready to spring from the car to the nearest bathroom.

Until I look around and realize that we're in the packed parking lot of a community center.

And the sign over the entrance to the building announces that today is the town's comic convention.

"What are we doing here?" I ask, my voice sharper than usual and my eyes narrowed.

"Last time we visited, your roommates talked a lot about all these different comic things and shows and we didn't know any of them, so your mom and I thought it would be a fun family outing to learn more about that stuff."

"I'd rather go anywhere else." If I go in there, all I will be able to think about is my ex-boyfriends, and I miss them so much that if I see a TARDIS I'll probably burst into tears. "We could go bowling."

"I don't think this town has a bowling alley," says Mom, getting out of the car. "Besides, you've been complaining for the last ten minutes that you have to pee. Well, here's the bathroom."

"Fine." I really do have to pee. "But then we're leaving."

"Sure, yeah." Mom isn't really paying attention, instead looking around the parking lot as if it's the most fascinating thing she's ever seen.

I hurry us inside, because we need to make this quick for a number of reasons. As soon as I've used the bathroom, I'm forcing my parents to drive us anywhere else. I can't believe that the first time they pick something for us to do as a family, it's this. They could have picked anything. What a shit time for them to take an interest in my life.

When I come out of the bathroom and head for the exit, Mom slips her arm through mine and spins us around so we're entering the gym instead.

"I want to leave," I hiss, my voice low but insistent. I don't want everyone around us to think this is a kidnap situation. I mean, it kind of is, but not in the way they should panic about. "Where's Dad?"

"I just want to look around," she insists. "Besides, your dad already went inside, so we have to find him."

"One lap and we're out of here," I say. "No stopping at any tables, and no talking to anyone."

Mom ignores me and practically drags me up an aisle. She'd better not make this take forever. This is in and out.

I try to pay as little attention as possible to what's going on around us until Mom halts in the middle of an aisle, pointing at something up ahead.

There's a small rectangle taped off on the floor and in the middle stands all five of my ex-boyfriends.

My heart is trying to escape my chest, and I clutch Mom's arm tight. What are they doing here? I didn't want to come in because I didn't want to be reminded of them, but I didn't realize I should also be worried about running into them. There were no public appearances listed on their website. They shouldn't be here.

"What the hell?" I whisper, panic creeping in. I need to get out of here. But Mom's grip on me is tight, and I'm rooted to the spot.

As soon as they spot me, Miles picks up a microphone and says, "Thank you all for coming out for our little competition today. We're super excited to be here with people we care about." His eyes are locked on mine, even though he's talking to the entire room. "We're going to get our live stream going momentarily here, and you'll all get a chance to play against us."

"While you're waiting though, we recommend you browse all of the amazing vendors here today. And we'd like to give a very special recommendation for one booth in particular." Lionel gestures at the booth right next to them. "Our girlfriend is selling her romance book today, and she's even here to sign them for you."

"We should warn you," says Quintin, grabbing the mic from Lionel, "that we were the inspiration for a few of the scenes in there."

I force myself to pry my gaze from them and glance at the booth. Fuck me, there is Sasha, smiling and waving at the gathering crowd of readers.

She seriously texted me that shitty apology, then moved in with my ex-boyfriends? And now she has them promoting her and her romantasy books? This is not okay, and I want to be angry, but I can tell that crying is going to win.

Yanking my arm out of Mom's grip, I fight my way to the back of the crowd. I need to get out of here before the tears start to fall. If Mom and Dad want to look around, they can, but I'll hide in the bathroom until it's time to go. I'd hide in the car, but Dad has the keys and I'm not about to waste time looking for him.

There's a commotion, but I ignore it. All I can focus on right now is the exit and getting away from this gym.

"I got you. It's okay." Long arms wrap around me, holding me against a solid chest as they stroke my hair.

When I glance up, I'm looking up into Ethan's face, and I try to break away. But his hold is too strong.

"Sorry, but we're not letting you get away again," he says.

"Come back to Chicago and be our girlfriend again," whispers Helix, stepping around Ethan and wrapping me in a hug sandwich.

"You going to fire your latest girlfriend and kick her out with only a couple hours' notice, too? Or were you going to schedule out my rehire date to give her some time to pack up, at least?" I snap, pushing both of them off of me. No matter how much I miss being cocooned in their arms, I'm not letting them play games with me like this.

"What girlfriend?" asks Ethan. "You're our only girlfriend."

"Don't be obtuse." I point back to the booth, my finger stabbing through the air as the anger I thought would lose out begins to surface. "Sasha is here with you. After the little show you put on when she tried to kiss you, now you're traveling around to comic cons with her?"

"Sasha *is* here with us," says Helix, looking confused, "but only to help sell books. She knows more about that sort of thing than we do."

The tears bubble back up, pricking at the backs of my eyes. *Great.* I'd hoped the rage would take over, but it looks like there's a two-for-one deal on emotions today. *Lucky me.* "I'm very aware of Sasha's ability to sell her books. I don't need to be shown. Thanks though."

Ethan and Helix both look at me, their foreheads creased in bewilderment.

"She's not selling her book," says Helix slowly.

"She's selling yours," Ethan adds.

Now *I'm* confused. "I saw her up there at the booth with her books."

"No, you saw her up there with *your* books." Ethan takes a step closer to me, and this time I don't back away, but I don't move toward him, either. "We came here to apologize to you for overreacting. We've wanted to for a while, but didn't know what to do to win you back."

"So when Sasha came by with an idea, we couldn't say no," Helix tells me.

I look from Ethan to Helix, my brain spinning like the loading circle on a slow website. "I don't understand."

"Clarissa, we want you to come back to Chicago with us and be our girlfriend again," repeats Ethan.

"But we're not hiring you this time," says Helix. "We'll still pay for everything because we can afford it, and because we want to take care of you, but we want you there because you want to be there. Not because we're paying you."

"You're ... not dating Sasha?" My brain refuses to process everything. There are too many people around and too many new pieces of information, and I'm completely overwhelmed and overloaded.

"We're definitely not dating Sasha," says Helix.

"You're the only woman we want to date," Ethan assures me.

"What do you say?" asks Helix. When I don't immediately respond, he says, "At least take a look at the booth we set up for you."

They each take one of my hands, and I let them tug me back through the crowd to the booth where Sasha is framed on either side by a tower of books, talking to readers. Now that I'm giving the space more than a fleeting glance, I notice that the covers are indeed my own. In fact, as I look around the space, I don't see a single one of her books in sight. Which is crazy, because this is definitely a crowd that would love a good dragon book, and she has a few of them.

"Look who we found, Sasha," says Helix, moving behind me and placing his hands firmly on both of my shoulders, probably so I don't bolt again.

"Just a second," says Sasha to a reader before coming around to this side of the booth. "Clarissa, I'm so sorry!"

Sasha throws her arms around me and pulls me away from Helix, hugging me tight.

"I tried to contact you again, but I think you blocked my number. Not that I blame you," she says, moving back to look me in the eyes. "You were right, that was a shit apology. I'm sorry that I was a terrible friend and let my craze for being the best author possible get in the way of that. There are more than enough readers for everyone and it's not a competition. We can help each other and both be successful." I open my mouth to respond, but she keeps going. "And by help each other, I don't mean share your boyfriends. They've made it very clear that you're the only woman for them. Which I completely respect."

Finally, I wrap my arms around Sasha too to hug her back, and then step away, bumping up against Ethan.

"I forgive you," I tell her. "But it's going to be a while until I can trust you again."

"Of course. I completely understand." Sasha wrings her hands, and she really does look sorry.

"This is a good apology though." I wave to the booth.

"Thanks." Sasha laughs sheepishly. "One of the benefits of being a romance author is that I'm a pro at the grand gesture apology."

"Sasha helped us brainstorm ideas for the best way to win you back," Ethan tells me, his arm snaking tentatively around my waist, "and we found that this town was having a comic con. From there it was easy to reach out and ask if we could partner with them for a live stream."

"Good thing we're so well-known, or it would have been harder to get them to agree," says Helix. "But they were eager to have us."

"And when they told us they wanted to win you back," says Mom, who has found my father and dragged him over to the booth, "all we had to do was wait until the day and then get you here."

"On time, of course," adds Dad.

I can't believe this. My head is swimming. "You were in on it?"

"We love you, honey, and we just want you to be happy," says Dad.

"Even if we don't fully understand what you're doing," adds Mom, glancing around at the other booths and all the people dressed in various costumes.

"Thank you." I grab Mom and Dad in a hug. "I appreciate you both so much."

"Does that mean you'll come home with us?" asks Miles, coming over from their little makeshift streaming area where he, Lionel, and Quintin have been watching this whole scene play out.

"Yes." I slide right into Miles's arms and kiss him full-on for everyone to see. It couldn't feel more right. "I'm so sorry for not being upfront with you from the beginning. I promise to be unbearably honest with you from now on."

Until Quintin comes over for a kiss too. "We forgive you. It's easy to forgive the people we love."

"All right, the live stream is set up and we have competitors," says Lionel. He nods in the direction of my booth. "Clarissa, looks like you have a line for autographs."

Turning around, I see that there's a line of people at my table, and my heart soars. My boyfriends and Sasha seriously set up all of this just to apologize. I've written a few apologies myself, but this one is easily the best I've ever seen. Sasha is a very good writer if this is what she came up with.

"Thank you!" I lean forward to give him a quick kiss too, then hurry around to the back of the booth so I can start greeting readers and signing books.

Epilogue

"How did writing go today?" asks Lionel, pulling me into his lap at his computer.

"Really well. I outlined three chapters." I wrap my arms around his neck so he doesn't spin me around again and nearly topple me off like last time.

"Is this the new sports romance one?" asks Ethan.

"Yes, and I already have a whole list of questions to research. Maybe one of these days I'll start a gamer one too. But I'd probably need your help with that one."

"Maybe you need us to help you with a few other things for your book too," says Helix, rolling his chair up next to us and tugging my shirt up over my head.

"Oh definitely," I agree. "If I'm going to have my heroine won over by two book boyfriends, then I'm going to need double the hands-on research for them."

"Perfect, because we're here to help," says Lionel.

"I don't know who keeps feeding Goobus all the extra treats, but he's getting chonky," says Miles, holding the cat as he comes into the computer den.

When we'd first brought Goobus home from the shelter, he was super skinny and underweight, but now he's overflowing in Miles's arms. His fur is long and flowing and his face is perfectly serene. He loves being carried around, and views all of us as his little lackeys.

"You know Goobus isn't allowed in the computer room," complains Ethan, but it's halfhearted. "He always tries to turn off our computers."

"It's not our fault that he insists he hasn't been fed," says Quintin, coming in behind Miles with an energy drink in his hand.

"Then when Goobus has a hard time getting up the stairs to bed, you're going to be the one to carry him," Miles shoots back.

"Wait, Clarissa's shirt is off," says Quintin, moving closer. "What are we doing?"

"Whatever we want," says Helix, chuckling.

Miles sets Goobus down gently, Quintin puts down his drink, and then there are five sets of hands on me, exactly the way it should be.

Bonus "Deleted" Scene

Thank you so much for reading *Bro Amazing*. Didn't get enough? Check out this filthy little deleted scene of how Clarissa was originally going to start DP-ing her boyfriends.

Don't forget to check out *Bro Smooth*, the next book in The Bro Series. An aspiring reporter, Rebecca, is all about her career and has no interest in dating. However, she does have a checklist of experiences to complete before college graduation. Luckily, a four man Rubik's cube relay team is there to help. Although they do have a few stipulations of their own.

About the Author

Alby Blake is a grant award winning, mid-west romance author who spends her days researching ways to embarrass her characters and trying to drink as much tea as possible. If she's not writing, she may be in the garden or admiring her cats.

Also by Alby Blake

Captured by a Knight

Welded Hearts

Love in Hiding